# Protection

A Steamy Small Town Romance

Shelley Munro

For Paul—my best friend.

# Introduction

I t's not every day a girl inherits a condom company, and to say accountant Alice Beasley is astonished and out of her depth is putting it mildly. For an almost virgin, she needs a quick education in all things condom because her inheritance is in danger. Someone is intent on sabotage and trying to destroy her new company.

Alice is suddenly getting down and dirty with charismatic James, the factory manager, all in the name of business and testing new condom designs. The sex is hot. Mind-blowing. It's a dark thrill and an erotic journey. Yeah, it's a difficult job, but she is the woman for the task.

The testing turns personal. Alice wants James. She craves his talented touch and sultry kisses, she desires passion and physical pleasure on a permanent basis but first she must convince bad-boy James to give up his fancy-free ways.

***Warning: Condoms were tested and a few harmed during the writing of this story.***

1

# Chapter 1

T hey were in the wrong place.

Alice Beasley stared around the crowded town hall feeling a little like her namesake Alice in Wonderland—lost and confused in a strange, foreign world. This bedlam reminded her of a storybook rabbit hole, not a small New Zealand country town called Sloan.

She gaped at a woman dressed in a bright orange turban and a long, voluminous, hunter-green gown. Another woman in a smart black suit teetered her way to the front of the hall, a small grubby boy in tow. His red, tear-stained face confirmed coercion and the same discomfit that slid through Alice's stomach.

The fish-out-of-water sensation persisted as she perused the colorful characters assembled in the town hall. This couldn't be the reading of her godmother Alicia's will.

Alice rifled through the black leather handbag at her feet and pulled out the scrawled details of the date, time and address. The lawyer had rattled them off at the end of a hurried phone call the previous evening. Frowning, she stuffed the paper back inside her bag, straightened and tucked her hands in her lap.

It was the right place.

A prickle of awareness jerked her upright. Alice glanced up from her clasped fingers, peeking through lowered lashes.

A man.

She hunched forward to appear less obvious but continued to scrutinize him. Wow, a gorgeous man surrounded by flirtatious females of all ages. Tall. A rangy build. Dark shaggy hair and bright blue eyes that focused on her and bore distinct interest. Alice wondered what it would be like to have this hottie at her side, touching her like a lover, then guilt assailed her.

He wasn't her sort.

Not with that wicked grin and his daredevil demeanor. No, despite this man's obvious attractions—her fascinated gaze darted back to scan his broad chest, his overlong hair and his...

Awareness pulled at Alice, her skin blazing with a flush of heat. She squirmed and tugged her white cotton cardigan. A quick jerk of her wrist pulled it away from her breasts but did little to cool the swelter of her body. She barely resisted fanning her face, smoothing the wayward strands of her hair away from her forehead instead.

*Oh my goodness.* She'd stared right at his...

Aghast at the way she'd ogled the man's crotch when practically engaged to another, she turned to Steven for distraction. His phone held his attention. Alice knew better than to interrupt since he'd come to Sloan under protest.

An ambitious man, Steven intended to advance to partner with his law firm. She admired his determination so she couldn't fault his plans for their future. With a sigh, she scanned the cavernous room, keeping her gaze clear of Mr. Hottie. Alice had read magazine articles about men like him, and they weren't suitable for a girl who desired security and a relationship to rival a happy-ever-after fairy tale.

Over to the side of the room, a group of elderly women operated a tea service. They had a steady stream of customers and worked together like a well-oiled machine. The clink of gold coins added to the general racket.

She noticed a podium on the stage at the front of the hall. Nearby, a sound system sat, ready for the speaker. Behind Alice, and in front of her, locals occupied rows and rows of wooden chairs, or at least they appeared to know one another.

Surely, they weren't all beneficiaries in her godmother's will?

"Are you sure we're in the right place?" Steven asked after three people in full white robes squeezed past them to take possession of empty seats on their left.

Polite and circumspect, no matter what the aggravation, this strange town seemed to rattle him. Hence his attempts to bury himself in work while they waited for the lawyer to arrive.

Alice didn't blame him. The people she'd met so far in the small town of Sloan were pure provocation. Ask a question and they gave a roundabout answer. No one, from the local police to the young woman walking the brown dog near the post office or the robed men and women who loitered outside the hall had wanted to discuss her godmother's company Fancy Free. Her request for directions and polite questions had led to smirks or icy silence. She'd quizzed the man when they'd purchased petrol and learned zilch. Their reticence reeked of a weird conspiracy.

"Alice?"

She huffed out an exasperated breath. She'd love to learn about her inheritance. Instead, she got this frustrating mystery.

"Yes, we're in the right place." Maybe she should have jumped on the internet and done some research after the lawyer's bombshell call. There hadn't been time since they'd both worked late then had to rush to a work function.

Steven bent toward her and whispered, his warm breath puffing against her cheek. "Are you sure the lawyer didn't give you a hint about your inheritance?"

"You could do a search on your phone," she suggested.

His appalled expression told her his decision. "It's a work phone. They monitor my usage."

She hid her grimace and feeling the weight of another stare, fidgeted. If she grew any hotter, she'd self-combust. She'd focus on Steven instead.

Her mother might consider him stuffy, but she was wrong. A pompous windbag, her father had stated the first time she'd taken the young lawyer home.

Alice knew better.

Despite her parents' opinions, Steven's ideals aligned with her own. They were perfect for each other.

And she'd have security, both financial and emotional.

"Alice?" Steven prompted again. "Do you know anything?"

Alice reconstructed the hurried phone call she'd had with her godmother's lawyer in her mind before shaking her head. "I asked Mr. Bellbooth when he rang last night but he said in accordance with the will, I had to come to Sloan to learn the details. He told me the date and time and hung up to take another call."

"Mighty peculiar." Steven spoke in a well-modulated voice. "I told you to let me handle it."

Irritation pierced her before guilt washed away her testiness. Although not officially engaged, they had an understanding, so she supposed his attitude spoke of concern. Really. They were perfect for each other.

A tubby man dressed in an old-fashioned pinstriped suit limped onto the podium and the locals ceased their loud chatter. The clamor diminished to a low hum.

Alice stared in fascination, her imagination taking flight. The man looked as if he'd stepped straight from a *Munster's* movie. After the show so far, flitting bats or body parts somersaulting across the floor wouldn't shock her. It had been that kind of day.

The lawyer, Mr. Glen Bellbooth she presumed, cleared his throat and silent expectation ensued. "If everyone is ready, I'll read the will." The man exuded confidence as he pulled a pair of spectacles from his inside jacket pocket, put them on and surveyed his audience before he began. "Alicia asked me to read the will in its entirety."

Alice wrinkled her nose. This torture would continue? The lawyer didn't understand the size of her student loan. The notion she'd be able to pay off her debts and save for the small house she'd always dreamed of refused to leave her mind.

She and Steven could start a family sooner rather than later. A home, a family and financial security was almost too much for her to comprehend.

*Oh please*, she prayed. *Please let my dreams come true.*

A life in the suburbs with an average two point four children.

She craved normal. After her topsy-turvy upbringing and the way her parents had dragged her and her siblings around the world from one worthy cause to another, she hungered for ordinary.

At first, she focused on every word. The lawyer droned on and she drifted into dreams of the future while various persons around the hall let out excited squeaks and jumped to their feet with cheers.

Financially independent and debt free. The idea, the potential benefits, filled her with exhilaration. Steven knew about her student loans. She'd confided in him about the house and how much she wanted her own home. Something that belonged to her. Steven wanted to rent a property so she hadn't raised the subject again. It didn't mean she agreed with his views. He was a good man. He'd see the sense in compromise and realize the importance of future security.

"What?" Steven gasped, his spine hitting the back of his chair.

Alice's head snapped up, her eyes wide with panic. Had she missed something important?

"To my goddaughter Alice Beasley, I leave my company Fancy Free," Mr. Bellbooth repeated. He studied Steven over the top of his glasses before continuing to read. "I am confident you, along with my manager James Bates can work together to grab a larger portion of the condom market share."

"A condom company?" Steven didn't bother to hide his horror. "Not bloody likely."

Heads turned to stare and several of the robed strangers whispered to each other, but shock held Alice in its grip. Condoms? Her breath hitched while her palms moistened with dread. What next?

One thing remained certain—it was weird in this rabbit hole called Sloan.

Mr. Bellbooth eyed them again, his brows an arch of silent inquiry, but when neither of them uttered a word, he continued. "I hope you will take an active part in the company management, but I understand if you wish to pursue your career in accountancy. I have added a stipulation to my will in the form of a codicil. If you run Fancy Free with the help of my manager for the term of six months, I will give you the sum of three hundred thousand dollars plus a share of the company profits. Should you find yourself unable to meet these terms, the money will go to the Foundation for the Blind, and you will receive ten thousand dollars."

Alice sat in stupefied shock. Her parents should have warned her. They must have known, but when she'd rung this morning to ask about Alicia's will, they'd told her they were running late for the church fundraiser.

They never stressed about money and lived from paycheck to paycheck. Alice suspected they'd wanted to surprise her with the news. Also, since her parents were big churchgoers, she'd bet they'd kept the news about a relation who owned a condom company quiet on purpose. Some of the people in her parents' church held conservative views and opposed any method of contraception. Given the beliefs of her parents' friends plus her parents' discomfort in discussing anything connected to sex, their reticence on the matter didn't surprise her.

She glanced to her left and her breath caught at Steven's distaste. He'd expect her to return to the Auckland suburb of Remuera and their jobs.

After all, they were almost engaged.

Alice let the rest of the lawyer's words wash over her while her mind drifted to her childhood and the horrid years after her father's bankruptcy. As a result, she'd grown up taking care with her money. Her student loan and the exorbitant interest charges made her stomach cramp, but there had been no other way to gain an education. She needed to train for a profession if she wanted security.

The lawyer concluded and straightened his pile of papers. He switched off the sound system and a burst of chatter filled the hall.

Steven made a gurgle of disgust deep in his throat and puffed out a hard breath that shifted the fringe off his forehead. "They have got to be joking. If any of the partners at my law firm get wind of your condom company, they'll shunt me sideways. I'll never make partner. We are a conservative law firm steeped in years of tradition." Distraught at the idea, he wheezed, each breath dragged from his lungs with a harsh gasp.

Alice fumbled in her bag for Steven's inhaler and handed it to him with a worried frown.

"I don't need my inhaler," he snapped. Each hoarse breath mocked his rejection of the medicine, and she arched her brows in exasperation. "All right. Maybe I do," he conceded. "It's this hick town. It's full of pollen and dust." An explosive sneeze punctuated his statement.

The lawyer stopped beside them and cleared his throat. The man who'd tried to flirt with her earlier stood at his side, a tiny smile playing on his sensual lips. When she stood, Alice noticed he had a dimple at the left-hand side of his mouth. The man was her fantasy come to life—the man she'd dreamed of as a teenager.

But not safe.

She'd stick with a steady man. A predictable man.

Alice gulped once she realized she'd stared at him for too long. She jerked her gaze away but still had time to notice his eyes darken and the corners of his mouth turn up in amusement.

*He knew.*

He knew she found him attractive and sexy.

Humiliation rushed heat to her cheeks. Chagrin filled her at her disloyalty to Steven. He was her boyfriend.

But still her gaze drifted to Mr. Hottie. Irritated, she attempted to concentrate on the lawyer. What was wrong with her?

The time to step into bad-girl shoes had been before her involvement with Steven. True, she hadn't planned to don a good-girl persona either—it had just happened—but she believed in commitment and loyalty. Steven was a decent, steady man and careful with money. They would have a perfect marriage.

"It's impossible. Alice can't run a company that makes money from *sex*." Steven's emphasis made the act sound dirty and despicable. "What will our employers think?"

Alice touched his forearm. "They don't have to know." She attempted to placate even though his attitude peeved her.

They might have an unspoken agreement but they weren't married yet. This was her inheritance. Alicia had left Fancy Free to her for a reason. Besides, an opportunity to pay off her debt and grab her dream with both hands didn't occur every day. Condoms might prove a noteworthy enterprise with the constant cry for safe sex.

Steven glared at her, his dark brows drawn together in a flat, bushy line. "As a lawyer and an accountant, our reputations must be spotless." The image of a caterpillar jumped into her mind and she had to bite her lip to stem her inappropriate humor. "You must walk away. Distance yourself."

Her amusement faded, replaced by irritation. Now he was treating her like one of the new lawyers at his firm. Her chin lifted. "I have a spotless reputation."

She and Steven had done nothing more amorous than kiss—a mere brush of lips and this had become a sore point. Sometimes a girl wanted to express herself. Sometimes sex came to mind, but every time she tried to take their relationship further, Steven jammed on the brakes. If they were committed, then surely they could make love. It wasn't a crime.

"Use of a condom is responsible. I doubt any employer would condemn safe sex," she said.

"Alice! Lawyers can't get involved in sex."

Alice closed her mouth with an audible snap. Did Steven have to spout his views in public? Heaven knows what the two men thought.

"Is this a private conversation?" Mr. Hottie asked.

Mortified, Alice blinked, her legs weak and shaky on hearing his husky voice. Up close, he was Mr. Dynamic. His strong, masculine personality shone from his tanned face.

And that voice...

It reminded her of rich, dark chocolate, the smooth and decadent type that melted in the mouth and tasted exquisite.

"Who are you?" Steven demanded.

"James Bates. I work for Fancy Free." He smiled at Alice, a gleam in his eyes as he extended his hand. Alice's pulse rate shot from elevated to fast and choppy. Slowly, she placed her hand in his and flinched.

11

Touching him was every bit as memorable and unsettling as she'd envisaged. The tingles, delicate at first, shot up her arm like a mild case of pins and needles. Then he squeezed, his callused palm abrasive against hers. The tingles morphed into a full-body shot, much like a pick-me-up tonic. Bad-girl thoughts crammed her mind with nakedness and tangled sheets.

With difficulty, she tugged to free herself of his potent masculinity. Breathless, she stared up at him and the scenario of a mouse cornered by a cat came to mind.

He worked for Fancy Free? With his personality and good looks, he probably spent a fortune on their products and took full advantage of staff discounts.

"Hello." To Alice's horror, her voice emerged breathless and low. A come-hither tone if ever she'd heard one.

"Alice and I will work together." James smirked.

Steven drew up to his full height of five foot eight. "I don't think so. Tell him, Alice."

Alice gulped. Okay, so James had emphasized the togetherness bit. Steven had noticed and Glen Bellbooth, as indicated by the lawyer's sly chuckle.

"I've called a gathering of the board for you to meet everyone," the lawyer said. "Tomorrow morning at nine sharp."

"We're not on an overnight vacation. I need to get back to Remuera," Steven protested. "I must finish preparations for my case that starts next week. You need to do the shopping and ironing. Isn't that what you told me?"

"I need to think." Steven's bossy, snippy tone flooded her cheeks with mortification. Had he always been like this? Or was she just noticing? She cast an uneasy glance at James and the lawyer and at the others witnessing the scene. Yes, she wanted security, but that didn't mean Steven could ride roughshod over her feelings.

"I don't know what's wrong with you. There's nothing to think about. We can't stay here."

He wasn't used to her contradicting him, but in this case, she intended to stand firm.

"I need more details before I can make an informed decision." She strove for calm even though her stomach jumped with anxiety. She'd get her friend Jennifer to ship some of her clothes. If Jennifer sent them by courier, they'd arrive tomorrow. Yes, that would work. Alice made eye contact with Steven. "I intend to stay."

"The idea is ludicrous," he said, his distaste discernible.

"Perhaps you'd like to discuss it in private." The lawyer's quiet words made Alice aware of people's stares, their whispers and amusement. Some had even slowed their departure from the hall to eavesdrop. Alice straightened, determined to grab control of her future.

"Good idea." For the first time in their relationship, Alice took the lead, grasping Steven's elbow to drag him from the hall. "We'll discuss this over coffee. I noticed a cafe when we drove into town." The snickers from behind brought a flash of discomfort but she kept moving despite Steven's resistance.

"I don't like coffee."

"I'm sure they'll have tea," she said. A hand on her shoulder made her jump and to her great chagrin, a squeak emerged.

James Bates' blue eyes twinkled and his dimple flashed into prominence. "I'll see you tomorrow." He didn't wait for her answer but strolled from the hall with the lawyer at his side.

"Alice." Steven's sharp tone pierced any chance of daydreams. "You can't seriously consider this ludicrous legacy is a worthy idea."

She drew a shuddery breath and turned to face him, her heart drumming against her rib cage. "It's a chance to improve my future. I thought you'd understand."

He stared at her for a long, drawn-out moment, his brows and mouth set in flat lines of displeasure. "If you stay in this hick town, our relationship is over."

Alice gaped at him. "I'm sorry." She pressed her lips together, irritated with her apologies when she had nothing to regret.

The legacy presented an opportunity, a chance to grasp her future in both hands. How could she walk away when she knew nothing about the company? She'd attend the board meeting tomorrow. "I intend to discover more about my inheritance."

"Alice, this is a strange place. Did you see the crowd camped on the outskirts of town? Did you notice the number of shops that sell airy-fairy souvenirs and emphasize the mystical forces present in the area? The town is full of wackos and weirdos. Add a condom company to the mix and it's downright peculiar."

Alice frowned at his behavior. This wasn't like him, since he never had a bad word to say about anyone.

"One last chance."

She shook her head.

"Very well." Steven stamped from the hall.

Alice watched him until he disappeared. Shocked, she walked outside to take in the people and sights of Sloan. She couldn't believe Steven's high-handed behavior and refused to pander to it. True, some of the town occupants were eccentric, but life would be a real bore if everyone behaved the same. A little color was a good thing.

She turned left and wandered toward the cafe she'd noticed earlier. First a strong, trim latte and then she'd make a list and find somewhere to stay the night.

"Down with condoms. Birth control is bad!"

The two white-robed women sprang from a side street. Alice started and attempted to back away, but they surrounded her. They waved placards in her face and pranced around with ungainly steps, both in advanced stages of pregnancy.

"No condoms. No birth control," one hollered. She handed Alice a business card before screeching, "Down with condoms."

Alice frowned at the business card. On one side it was plain white and the other bore a picture of a dog. The absence of further details, names or phone numbers to say who it belonged to or what it represented surprised her.

"Bad, bad birth control," the other shouted. She also handed Alice a business card before resuming her protest. "Down with condoms. Down with condoms. No birth control."

The second business card depicted a clown but nothing else. More bemused than frightened, Alice stuffed them into her handbag and continued to the cafe, hastening her steps to outpace the pregnant women. She slipped inside the cafe, the plaintive sounds of a country ballad almost loud enough to drown the shouts from outside.

Alice took possession of a table tucked away in a corner and let her breathing ease to normal while she waited for the waitress. She relaxed until her mind drifted to condoms. Things kept becoming weirder by the minute while her life raced out of control. The parallels between her day and the adventures of the original Alice were plain scary. A sudden thought brought a choked gasp. Perhaps she should have stayed away from the cafe because wasn't there a tea party somewhere in the story? And hadn't Alice almost lost her head?

# Chapter 2

After a restless night where work problems encroached on sleep, James had come into the office early to take care of paperwork. Instead of an empty in-tray, Alice Beasley had intruded on his concentration and he hadn't finished a damn thing. He tapped his pen on the desk, the staccato beat an echo of his irritation.

The girl didn't possess a quarter of the spunk of her godmother. James was surprised she'd shown enough backbone to stand up to her pompous boyfriend. He'd scrutinized her before and throughout the reading, trying to understand what made her tick, to gauge her character, the type of woman he'd have to deal with for the next six months.

The answer screamed at him, as obvious as the nose on his face. He rose and paced to disperse the jumbled-up energy and pent-up frustration that had stalked him from the moment he'd climbed out of bed this morning.

A prude.

What the hell had Alicia been thinking?

The woman had seemed shocked to the core when she'd learned Fancy Free sold prophylactics. A pity, because she was cute in a next-door-girl kinda way with glossy brown hair, cut in a style that framed her face and made her resemble a pixie.

Her eyes were pretty, an unusual shade of brown. James clicked his fingers. Cognac. Yeah, they reminded him of the color of expensive brandy. Golden freckles danced across her nose and cheeks, reinforcing the pixie image, while her pink rosebud mouth cried out for kisses. The rest of her body had remained hidden beneath a baggy woolen skirt and voluminous white cardigan. It was only a guess but he suspected her body would be neat and compact like the rest of her.

James checked his watch and sighed. Let the fun begin. He plucked a purple folder from his desk and strode down a short passageway to the boardroom. Once inside, he closed the door behind him.

The other board members, Richard Morgan, Sam Glengarry, Harriet Te Whare, Katarina Wilson, Ben Kumar and Joseph Craig already sat around the oval table, cups of coffee at their elbows. All retired, apart from Richard, most of them had grandchildren.

James thought they'd reverted to childhood because some days he felt like a babysitter instead of the company manager. He slapped the folder on the table and grabbed a coffee before taking a seat.

An empty white china plate sat in the middle, the dark crumbs evidence of its previous contents. Everyone pored over the latest edition of the *Sloan Gazette*, the gossip column in particular. No one knew Ms. Knowall's true identity but she seemed to have the inside scoop on lots of juicy secrets.

Since his arrival back in Sloan, James had gained playboy status because Ms. Knowall sprinkled details of his private life through her column. Between Ms. Knowall and the cult that protested the use and manufacture of condoms, his life reverberated with conflict.

"James has been a busy boy," Joseph Craig said.

"Oh, we've made this week's column," Katarina Wilson declared with a hint of glee. She placed her cup down and *tsk-tsked* under her breath. "Bother, I didn't come out in my scarlet-woman costume today. It's at the drycleaners."

James scowled. He'd like to wring the gossip columnist's neck. Thanks to her, his sister didn't speak to him except for the occasional lecture. Things had been bad before but now...

The constant aggravation from the Children of Nature cult didn't help matters where his mother was concerned. "Have I missed out on the chocolate cake again?"

"Saved you a piece." Rita Jamieson, Fancy Free's administrative wonder winked at him. "I know what this lot is like. Human vacuum cleaners. I saved one for our new boss too."

"She didn't look like the condom type." Sam Glengarry dropped his coffee cup on his saucer with a clatter. He stretched his arms above his head, groaning at the creak of bones.

"Huh." Harriet Te Whare snorted, her knitting needles clicking as she worked on her current project, a striped scarf for her granddaughter. "You weren't the condom type when Alicia approached us to help her raise the money to float the company. You're sure as hell in favor of condoms now."

Sam puffed up with indignation, making James grin. They'd all gone to school with Alicia and settled in Sloan to have families. Now years later, they'd taken a risk with their investment in Alicia's foolish idea to start a condom company. Fierce pride filled James. A pity his mother wasn't part of the same group.

"Have we received the test results for the X-100?" Katarina Wilson asked.

James nodded, thankful he'd diverted a rundown of Ms. Knowall's column. He didn't want to know which of his latest exploits had hit the gossip column. No doubt he'd piece it together over the course of the day. "Yes, that's what I wanted to discuss—"

The door flew open and Glen Bellbooth and Alice entered the boardroom. Alice, his new boss. James let his gaze skim her body. Once again, she'd arrived in disguise, a black skirt today with all-encompassing layers of fabric. James cocked his head, curious about the hidden curves.

Did she have something to hide?

"Morning all," Glen Bellbooth said. "Coffee, Alice?"

She nodded, her distraction allowing James to look his fill. His attention strayed to the golden speckles on the bridge of her nose before his gaze drifted downward to the creamy skin at the base of her throat. Did she have freckles on her breasts as well? And what about size and shape? Hard to tell with the baggy clothes.

A soft, choked sound brought a grin. He winked at her, chagrined when she didn't respond. Most women blushed or flirted in return, unable to resist his charm and his sexy dimple. Miffed, he realized this woman had slipped into his mind yesterday and hadn't left. He was at a loss to explain his fixation since she wasn't his type. James admitted it—he normally went for obvious. Long legs and big breasts, women who knew how to highlight their assets. He shot another glance at the new owner. The sleeplessness of the previous night hadn't just been work related. This woman had intruded, in a graphic, sexual manner that left him hot and eager and desperate. A series of intimate images flickered through his mind.

James cursed. His body had no such qualms, suddenly tense in places that had no business reacting in the middle of a board meeting. He redirected his thoughts to the more mundane and away from dangerous territory. When he added Ms. Knowall to the equation, his dick subsided.

"Have a seat." Rita motioned to a chair. "I saved you some cake. You too, Glen."

James grabbed a pen from inside the folder, his mind on the future. He wasn't staying in Sloan for much longer. Just the six months his contract stipulated, the six additional months he'd promised Alicia. Although his main aim remained, to catch the person responsible for the sabotage of the trials for the X-100, he'd agreed because of family.

A stupid idea. His mother disapproved of everything he did. Some things never changed, but Alice might create a welcome distraction and he could discover the body beneath the layers before he left...

Richard Morgan, one of Sloan's cops, nudged him in the shoulder. "Mind out of the gutter, boy," he said gruffly.

"What? I'm not doing anything." James summoned an innocent and wronged expression as he turned to the older man.

"Huh." Richard gave a snort, half laughter but laced with disapproval too. "I've seen the same look on Luke's face. You have mischief on your mind."

"My mind is on condoms," James countered. "The X-100—"

"Yeah, but not in a business sense. I wasn't born yesterday. Don't hurt that girl, James."

James scowled, irritated now. "I don't intend to hurt her. We have to work together." But exploration of mutual pleasure wasn't out of the question. No pain involved in a little consensual sex. Before Richard added to his lecture, James changed the subject. The genuine care in the older man's voice brought the rush of memories of lighthearted childish days spent roaming Sloan with his friend Luke Morgan. Richard and Luke were like family to him, more supportive than his own. "How's Luke? I've spoken to him a couple of times, but he seemed preoccupied. Muttered something about crime sprees and damn cults. At least, the demonstrations against Fancy Free have died down. I half expected a protest inside the hall when Glen read the will but they behaved for a change. I heard via the gossip vine they accosted Alice. Has the cult been up to something else?"

"Yeah, rumor says cultivation of wacky weed. They've been baking it into cookies for sale to the local teenagers, or at least that's what we think. We have to prove it first, catch the blighters red-handed. Yep, we're busy. The newspaper story about mystical powers in Sloan has brought a new batch of weirdos into town. A few strange things going on."

"Is everyone ready to start?" Glen Bellbooth asked, interrupting the questions James had intended to ask. "Alice has agreed to stay for the six months stipulated by the will, which will work out well since James can show her the ropes before he leaves. Once Alice knows everyone, you can conduct your regular meeting and I'll leave to prepare for my court appearance." He nodded at Alice. "James will cover the day-to-day procedures with you later. Don't worry. By the time his contract ends you'll be an expert."

That sounded fine to James since he wanted to learn what made the woman tick. Time spent together would give him that opportunity. A quick glance around the six board members confirmed their acquiescence. James conducted the introductions and opened the purple folder he'd placed on the table in front of him. "I want to talk about product development. The new condom design is complete and we're ready to begin trials to test the X-100."

"I still don't know why we need this new one," Joseph Craig grumbled. "We've got glow in the dark ones, varied sizes, flavored ones and who knows what else. Why do we need to develop more? Who wants another condom?"

James bit his tongue. Alicia had explained everything to the board, discussed things in old-fogey terminology. The elderly board members didn't like change. Sometimes he wondered how Alicia had talked them into their investment in the sex industry, although he had to admit they showed more interest and asked insightful questions these days. "Our opposition brings out new products regularly. If we want to keep our market share, we must do the same," he explained in a calm voice. Some days he felt like a parrot.

A cough attracted his attention. Alice's face had turned bright red.

"Are you all right?" he asked, although James suspected the reason for her unease. Her gaze focused on the photo of their newest condom design. Stretched out in all its glory over a fiberglass penis, the X-100 looked high-tech and very impressive.

Alice nodded and reached for a glass of water. The tremor of her right hand brought a self-conscious frown. "I'm fine. Please continue."

What on earth was she doing here? She pushed a lock of hair off her face and wished she could fan away the fiery heat. And she still didn't understand why her godmother had left her the condom company. When she'd attempted to ask her parents, they'd brushed her off with excuses about church and religion. Even the lawyer Mr. Bellbooth had said he wasn't sure of her aunt's reasons, but did it matter? An unladylike snort emerged.

"Is something wrong?" James asked in a husky voice.

"I'm fine. No problem." She barely halted the telltale shiver of bliss at the sound of his voice. As one, everyone turned to stare at her and that heightened her awareness of the wretched man.

This was ridiculous. How could an almost virgin run a condom company? She couldn't count her one time at university as experience. The heat in her cheeks intensified even farther when she sneaked a look at the photo on top of the folder. Half expecting a voice to shout, "Off with her head," she swallowed and wondered if they'd notice if she ran from the room. Her gaze wandered to the photo again without waiting for her brain to give permission.

The condom was a delicate violet color and had tiny raised dots all over the surface. It looked like an alien creature with chicken pox. There were strange appendages attached. It was hard to say what that round bit did. Dragging her gaze from the photo, she turned her attention to James' run down of the product and the current state of play. Tests. Trials. Okay, that made sense. They had to know if they worked.

But how did they conduct the tests?

Her mind jumped into overdrive as she visualized a typical condom trial. A man and woman naked on a huge bed while a man dressed in a white coat stood with a clipboard, snapping out pertinent questions and ticking off the questions in his survey. How did the latex feel? Did it fit to the penis? Was it too thick? Too thin? Was it big enough to catch semen? Did it stand up to vigorous thrusts? Is there significant loss of sensation?

A tight band constricted Alice's chest, affecting her breathing. She furtively tugged at the underwire of her bra while a wave of heat engulfed her body. She squirmed, warmth growing in her nether regions because of her sexual thoughts. Alice bit into her bottom lip. She had questions, but nerves and uncertainty made her hesitate. A sharp inhalation did nothing to steady her trepidation. This was stupid. She had a vested interest in this condom company and had every right to ask questions.

"Um, how do you conduct trials?"

"We ask for volunteers, dear." The elderly lady in the seat next to her stopped her knitting to lean over and pat her on the hand. "Thankfully, our team of volunteers likes sex."

"That's after using our special machines for the initial tests," an elderly gent added.

"Oh." Alice bit her lip again. None of the elderly board members appeared embarrassed while nerves caused her stomach to twist enough for all of them. It was that man's fault. He made her thoughts veer to naughty and forget her problems with Steven. Her gaze speared to him and clung.

James Bates.

His husky voice and handsomeness had spilled into her dreams last night. She could barely look him in the face after she recalled her nakedness, wantonly sliding her well-endowed chest across his face. Begging for it. Begging for him. Tension gathered low in her belly as she recalled the exquisite sensation of his mouth closing over her nipple. He'd drawn her tip deep into his mouth and sucked hard until a corresponding tug echoed in her...

Pussy. Huh, she might as well think bluntly since she'd dreamed in Technicolor with no holds barred. He'd stripped off his jeans and white cotton shirt and displayed tanned muscles. Smooth skin. A huge erection. Alice groaned and imagined his cock sliding deep into her body. Or at least she tried since she remembered only the barest mechanics and sensations.

She shifted on her chair and sighed, her feminine flesh pulsing. It had been so long since that one foray into sex. Maybe it was time to explore again?

"Are you all right, dear? You look flushed." The knitting lady again.

Alice jerked back to the present to find every one of the six board members staring at her again plus the admin lady, and worst of all, the manager James Bates. He sported a grin, almost as if he knew what she'd fantasized about and relived only seconds ago.

*Oh my.* Steven was right. Her morals had fallen by the wayside. She was a wicked woman and was going to hell.

Realizing she had yet to answer, Alice blurted, "Fine. I'm...ah...focused on the business." And how. If she concentrated on sex and condoms any harder, she'd self-combust. An X-rated version of Alice in Wonderland. Who'd have guessed?

"How's the security?" Richard Morgan asked. "Have we had any more breaches since we installed security cameras on the roof?"

"The alarm wasn't tripped, but we've had problems on the production line. Missing supplies, and Scott, the floor manager, discovered someone had changed the settings on the packing machine. Most of the boxes packed this week went out one condom short. We only discovered this after they'd left the warehouse. We've had to recall them."

"More money off the bottom line," Sam Glengarry muttered, fingering his chin in a thoughtful manner. "Not good."

"We'll have to set up covert cameras on the floor." Richard frowned. "I didn't want to do that."

"We'll do what we have to," Katarina stated. "Besides, I want to buy a red coupe with my next payout. Can't do that if we don't have profits."

"Red?" Ben asked. "I'd get a black one. I heard on the radio today that the most desired car color in Britain is black."

"Humph," Katarina said. "It's a bugger to keep clean. Fingerprints all over the paintwork. There's nothing worse."

"Can we get back to condoms?" James demanded with a trace of impatience.

Joseph Craig nodded, even though his mind was clearly on bonuses. "That's rough. Too much money invested in the X-100. We must sort out our security problems before the public gets wind of the trouble. Can't have the consumers' confidence in the integrity of Fancy Free's products dented."

Everyone around the table nodded. The board moved on in discussions.

Rita Jamieson, the admin lady, produced a life-sized penis made of fiberglass from a padlocked wooden box, placed it on the table and rolled on a teal green condom with purple dots.

Harriet Te Whare glanced up from her lime green and canary yellow knitting. "I'm not sure about the color selections."

"Rubbish," Ben Kumar stated. "Purple is the new black. I suppose we could have black dots since that color is so popular on cars."

"We'll have several colors," James said. "A matching palette. These are just two examples."

"I'm more worried about the design." Joseph Craig accepted the model from Rita and surveyed it from all angles. "And I'm still not sure about these dots. What have the people in the trials said about comfort?"

"The raised dots are fine. Do you have another one there, Rita?"

Rita rolled a condom on a second penis model and handed it to James.

He ran his fingers over the dots. "I've used it myself. See the way they move when I touch them? It's like a mini massage when it's in use."

"But they're much bigger than our regular raised dots model," Joseph argued. "We need to use extra latex in the design because the dots are larger."

"No. We have the right amount of latex. Pretend my hand is the woman's vagina. See how the dots fan outward like tiny brushes?"

Alice gaped, her eyes wide as he showed the rest of the board how the new condom functioned. His fist acted as the woman's vagina while he used his other hand to demonstrate how the raised dots worked. They didn't bat an eyelid but paid close attention and asked intelligent questions. Alice leapt from one revelation to another and learned more about the theory of sex and the practical application of condoms during the day than she'd soaked up in all her twenty-five years.

But she made it through the day—just—despite the heat controls of her body jamming on hot and fiery. Her mind drifted in the gutter with her consciousness of James Bates. Big and male, his crotch seemed level with her face for a good deal of the meeting as he stood to demonstrate various things for the board members. She had never been so aware of her body. Her nipples were more tender than normal, brushing with exquisite friction against her sturdy cotton bra. She'd never think about condoms and sex in the same way again. *Never*.

By the end of the day, Alice needed a drink. Too bad if Steven didn't approve of women and alcohol. Besides he'd given up all rights when he'd walked away yesterday. He wasn't there to see, and in this day of firsts spent in the Sloan rabbit hole, what did a few more steps on the wild side matter?

# Chapter 3

Instead of returning home to the bed and breakfast on Griffin Street, Alice turned right onto the main street of Sloan and marched through the front doors of The Thirsty Cricket pub before her courage deserted her. Outside, darkness started to fall since they'd worked until seven. Her stomach rumbled in a plaintive protest. Food. She'd have dinner here along with a drink to calm her ruffled nerves.

She bowled up to the bar and waited for the barman to finish serving a customer. She stared at the array of bottles and ignored the drunken chat-up lines from the table of men over to her right.

Elvis sang about being someone's teddy bear. His husky voice poured from the loud speakers and wrapped around her like a comforting cloak. Her first visit to a real pub rather than a café, and one without Steven.

A day of firsts turning into a night of firsts. The sense she'd strayed into a rabbit hole with a parallel universe heightened.

"Gin and tonic please." Alice climbed onto a barstool and handed the man a ten-dollar note when he placed the drink on a cardboard coaster in front of her. After a sniff of her drink, she took a cautious sip. It tasted clean and crisp with a hint of lemon. Very refreshing. It cooled her parched mouth, and when she rolled the glass against her cheek, it acted like an ice pack, a diffuser for the heat in her face. She took another sip then another until only ice cubes remained. She set the glass down and replayed her extraordinary day.

Condoms.

The flush in her cheeks returned as she recalled James asking her opinion of the X-100.

"Like another?" The barman straightened from stocking the small chiller behind the bar.

Alice considered it for seconds before nodding. The second drink slid down as easily as the first. Steven would have kittens if he saw her at a bar. Not that he had a say how she spent her time. He'd given up that right when he'd walked away without a backward glance the previous day. Alice scowled about his pompous, conservative attitude, and fifteen minutes later, she ordered a third gin and tonic along with a whiskey. The amber color looked pretty but the strong, peaty scent gave her pause. Cautiously, she sniffed it again, screwing up courage to try the drink.

Time to try new things and experience sin.

No place for hesitation.

Alice tipped back her head and swallowed a healthy mouthful. It burned all the way down her throat with a blaze that spread through her belly. A harsh gasp of shock escaped and her eyes watered. Fire water indeed.

"Hello, are you on your own? Mind if I join you?"

Her head whipped around and her mouth fell open for long seconds before she realized she was gaping in an unattractive manner. Her teeth clicked together with an audible clunk.

James. Mr. James Dangerous AKA Hottie.

Alice's eyes widened even as she struggled for breath. Potent stuff that whiskey. Her heart pounded in an erratic manner. After experiencing the same irregular thud for most of the day, she should have become used to it. She hadn't, and each time the sensation created more havoc, especially when an infuriating internal shimmy accompanied the *thud-thud-thud*.

This man drove her to distraction.

She couldn't even indulge in the sinful pastime of drinking without his intrusion. Maybe she should rip open her suit jacket, her blouse and heavy-duty bra and offer him her body.

She groaned as the idea registered. As if she'd have the guts to offer herself to Mr. Hottie. Alice glared at the remains of the whiskey on the bar in front of her. What was she doing here?

Steven was right. She wasn't cut out to inherit a condom company.

"You had enough fun at my...my expense to...day." She formed her words carefully. Funny how much energy it took to talk. "What do...do you th-ink of the X-100, Ms. Beasley?"

He had the effrontery to grin. "You're in the condom business now. You need to get used to our discussions."

"Are they always so...so frank?" Alice avoided his gaze. The wretch looked so pretty she squirmed with the urge to touch. And his sexy dimple...

She'd have to deal with him if she wanted her inheritance. She was in this for the money, she reminded herself. Yeah, she admitted it. Six months. She could handle six months but only if she kept her distance from this disconcerting man.

James shrugged and gestured at the bartender for a beer. "It's a serious business. All the board members have invested money and want to make the best decisions for the company." He watched her until she felt as naked as a bug under a microscope, his mouth curved in an infuriating grin.

"It's not my fault this is all new. Anyone would find the frank discussions cause for embarrassment."

His eyes narrowed. "How new?"

A pregnant pause highlighted the question. Alice gnawed her bottom lip and winced at the tenderness while she considered how to answer.

"I'm an almost virgin." The words burst from her, and horrified, she picked up her glass and slurped down the remnants of whiskey. It didn't taste much better this time and a burn seared her soft palate. She coughed and spluttered.

"Go easy. You'll choke if you're not careful. Here, have some beer. It will soothe your throat."

Alice accepted the glass of beer and chugged it down. "That tastes good."

"I'll get another one," he said, his tone wry when she lifted his glass to her mouth again. "How the hell can you be an almost virgin? You either are or you aren't."

Horrified, she gawked at him. Oh my goodness. She'd confessed an inner secret.

James gestured at the barman and ordered another beer before turning back to her with a grin that lit his blue eyes and made her want to test the dimple in his cheek. "So what's the answer?"

"I refuse to tell." Why would she bare her soul to him? He was a stranger. A sexy stranger, who if rumor could be believed—as per this morning's paper—had a parade of beautiful, leggy women strutting through his bedroom. Alice glanced at her cloth-covered knees with a rueful sigh. No way did she qualify in the leg department.

James Bates wasn't the right man for someone wanting security. She had to ignore his pretty face and sexy smile. His tempting muscles and cute dimple.

She shook herself and almost fell off her barstool. James slipped his arm around her waist, and she shrugged him off. She had a boyfriend.

Steven.

She drummed the fingers of her right hand on the bar. Steven had refused to speak to her when she'd rung him at midday. They'd dated for over a year and had so much in common, but she couldn't believe his tantrum and now his sulky attitude. She wanted—needed—a partnership. Someone to rely on and a man who held the same values as her. A secure future with no financial hiccups. A partner who stood at her side—no matter what happened.

She picked up one of her glasses, peered at the dregs and placed it back on the bar. The gin and tonic looked more promising. Steven had failed her, and it hurt. No, his lack of support irked her.

James brushed her arm as he shifted on his barstool and every one of her senses went on high alert, diverted from her Steven problem. She smelled his citrus and spice aftershave and heard each one of his deep even breaths. A heavy sigh drifted past her lips as her gaze zapped back to study his sexy mouth and his sparkly blue eyes...

He was so pretty.

Oh boy. Eyes front. There was something wrong with her. Every inch of her skin tingled and her mind drifted to sex with alarming ease. She consoled herself with the fact that anything sexual rated as work-related. That helped with her guilt except she kept fantasizing about sex with James. Close and very personal sex.

Somewhere, somehow during the day, she'd shoved Steven aside and replaced him with Mr. Hottie. Her actions reminded her of a desperate woman. Heck, she was a wanton woman, a little voice in her head whispered.

Alice straightened and wobbled on her barstool. Her shoulder and the outward curve of her breast brushed James' arm before she grabbed the bar and righted herself. The friction between their bodies set off a series of pleasurable explosions inside her. Despite one audible pant, she attempted calm and cool. Okay, that had never happened when Steven touched her.

Alice gulped and risked a glance at James. Warmth and heat radiated from his expression, and she wanted to bask in the masculine attention. Then she noticed the twinkle in his blue eyes and indignation surfaced.

"You're laughing at me." Alice drained the last of her gin and tonic and set the glass on the bar with a distinct clunk.

"No, I'm not," he said. "What you see is admiration. Not every woman would take work at a condom company in her stride."

"Oh." Alice peered closer but his eyes moved across his face. All three of them. She winced as her head whirled. With a shocked gasp, she screwed her eyes shut before opening them again.

"Are you okay?"

"Did you know you have three eyes?" Alice blinked. "All blue like the sky. And two noses. What on earth do you do with two noses? What do you do when you have a cold? How do you know which one to blow first?"

James placed his arm around her shoulders. "Your parents named you well," he murmured, a chuckle underlying his words. "You're very curious."

"Will you come back to the bed and breakfast with me?"

"Sure, I'll walk you home. Make sure you get there safely."

Alice attempted to focus on his middle eye. "No, I mean I'm tired of wondering what the fuss is about. I want to learn the mysteries of sex."

James spluttered before he looked back at her. "That's a bad idea."

She puckered her lips into a pout, a seductive one, she hoped. It was difficult to concentrate with that number of eyes scrutinizing her. She had an argument ready to refute him. "An owner of a condom company should know how to work the apparatus." She nodded and regretted it since the movement doubled the number of eyes. "There's something wrong with your face. It keeps sprouting eyes. You've got six."

His mouth twitched. "Do you drink often?"

"Waz that got to do with eyes?"

"Absolutely nothing," he agreed. "Are you ready to go home now?"

Alice checked her drinks. No whiskey left. No gin left. But the glasses. Ye gods. They had gone forth and multiplied. There were four of the blighters. She shuddered, the unpleasant gulp of the whiskey still a recent memory. "Finished."

"Let's get you home then." James jumped off his barstool and waited at her side.

When Alice attempted to emulate his feat, she teetered, toppling sideways and ending up with her nose pressed into a muscular chest.

"You smell of lemon but you're not prickly like a tree." She pulled away to study him. "I'm sure you'll feel nice against my naked skin."

A man clapped him over the shoulders. "You're in there, James."

Alice frowned at the bearded man who spoke. All four of his eyes winked and that beard grew out of control. With fierce concentration, she leaned on James, a firm grip on his arm for balance while she savored the play of hard muscles beneath her breasts.

James sucked in a hasty breath as Alice wriggled one warm hand beneath the collar of his shirt. The minx was as drunk as a lord, and so, so sexy with it. Talk about temptation on two wobbly legs.

Ignoring the regulars and their smart-arse comments, he steered her out the front door of the pub, conscious of how well she fit in his arms. She smelled great—of cinnamon and whiskey. After an afternoon with her, he appreciated her intelligence. When he'd seen her disappear into the pub, he'd made two calls and joined her. In the back of his mind, he'd hoped to move from business acquaintances to intimate friends or at least nudge the relationship in that direction. He hadn't figured on squiring a drunken female to safety.

A virgin. Almost virgin.

He wondered at the story behind the almost bit. Why the hell had she told him that? Now his imagination worked overtime while he pondered the color of her nipples and how her breasts would fill his hands. Not that he could do anything tonight. His cock lengthened, exerting a clear opinion on the matter, unhappy with the gentlemanly notions crowding his mind.

But hell, no way could he take advantage of a woman in this condition. Despite his reputation, he had principles, a code of conduct. He snorted. And wouldn't Ms. Knowall fall over in shock if she discovered this truth.

James propelled her from the Cricket into the main street. Night had fallen and streetlights lit the cobblestone footpath. Apart from the corner dairy, which did a brisk trade in their small games room, the shops had closed for the evening. A group of teenagers lingered outside, the telltale haze of cigarette smoke giving away their purpose. Although he knew them, James steered Alice past with nothing more than a curt nod. He ushered her down the street past the post office and the florist's with its dramatic spring window display.

The Children of Nature shop highlighted baby-wear in their window. A snort emerged and for a few seconds he considered sprinkling the footpath with condoms. He chuckled. Ah, perhaps not. After dodging a couple outside the jeweler's, he

35

guided Alice past the police station and headed toward Alice's Griffin Street accommodation.

"Can you skip?" Alice demanded.

"No."

"I wanna skip. Never done it before." Alice spoiled her dignified reply with a loud hiccup. "Wanna skip." She struggled.

"James Bates, hands off that woman."

Oh god. His mother. They'd almost made it to Griffin Street. Why couldn't she have waited for a few minutes longer before taking the dog for a walk? Dredging up patience, he turned to face her. Gypsy, his mother's dog, growled low at the back of his throat. The fluffy white rat had never taken to him.

His mother scowled. "Unhand her this instant."

Alice chose that moment to come to find her tongue again. "No, no," she chided, waving an unsteady finger through the air. She almost whipped off his mother's nose. "I might fall over. I'm almost a virgin, you know. We're going to my place to take care of that wee matter."

James groaned. His mother already considered him a wastrel. She'd told him often enough he was a disgrace to the family and should emulate his older lawyer sister.

"James!"

"Think what you like, Mother. Nothing I say will sway you." James tried to keep the bitterness from his voice and failed. Without another word, he directed Alice down the street. His mother's hard stare bored into his back until they turned the corner onto Griffin Street. One more transgression to add to the long list his mother kept on his behalf. James sighed.

The old Victorian house where Alice had chosen to stay was halfway down the street. He opened the white gate and they ambled up the footpath to the front door. The owners—Jake and Lindy Redcliff—kept the place immaculate. Tidy beds of red petunias and white pansies contrasted with the duck-egg blue paint of the house.

"Do you have your key?"

"In my pocket. Lucy Locket had a pocket, ya know? Kept her key there."

"Clever girl." She made him laugh, but he'd bet she wouldn't chuckle much tomorrow morning. "Which room are you in?"

"Sunny one." She blinked like a sleepy owl and pressed even more firmly against his side.

James assumed the Sunflower room. Luckily, he knew the location since he'd stayed in the same room for two weeks when he'd first arrived back in Sloan.

"Alice. Alice, are you awake?"

"No," she whispered.

With a soft chuckle, James searched for a pocket and found her key in the second one he tried. He unlocked the door and maneuvered her inside. After shutting the door, he scooped her up in his arms and headed to the Sunflower room. The stairs creaked a loud protest. James froze, positive Jake and Lindy would cry intruder. When it didn't happen, he continued up the stairs, glad they'd left night lights on for her.

James reached Alice's room and fumbled the door open. He shouldered his way inside and flipped on the light before closing the door.

"Can you stand on your own?"

"Course I can," Alice warbled. She lurched forward and almost fell flat on her face.

James lifted her off her feet and dropped her on top of the white lacy bed cover. Lindy had changed the room, the décor more feminine since he'd stayed here.

"I'd better go."

"No, you can't leave yet." Her pink lips formed a pout. "I need you." Her voice rose.

"Okay." James agreed to stay and prayed she didn't wake Jake and Lindy. In all honesty, he didn't think they'd mind, but he'd prefer not to experience their reactions when a clean getaway would work better. "I'll sit beside the bed for a while."

Alice glowered at him then kicked off her shoes, pulled back the covers and lay full length on the bed. "My head's all a spin."

"Close your eyes and breathe. It might help if you lie on your side." But it probably wouldn't. Hopefully she wouldn't throw up. James covered her, watching while she followed his instructions and relaxed when he heard her soft sigh. A clock ticked and he closed his eyes. He'd stay until she fell asleep.

The crick in his neck woke him. James winced, coming to full wakefulness and stretching out the kinks. A soft snore drew his attention and early morning light shone through the net curtains. What the hell? The previous evening rushed back to him.

*Alice.* He'd only intended to sit with her until she'd gone to sleep, but he must've dozed off. James rose from the chair and stretched his hands above his head.

The figure in the bed stirred and woke quicker than he had. "James, I'm still dressed. I'm still an almost virgin, aren't I?"

Her question rubbed him the wrong way as did her hopeful expression. "What sort of man do you think I am?" Perhaps she'd listened to the rumors.

Alice stared at him with a solemn expression. "A sexy one."

A surprised laugh escaped. "Why me? What about your boyfriend?" James dropped back into the chair. Despite good behavior last night, he'd seen a little more of her body. She was curvy in the old-fashioned film star kind of way. Large breasts, a trim waist and curvy hips for a man to hold on to. A pocket Venus. "What the hell is an almost virgin?"

"Steven doesn't enjoy sex. He has done nothing but kiss me. Doesn't seem to like that either. You have more experience with women." Alice's gaze shifted across his face before drifting lower, devouring him with an innocent hunger that made his cock rear to attention. "Besides he doesn't like me anymore."

James reacted to her even though she'd pissed him off with the implication he slept with every woman who walked into his life. Or maybe he was extra touchy because of Ms. Knowall's frequent digs at his love life in her column. He led a productive life, dammit, and he liked it fine without changes. He could do what he wanted, when he wanted. Footloose and unencumbered remained his motto. Who the hell wanted settled and stagnated?

He stood and prowled across a blue Persian rug until he reached the bed. "Are you sure I'm not the big, bad wolf? You've heard the rumors about me, right?" He took his time, moving nearer and nearer to her until he lay on ruffled lemon sheets.

"No." Her voice sounded a trifle uncertain now and he watched her teeth tug at her bottom lip. If she kept that up, it would soon look swollen and puffy, as if she'd kissed a man for a long time.

The need to make it so surged within him, biting with an intense ache. James leaned over her, caging Alice between his arms and the bed. He closed the distance between them, the beat of his heart loud to his own ears. He might not be a saint, but he had a conscience, his own set of morals. One last chance. "Are you sure you want this?"

# Chapter 4

"Yes." Alice swallowed. This close, James appeared big and strong and not as tame as she'd prefer. "Yes, I'm sure."

What would her friend Jennifer do in the same situation? Something devious, but what? *Quick, decide.* She couldn't dilly-dally here all day because he'd leave.

She'd have to go to the restroom at some stage. After a fight to free herself from the constraints of the sheets and his muscular arms, she wriggled one hand from captivity. The force of her struggle slammed it into his collarbone.

He winced but when he tried to back away, her fingers curved around his shoulder and clung. His scent tickled her nose and made her think of the outdoors—trees, grass and trickling streams all tangled up with lemon. His body warmth seared right through the fabric of his shirt and the man froze at her touch.

Good? Bad?

Alice wasn't certain, but she let her hand slide toward the open collar of his white shirt. Her fingers slipped underneath the fabric and met warm flesh. Her breath caught at her daring. She'd never been like Jennifer, one to grab what she wanted from life. Alice inhaled, steadying her attack of nerves.

All that would change, and soon.

"Let me go," she demanded.

"This is not a good idea. I'm not nice when it comes to sex."

What did he mean not nice? Did he beat his women?

She peeped at him between lowered lashes and decided no. Perhaps he meant he enjoyed unusual positions. Did she need to purchase a sex manual and hit the research trail? She'd noticed a bookstore on the main street. No wait, the internet would present less of the embarrassment factor.

With a toss of her head, one hard enough to make her hair swish across her forehead, she licked her lips.

"Mad, bad and dangerous to know." Alice's voice entered sultry territory. An alien had taken over her body. There was no other explanation. "Take off your shirt so I can touch you."

James stared at her, his blue eyes dark and unfathomable. Finally, he levered away from the bed.

She held her breath, afraid to move. If he walked away, she didn't know what she'd do. Hopefully, the alien inside her body had a plan of attack should the need arise.

He stood by the bed, his hesitation obvious. Then, in a flurry of movement, he stripped off his shirt.

Alice inspected him, frissons of excitement tugging her breasts, her nether region, her entire body. That would be pussy, the alien inside snapped. Don't act prissily. Men don't like prudes. They want real women.

James continued undressing. With rapid movements, he stripped off his jeans and black briefs. He kicked them aside and stood in a statue-like pose.

A naked man.

Oh. My. God.

He prowled toward her.

Alice gulped, her gaze zeroing in on his erection. It bobbed up and down, only stopping when he halted by the bed, mere inches from her head.

"Now that you've got me naked, what do you intend to do with me?" he asked in a sexy drawl.

A challenge.

Alice glanced away from the thick cock. Good question. Her gaze drifted back to the veins beneath the surface and the darker-colored head.

Without warning, it felt as though someone had sucked every particle of oxygen from the room.

"Why don't I give you a hint? For this to go any further, both of us need to remove our clothes. We can't have down and dirty sex if you hide under there."

Now that was a dig at her. Alice flung back the sheet that covered her bottom half. She still wore her black skirt, her matching top and black cotton socks. She stood and peeled off her socks.

"That it? All I get to see is your toes?"

Alice grimaced and, despite a tremble of fingers, undid the top three buttons of her shirt. It gaped to show the generous curves of her breasts. Doubt struck hard and shot terror through her veins. What would he think? Ever since her early teenage years, males had fixated on her breasts because they were so big.

It was the reason she dressed in layers with clothes that disguised the size of her chest. It was why she'd accepted Steven when he'd asked her out on a date. He hadn't studied her breasts first. She laughed, some of her humor directed at herself. Steven didn't like to look at all. Something ironic in that.

"Changed your mind?"

"No." Alice unfastened the last buttons and shrugged the baggy black shirt off her shoulder, baring her sturdy bra to his gaze. Without hesitation, Alice peeled her black skirt over her hips. With a deft twist of her wrist, she flicked her bra closure and removed it. For an instant, she paused then shucked her panties. After a deep breath, Alice straightened. She stood upright, her shoulders back so James saw her clearly.

His expression didn't change for a long, drawn-out second. Then his brows rose. "Is there a problem?"

"Um, I need to go to the bathroom." She couldn't maintain his gaze and scanned the room. Two suitcases sat in the far corner. Ah, her clothes. Thank goodness the lost case had arrived. The courier had promised her he'd recheck the depot. They must have found it. Her gaze flitted back to James and away.

"I'll be here when you come back."

Alice cast another doubtful glance in his direction before scuttling to her en suite and shutting the door. He'd seen her naked. The thought ran through her mind in a constant loop while she took care of business. What if he left? What if one look at her naked body had appalled him?

She grimaced as she washed her hands and cleaned her teeth. Her head ached a little. A hasty breath later, she opened the door.

He was still there.

Relieved, she closed the distance between them and let her breasts brush his chest. He'd had his chance. It was too late for him to flee now. Delight zapped her, a jolt of pleasure as her nipples dragged against the muscled planes of his chest.

James shuddered, grasped her shoulders and drew her even closer. "Hell."

"Something wrong?" He'd seen her now. If he left, she'd have to kill him.

"Why do you hide your stunning body in those godawful clothes?"

43

"People gawk at my breasts. They don't see *me*. I hated my teenage years and my appearance." She gestured at her chest.

"So you hid."

"Self-protection."

James lowered his head. Alice closed her eyes and puckered up, her heart pounding so hard she could barely hear herself think. Their mouths slid together and clung. She sighed, loving the hardness of his lips as they shifted against hers.

He pulled back and smiled down at her. "Open your mouth for me."

Alice puckered up again, rounding her lips so they parted. "Like this?"

He chuckled. "Relax your lips. I won't hurt you. Kissing is enjoyable. Pleasurable."

"Prove it," Alice dared.

With a laugh, he cupped her face and dipped his head to nibble her lips. Alice attempted to relax but it wasn't easy with his naked body pressed against hers. His tongue slid over her bottom lip, then his teeth bit down. She gasped, and he took advantage, coaxing and urging her to open her mouth farther. His tongue slipped inside, teasing, sliding against hers.

Kissing Steven had never thrilled her like this. Her breasts ached even though he'd hardly touched them. She shuddered, aware the best was yet to come.

Without warning, he swung her into his arms and walked over to the bed. Alice was so startled she didn't have time to squeak. She bounced on the bed before James leaned over and fixed her body in place.

"Will I get in trouble if I pay attention to your breasts?" James kissed the corner of her mouth, the tip of her nose.

"Just do the same thing you'd do with any of your women," she said, striving for an airy tone when acute embarrassment filled her. No one had scrutinized her chest like this since age thirteen when she'd fallen into her friend's swimming pool at a party. To this day, she didn't wear T-shirts.

James froze, the rub of her luscious breasts against his chest a kind of torture. For the second time she'd implied he had too much experience. He studied her innocent expression and released his indignation as he took in the sights. With a finger, he traced the base of one breast before following the feathering of veins beneath the surface. Not one freckle. She possessed skin the color of rich cream, and he wanted to lap every inch. Her breast quivered at his touch, her pretty pink nipple pulling tight. The whisper of pleasure from her lips made his cock perk to attention.

Hell, she was beautiful, from her full, creamy breasts to her slim waist and flaring hips. Not fashionable, but her body would make any red-blooded man howl with joy.

His affronted mood subsided as he concentrated on her. He trailed his hand across her collarbone, savoring the petal-soft skin. Desire filled him plus the need to give her pleasure and make her first time with him one she'd remember. Selfishly, he didn't intend to give her another opportunity to say no. He'd tried to do the right thing, to warn her and his conscience remained clear.

She was willing.

She wanted him, and that was a powerful aphrodisiac.

"If there's anything you don't enjoy, let me know." His voice emerged gritty while his cock tightened with pure lust. Fighting the urgency thrumming through him, he splayed his fingers across her breasts to lightly knead and pluck her nipples.

Alice jerked before stilling, her eyes wide. The reaction told him she didn't believe she was a treasure worthy of exploration. James bit back a groan. He could explore sexuality with this woman for months, for years, and never get tired. A frown surfaced at the oddball notion.

He wasn't settling down with anyone. Damn if he'd stay in Sloan so his mother could sneer at him whenever they met. He had no idea why he'd returned to Sloan anyway—some misbegotten idea his family would welcome him back into the fold.

"Is something wrong?" Her voice held anxiety, the emotion underlined in her golden-brown eyes.

James summoned a reassuring grin and leaned over to blow on her nipple. Large, to match her breasts, they puckered and colored to a rosy pink. James licked around the circumference of her nipple, testing her reaction. She took a hasty breath and held it for long seconds, her golden eyes wide and uncertain.

"You're beautiful," James murmured, the reassurance she needed to gain confidence easy for him to give. "So responsive." He blew on her other nipple and watched her reaction. "See?" Unable to deny himself any longer he drew her nipple into his mouth.

Alice jerked and issued a soft moan.

James used one hand to tease a nipple while his tongue swirled over the other one. Another low moan sounded, and her hands clamped on his shoulders. Fingernails dug into his skin.

His mouth quirked and he let go with an audible pop. "Did you like that?"

Alice seemed to consider her answer before she replied. "Yes."

"What did you feel? And where did you feel it?" A test. James waited to see what she'd say. A test of his willpower too. He kissed and nibbled her breast while maintaining eye contact. An easy-to-read expression shimmered across her face and she clamped her bottom lip between her teeth. He couldn't wait to see her reaction when he kissed her intimately. "Alice?" he prompted.

She released her lip and moistened the plump curve with her tongue. James savored the innocent gesture, and his gut jumped with awareness. Innocent but oh-so sexy.

His.

Awe filled him. Possessiveness, but reality followed swiftly.

Hell, had he thought that? This—whatever what might be between them—must remain a temporary thing.

Yeah, temporary.

He shook himself to emphasize the fact. "Alice?"

"When you," she paused, her cheeks going pink, "sucked, the sensation traveled all the way down there." She gestured with her hand.

"Show me," he whispered, intent on pushing her from her comfort zone.

Alice hesitated while gathering her courage. Her pale hand crept from his shoulder and skimmed across her quivering belly to halt half an inch from the short curls guarding her femininity.

"Go on."

Her fingers moved downward. Her legs parted.

James smiled. Innocent and sexy. That was test enough for now. He'd take it from here. He slid his hand down her torso, following the same path as her fingers. But he didn't stop. Instead, he parted her legs farther, his fingers skimming across her swollen folds in an exploration of her moist flesh. Her scent rose, teasing him. James inhaled and couldn't resist a pass over her clit. The tiny bud peeked from its hood and pulsed beneath his caress. Soon he'd drive into her sweet flesh. His cock jolted, and he rocked against her upper thigh, teasing himself and pushing his need higher.

Alice's hand slid across his shoulders, hesitant and a little shy. Her hand slipped downward and she seemed to gain confidence when he didn't protest. Alice squeezed one buttock and earned a quick kiss.

"Please," she whispered. "Please, I need you."

"Where? Tell me. Describe what you want," he ordered, forgetting he'd decided to take control.

She worried her bottom lip, her brandy-colored eyes apprehensive.

"If you don't tell me, I might do something you hate."

Alice hesitated for so long he thought he'd pushed her too hard and fast. Finally she released her abused lip and the pale column of her throat moved in a swallow. "I want to explore your body." Her warm hand squeezed his arse again, the innocent touch reverberating throughout his body and mind.

Giving. So bloody giving.

Her first lover had rocks in his head.

His pulse thumped as he rolled off her. He positioned himself on his back, an offer of free access and silent permission to study him as she wanted.

Trembling fingers skimmed his stubble-covered jaw, dipped into his dimple and traced his mouth. James parted his lips a fraction and sucked her forefinger inside. Her gasp was loud. Startled. And it made him want to laugh. Instead, he drew on her finger and cupped her head. The silky strands of hair tickled his palm, bringing a desire to touch and stroke and soothe away her jumpy virginal nerves. His tongue smoothed across her fingernail and ran across the delicate skin between fingertip and nail. Alice gasped again, golden glints shining in her eyes. He captured her gaze with his and released her finger. James nipped her earlobe and surprised a yelp out of her.

"Ouch." She pulled away to finger her ear. "I thought I was in charge."

"That can be arranged." After brushing another kiss across her lips, he kissed the tip of one breast and glided his hands across her rib cage.

James smiled when she plucked up the courage to curl her hand around his cock. Her fingers traced the flared head, her curiosity endearing and arousing. She explored his tender balls and wrapped her fingers around his shaft. She pumped, focusing so hard her tongue poked between her lips. The innocent exploration dragged a soft curse from him.

"Enough. This is torture," he added before she put a different interpretation on his words. Discouragement was the last thing he intended.

He took a moment to kiss her again. Good girl. She learned fast, opening her mouth to him in participation rather than her previous passive behavior. Their tongues tangled. James felt the rapid beat of her heart, saw the flush of rosy arousal on her face and chest. He wanted to go slow, to arouse her, teasing until she throbbed in need, until they both ached for the conclusion.

But it wasn't going down that way. Not today.

At least they wanted the same thing.

James pushed one leg between her thighs, silently indicating she should part her legs. So beautiful. So sexy. He dipped his head to nuzzle her breasts, moving over Alice and guiding his cock to her pussy. Moist warmth met him as he pushed the tip of his cock into her heat.

"Fuck." James froze, a heavy jolt of disbelief coloring his voice. He jerked away from her, horror in his stare.

Through his dismay, James saw her flinch as if he'd struck her. Another abrupt move on his part and she'd run for the hills surrounding Sloan.

He cleared his throat. "I don't suppose you have a condom?"

A surprised burst of laughter bubbled from her, diluting the alarm he'd seen seconds earlier. "A condom?"

"It's not funny," he said stiffly. His body ached for release. Without a condom, he'd have to take care of the matter himself when he wanted the satisfaction that only a woman's snug pussy would ease. He'd end up with blue balls for hours if he couldn't have her now. His hand just wouldn't be the same.

"You work for a condom company, right?" Her breasts jiggled in a distracting manner. "Manager, isn't it?"

"Give it a rest." A tinge of heat settled at the tips of his ears. "If you're offering sex, shouldn't you have condoms?" More than a trace of accusation shaded his words.

"Oh sure. All I've seen is the X-100 in its inflated glory." She giggled, her cute button nose wrinkling at the same time. "I guess we'll have to do this later."

James scowled. "You realize my balls will ache for hours." He dragged a hand through his dark hair while irritation simmered inside him. Yeah, there was a funny side to this but he didn't appreciate it at present.

Alice stirred beneath his tense body, brushing against the sensitized tip of his cock. The scent of aroused female filled his senses. Her silky-soft skin tempted. James groaned, knowing he'd act the gentleman.

No need for both of them to leave the room frustrated.

He trailed his fingers across her rib cage and leaned over to lick the fragrant skin below her belly button.

"You make me feel hot," she whispered when he glanced up to see her reaction. "Inside." She pointed vaguely to the juncture of her thighs. "I've never felt this way before."

"When you said almost, what do you mean?"

She squeezed her eyes closed. "I don't want to talk about it."

James hated that a man had hurt her and pricked her confidence. Anger bled away some of his frustration. The mystery man had pricked something else as well, but he'd done a piss-poor job of it. He'd do his best to boost her self-assurance. And, he promised himself, he'd prize the story out of her somehow.

He rimmed her bellybutton with his tongue before prodding the tiny indentation. Suggestively. Yeah, he had to thrust into something or he'd self-combust.

"That tickles," she protested.

"I live to annoy." According to his mother and sister.

James levered his body upward and parted her legs so he could slide between. After initial resistance, she followed his non-verbal instructions, but her brandy-flecked eyes held uncertainty.

"Know this, sweetheart." His voice contained anger toward the man who had wounded her confidence. "I won't hurt you. I like women."

"You have experience. That's why I asked you to...to..."

Irritation swept him at her words. Why did people harp about his reputation? He wasn't a bloody playboy. James bit back the sarcastic retort burning the tip of his tongue. Nothing wrong with not wanting to settle down. It might be a habit for his family members to marry in their early twenties, but he wanted none of the tradition. He hadn't loved Carol—too bad if their parents had wanted to cement their close friendship.

James pushed aside memories of the spirited arguments to concentrate on Alice. She deserved the attention. Even though she'd judged him the same as everyone else.

He pressed a kiss on her upper thigh.

Alice jumped. "What are you going to do?"

"Pleasuring you, my dear." He winked before returning to the task at hand.

Pleasure. Alice bit her lip to stop the escape of a loud groan. From the second her clothes had hit the ground she'd enjoyed every touch. Oh, there was a little embarrassment, but that was to be expected. It wasn't every day a girl found herself up close and personal with a genuine bad boy.

James planted a kiss on the inside of her thigh. Her heart thudded. He parted her legs even farther until air washed over her private parts. She swallowed, and her tongue flicked out to moisten dry lips.

"You're beautiful," he said in a husky voice. He glanced up at her and smiled, but she knew he wasn't referring to her face. Pleased but shy at the knowledge he'd studied her so intimately, heat crawled across her face and down her chest.

"I'll take your word for it."

"Haven't you ever looked at yourself?" He sounded surprised.

"No." How the heck was she meant to do that?

"You should. We'll do that another day."

Oh my. A second session with the bad boy. *Go ahead, bad boy. Make my day.* Alice giggled.

"Something funny? Am I not doing this right?" He used his fingers to part her folds and leaned closer to blow a stream of warm air across her exposed flesh.

Alice shuddered. "No complaints. Please continue." She did not understand where this mouthy wanton inhabiting her body had come from, but she liked her.

The stream of warm air centered on an achy part. Her clitoris? *Interesting.*

His fingers trailed the length of her cleft, following the same path the burst of warm air had taken. He caressed, his fingers dragging on her flesh. A sharp jolt of energy speared through her. She gasped, desperate for a repeat of the delightful sensation.

James grinned up at her. "You like that?"

"Yes." No point lying. A blind man could tell she was out of her league and going on instinct.

"There's more."

*Oh goody. Bring it on.* Alice closed her eyes to concentrate. His fingers moved downward and liquid arousal broke the silence. Her eyes flew open in consternation.

"You're soaked." He smiled. "You want me."

His words held masculine pride and satisfaction, so she waited for his next move.

His finger dipped into the mouth of her pussy. When he removed his finger, she wanted to protest. Just when things were getting interesting.

Without warning, he slipped both hands beneath her butt and lifted her hips. Her legs gravitated to his shoulders. Startled, she wondered what James would do next. Her heart thudded against her breastbone and raced faster as he lowered his mouth. He licked the length of her cleft, following the same path as his finger. Alice shivered, shocked rigid but honest enough to admit his touch thrilled her.

Oh, she knew about oral sex.

In theory.

Theory was light years away from practical.

The return journey of his tongue and lips shot spasms of enjoyment charging through her body. She tensed, ready for more. There had to be more, right? Then his tongue teased an achy spot. He lingered. Teased a little more.

Her clitoris. Yep, she was positive when pleasure surged, a soft wave pulsed deep inside her. But instead of ending, James continued to tease her swollen flesh. With considerable skill too. *Oh yes. Please. Right there. Don't move. Continue. Please.*

To her relief, he followed her silent directions. The sensation deepened. A few more pulses then the pleasure swelled and she soared. One more swipe of his tongue and she split apart, the wonderful sensation fracturing into a series of rapid waves.

"Ooh," she murmured as she floated back into her body—because this had been a magnificent out-of-body experience—and relaxed like a cooked spaghetti noodle.

"Was it good for you?" James asked.

Alice belatedly remembered that she had and he hadn't come. A tactful answer required. Guys, she'd heard from various gossipy sources, became a little tetchy when it came to sex and not getting any. She stared at his erect penis. It looked large and red and bad-tempered. It gave an angry twitch as she gawked.

"Um..." Alice glanced up to scan James' face. "I...yes..." She stared. The man's face screwed up as if he suffered great pain or else he—

The wretch was laughing at her. She tapped him on one bulging biceps. "Yes, it was good for me," she snapped. "Why are you laughing?"

A tentative knock sounded on the door and his amusement faded. They glanced at each other in silent communication, Alice wrinkling her nose in answer to his raised brow.

"Alice? Are you awake? Breakfast is ready."

She stared at the wooden door in horror. Had she made a lot of noise? Her gaze darted to James and he pantomimed for her to answer.

"I'm up. Won't be long," Alice called out. She strove for a woman-of-the-world tone, but her reply fell into the feeble, scared zone. It must have reassured Lindy because she heard receding footsteps before silence fell. She turned to stare at James.

He shook his head, a rueful grin on his lips. "Well, Ms. Beasley. You're not the only one who's up. A fine mess you've got us in this time."

"Why is it my fault? I've heard you're a playboy and a cad." The minute she said the words she wanted to take them back.

"Ah, you've read Ms. Knowall's column. You're right. I am a playboy and a cad." He stood and picked up his clothes, dressing with an elegance she admired. "You should remember that and stay away from me."

"I'm sorry." She'd said the wrong thing.

"No problem. I'll see you at work." He strode over to the door, opened it and stepped into the passage. A soft click sounded when he closed it.

Alice heard footsteps and the murmur of voices. Color swept to her cheeks as she imagined what Lindy would think. If inheriting a condom company hadn't already ruined her reputation, then she'd done the job now by letting James Bates, sexy bad boy, spend the night in her bedroom.

# Chapter 5

Alice climbed from the bed, self-conscious of her nakedness. Avoiding her reflection in the mirror, she scuttled to the small en suite and jumped under the shower, letting the water pour over her hair and face. Five minutes later, dressed in a gray trouser suit, she made her way into the kitchen for breakfast.

The wooden table was set for three with floral placemats and coordinated napkins. A posy of spring flowers in the center of the table added to the Victorian theme. The rich scent of coffee floated in the air. Lindy Redcliff stood at the stove, spatula in hand, humming along to a top-forty hit. Jake, her husband, sat at the table and had already started on his breakfast.

"Morning," she mumbled. "Sorry I'm late."

Jake glanced up from his scrambled eggs. "We know why you overslept. You've been doing the wild thing with Sloan's playboy."

"Jake!" Lindy put a world of remonstration into her husband's name, but it didn't dampen his smirk.

"No," Alice said. "We were discussing work." The first thing that came into her mind.

Jake's lips quirked. "Condoms. Care for some eggs and toast. Muesli?"

Alice met his gaze with difficulty. "I'm not hungry." The truth. She'd lost her appetite. "And yes, we discussed condoms as part of our business meeting. Fancy Free sells condoms."

Jake set his knife and fork across the center of his plate. He lifted his wrist to check his watch. "Hmm, I hope your company pays overtime for such a long meeting."

"Leave the poor girl alone or we'll lose our guest." Lindy propelled Alice to an empty chair. "Coffee? A package arrived for you."

Alice nodded, afraid to speak for fear of blurting out something to cause more embarrassment. Her face emanated heat, which, given her sudden leap to femme fatale status, she should expect. If only her brain would get with the program and give her the nous to act cool as a cucumber as a good femme fatale should. She snorted. Yeah, like that would happen. Her friend Jennifer was the poised one not her.

She picked up the package and studied the writing on the label. It wasn't Jennifer's. Mystified, she unfastened the string and unwrapped the plain brown paper to reveal a square white box. Alice peeled back the sticky tape that held the box closed and lifted the lid. Something jumped from the box straight into her face. She let out a shriek of surprise and shot backward, her chair toppling over in her haste.

"Alice? Are you all right?" Lindy asked.

Alice stared at the box and the lurid colored clown face that leered at her. It still moved, jiggling from side to side on a shiny silver spring. Her heart fluttered in an erratic manner and her legs shook so much she had to sit. She righted her chair and the seat cushion that had fallen to the floor and sat, studying the box with distaste. "I'm sorry. It gave me a fright."

"It's a jack-in-a-box." Jake's lips curled in a delighted grin. "Who's it from?"

"I don't know." She stared at the red envelope sitting beside the clown box. Her skin prickled as she ripped open the flap and pulled out a card. The front depicted the same dog picture she'd noticed on the business card handed to her after the reading of her aunt's will. Inside the card was one word. *Surprise.*

Trepidation hit Alice. She'd received a surprise all right, but what did it mean? She reached for her coffee with a trembling hand. Fancy Free. That had to be the connection. The women who had given her the business cards both belonged to the cult. This must be something to do with condoms.

The shrill of the phone broke into her reflection. The noise shut off when Jake leaned back in his chair to snag the phone off the marble counter. "Hello. Sure. She's still here." Jake handed her the portable, his dark eyes twinkling. "It's for you. The playboy." His smirk said more but after a brief glance at his wife, he returned to his breakfast.

"Hello?"

"Alice, we have a problem. How soon can you get here? I've called an emergency board meeting." Not a hint of the lover shaded his voice. This was the businessman and he sounded worried.

"I'll be there in ten minutes." She could do businesslike and professional too.

J ames tapped his foot and waited in the boardroom for everyone to arrive. How the hell had this happened? He glanced at the brochure spread out on his desk. It belonged to their main competitor. Their opposition's new condom, a replica of the X-100, went on sale to the public today.

The X-100 wouldn't ship from Fancy Free for another two weeks since they hadn't finished tests and the final design of the packaging still required tweaks. He cursed under his breath. Someone, somehow had stolen their design.

Loud shouts attracted his attention and he strode over to the window. A group of cult members loitered outside the premises, placards held aloft. Their white robes flapped in the stiff breeze but the cool start to the day hadn't deterred their enthusiasm. With turban-covered heads held high, they marched in a tight circle, chants loud and strident.

"Condoms are evil."

"Make love and babies!"

"Down with Fancy Free!"

James frowned. The cult had moved into town about six months ago, around about the same time small, niggling problems had started at Fancy Free. They opposed contraception and judging by the number of kids around the property they'd purchased, they practiced what they preached. James' frown intensified. Was it possible that one of the cult had infiltrated the company? No, too far-fetched. He swung away from the window, knowing there was nothing the company could do about the protest in front of their building. Richard and Luke said the cult weren't breaking any laws. They had a right to protest.

Richard Morgan and Sam Glengarry wandered into the boardroom first. One look at him wiped the grins from their faces. They dropped into chairs.

"What's up?" Richard asked. "Has Ms. Knowall attacked Fancy Free in her gossip column again?"

Ms. Knowall—yet another person who wouldn't shed any tears if the company failed.

"Worse," James muttered. "I'll wait for the others so I don't have to repeat everything."

Alice hurried into the boardroom, flushed with her luscious body hidden beneath another of her shapeless suits. This time it was gray. She wore a white blouse underneath but a large maroon scarf hid her best assets. A short ponytail emphasized the cuteness aspect. James now knew the freckles only covered her nose and her skin was pale and petal soft. The rest of the board followed not long after, redirecting his thoughts from Alice to the X-100.

His gut tightened while the board members ambled to their chairs, as if they had all the time in the world.

"Where's the coffee?" Richard asked. "I didn't get much sleep last night."

Ben smirked and it hit sly with bells on. "I bet it wasn't work. I saw you with that woman last night and you looked mighty cozy. Yes sir, mighty cozy. Mark my words, we'll see a mention of you in the *Sloan Gazette* any day now."

James cut in before the oldies went off on a tangent and started in on the local gossip. "We have a problem."

"I'm missing my bowls tournament," Harriet said. "I have a good chance of winning today since Mildred Walker is sick. You're the manager. I can't see why you don't manage the problem."

The board members nodded and talked at once.

James bit back an uncomplimentary curse, trying to remind himself he must tread warily. He inhaled and then exhaled before attempting to get his point across. "T.J. and Co have a new condom out on the market today." James spoke above the chorus of complaints. The noise abated, and he lowered his voice. "It's a replica of the X-100."

"The same?" Alice asked, grasping the implications.

James sighed. "Yeah. Our edge is shot to hell. The company will lose its shirt on the X-100 because after the problems we've had, it's still not ready to hit the market. It will be another two weeks before we ship."

Ben opened his mouth, hesitating before he spoke. "No dividends for the shareholders this year?"

James closed his eyes and wished for Alicia's calm presence. She had a way of cutting through the crap. He missed the way she managed the board in times of crisis. "Not after this."

"What are our options? How did it happen?" Alice asked. She hadn't joined in the general outcry. Her eyes were huge and the freckles stood out against her pale skin. At least he didn't feel so alone at the top. He shoved aside a sliver of concern as his suspicions took another turn. He hoped Alice wasn't doing this for the money. Contrary to his parents' beliefs, there were more important things than accumulating wealth. He scanned her face again. It was full of quiet determination. Instinct told him she would do whatever it took to help the company succeed. Just as he would. Neither of them could afford failure.

"Our development team has another possibility they could develop."

"But that's more money down the drain," Katarina stated. "It's a risk we can't afford."

"But if we don't take a risk, we'll end up with nothing," Alice said quietly. "Let's give James an opportunity to tell us his plans so we can make an informed decision."

James had the urge to grab Alice and kiss her, especially when the rest of the board nodded in grudging agreement. Perhaps there was more of Alicia in her than he'd realized.

"I'll admit this will hit our cash reserves hard. I'll work with Rita to redo our budgets and arrange for extended overdrafts at the bank. There shouldn't be any problems there. Meanwhile, we need a plan to minimize our losses. I've asked Rodney to come up to discuss his ideas for a new product. Richard, can you review security and find out how the hell our innovative idea ended up in the hands of the opposition? We want to make sure it doesn't happen again."

Richard nodded. "No problem. I might need a helper since I've got a few other things on my plate. Joseph? Ben?"

"We can help," Joseph said.

A tap sounded on the boardroom door. James strode across to answer, ushering Rodney, their chief product inventor, into the room.

He dropped into a seat next to Ben and ran his hand through his curly brown hair. The unruly tufts of hair indicated he did this on a regular basis. Next, he took off his glasses and polished the lenses.

Harriet pulled out her knitting, seeming to accept she wouldn't get to bowls today. "Tell us about your new idea, young man."

"I c–c–all it V-vibrations!"

The board let out a collective sigh of relief. James hid his grin. It always took Rodney a while to warm up, as if his enthusiasm oiled his voice and helped with his tentative disposition.

"Vibrations. Weird name for a condom." Richard stood, checked the coffee filter and then switched on the machine. The *drip-drip* began, and the invigorating scent of coffee soon permeated the boardroom.

"This is a–a deluxe model. It has a dual purpose to function as a condom and a vibrator." Rodney glanced around the table with a proud grin. "Good, uh?"

Doubt seemed the major reaction. Exactly his response when Rodney had first told him about the new idea.

"Have you done any trials yet?"

Rodney's grin faded. "No, not yet. We decided to wait for the X-100 to launch, doing final tests on that first."

"How soon can the trials start? How much will they cost?" Joseph asked.

Alice listened with a sense of dread. Thankfully, she hadn't swallowed more than coffee this morning. The knowledge that her inheritance was in dire danger wasn't doing much for her security levels. The shiny picture she held inside her head of a three-bedroom house with a husband and family was slipping from her grasp. Alice swallowed the lump of terror in her throat and decided to face the problem instead of trying to hide from the truth. She needed to act and fight for her future.

"Can we be sure that the same thing won't happen with the new product? That the idea won't be copied by an opposition company?" she asked.

"Excellent point." Sam Glengarry shook his mane of grizzled hair. "No sense throwing good money after bad."

Richard tilted back on his chair until two feet left the carpet. "Did we use the group of final testers we normally use?"

The image of naked couples in a lab, lying on a sterile white bed with discarded X-100s surrounding it popped into Alice's mind. She suppressed a snort of humor and forced her mind to the current discussions.

Joseph straightened from his slouch, looking more like an ex-property tycoon than a retiree. "Do you think that's where the confidential leak is? The people who test our products?"

"It's one possibility. They've signed confidentiality clauses, but maybe someone isn't sticking to the terms." James rose to pluck the full carafe of coffee off the coffeemaker. He filled several cups and passed them round.

"We need to do everything differently this time," Alice said.

James nodded, his gaze caught hers and held. Heat seared between them. It was like putting her fingers in an electrical socket, or at least how she imagined it felt. The heat traveled from her face, down her throat and lingered in her breasts. The tips reacted, pulling tight. The exquisite sensation shot from her breasts to her sex, tingling with possibilities and bringing a rush of moist arousal. Oh boy.

"Well, who will test the condoms?" Rodney asked, drumming ink-stained fingers on the polished tabletop. "They can't go to market without trials. I need human guinea pigs to run tests in conjunction with the machine tests, especially since I'm experimenting with different latex processes. I'd offer to test, but I'm so busy with design work I don't have a life. I can test them on myself but that's not enough. We need male and female testing."

"Don't look at me." Harriet's knitting needles flashed silver in the stream of sunlight coming through the bank of windows. "I'm too old to test condoms."

"Ask Richard. He might want to test some with the mystery woman," Joseph said.

"Leave me out of this," Richard snapped.

"The way I look at it." Katarina's voice was firm. "There's only one sensible solution. We need to keep this in-house. James and Alice can test the condoms for us."

# Chapter 6

A rusty bark of laughter escaped Ben. "Better shut that mouth, girl. A fly will happen by and will think it's an invitation to come inside."

Heeding the warning, Alice pressed her lips together, her teeth meeting with an audible clack. They didn't expect...

She scanned their lined faces. Their expressions ranged from grim to determined. *They did.* They expected her to help test the condom. With an inward eye roll, she glanced at James and found him observing her. His expression told her nothing. She didn't know him well enough to tell if he favored the idea or not.

"Alice, we wouldn't make the suggestion but it's obvious there's chemistry between you and James," Katarina said.

Joseph nodded. "You didn't get those swollen lips from sucking lemons."

"I hear the two of you left The Thirsty Cricket together last night," Ben said.

Alice's cheeks burned. Was nothing sacred at Fancy Free? "I don't think—"

"It's a great idea." Rodney interrupted before she voiced her objections.

Harriet paused her knitting to nail her with an intense stare. "The thing is, we will lose our shirts if we don't take drastic action. Alicia drove this company and we're drifting without her." She wrinkled her nose. "Like a rudderless ship. We need you. No offense meant, James. We need you too."

"Stop the pressure, guys." James' gaze rested on her for an instant. "Alice and I will discuss the testing later. Meantime, are you in agreement about the development of a new condom model?"

"Take a vote," Rita suggested. "All in favor raise your hands."

Alice watched the hands go up one by one. Officially, she was still almost engaged to Steven. He'd made his views clear about condoms and hadn't returned her calls. Perhaps she'd try to ring Steven again and ascertain where their relationship stood and she'd arrange for an extended leave from her job. She'd put that off because it felt as if she were closing the door on the security she knew in exchange for something unknown. Yes, there might be money in the future, but risks littered the way.

Scary risks.

"Alice, are you voting?" James cocked his head, his bright blue eyes full of questions and something more difficult to discern.

Alice had difficulty breathing as she stared back.

"If we go ahead, we'll stretch our financial resources, but I believe we can weather this rough patch," he added.

Risk. Huh! Losing her inheritance, after walking away from her accountancy job, made her stomach roil. But what were the options? Now that she'd told the lawyer she agreed to the terms of the will, she had to support the company. Time to join the tea party or leave the rabbit hole.

She raised her hand.

"That's all of us. Okay. We proceed." James stood. "Rita and I will start with the budgets and the bank. I suggest we meet tomorrow morning at nine. I should have an update by then."

Rita and the board members dispersed to take care of their daily activities leaving Alice alone with Rodney and James.

"I have several of the prototypes ready to test," Rodney said. "Should I get them?"

"Please." James smiled.

Rodney hustled from the room.

The oxygen leached from the boardroom with him. Alice swallowed, aware of her body's heightened reaction to James. She gasped to fill her lungs. A scoundrel, her mother would have said. She agreed, and she should keep her hands off. Except after one taste she wanted more. Every instinct demanded she move closer and take everything he offered. So, he'd leave, but she'd have memories to drag out when she moved into her own home. She'd learn about sex and passion and how to run the company.

"You don't have to do this. It's a stupid idea. I don't mind doing the tests—it's a good plan since it cuts down on the possibility of information leaks. But you don't have to help."

*No.* Her reaction came instantaneously. Pain, layered with a slice of jealousy, pierced straight through her heart. The idea of James testing the condoms with another woman...

No! If anyone tested condoms with James, it would be her.

"I'm up for this crazy scheme."

"Well, let's hope I am." James gave one of his sexy, bad-boy grins. "We'll be in trouble if I can't rise to the occasion."

After this morning, it wasn't difficult to imagine the scenario. Long. Thick. Blunt-tipped with a reddish crown on full arousal. Her body tingled, and she wished she was brazen enough to undo the row of brass buttons on the denim blue shirt he wore and slide her fingers beneath to touch warm flesh. Even better, she'd like to strip the clothes from his body and explore. She'd search out the tender places—his flat masculine nipples, the soft skin below his ear, his belly. Alice fought a smile. She'd work out what made this rogue tick.

"Earth to Alice!" His hands curled around her shoulders and he shook her. "Are you sure you're okay with this damn-fool idea?"

An imp of humor broke free. She leaned closer until the tips of their noses touched. His eyes widened, the irises deepening in color until they reminded her of mysterious rock pools she'd played in at the beach as a kid. "Tick-tock," she said seconds before she leaned right in and kissed him.

At first, he didn't react, his lips remaining slack beneath hers. She hesitated. Okay, so she was still an almost virgin, but she knew a thing or two about kisses.

She opened her mouth a fraction and let her tongue dart out to moisten his lower lip. She nibbled where she'd moistened before sucking. James tightened his grasp on her shoulders, a silent acquiescence for her to continue. She gave his top lip the same attention, a nibble at the upper right corner, a nip and the touch of her tongue to soothe the sting.

James growled, the sound vibrating right down to her breasts. Her nipples rubbed against her plain, super-strength cotton bra, each breath an exercise in torture. She wanted to rip off the hateful garment and slide against him like a cat, letting him torture her at will.

Her tongue slid across the smooth enamel of his teeth and cozied up with his, twining together. She wound her hands around his neck and sank her fingernails into the delicate flesh there. Her breasts brushed his chest with each breath, each move. She needed...she wanted...

With trembling fingers, she slid several of his shirt buttons undone and slipped her hand inside. Her nails scraped across one of his nipples. The flat disc reacted to her touch as she teased it to prominence. James growled again, his hands skimming her body. They came to rest on her butt when he gathered her closer.

Alice ended the kiss and the little imp inside came out again. "You have an erection. I didn't think you'd have a problem."

James chuckled, the sound rich and sexual. The humor pulled at her breasts, making them harden while other parts of her softened. She craved his touch on her naked skin. She stroked his chest, pressing her fingers into his smooth muscles.

"Touch my breasts. Please. I need..." Hard to sum up the strength of her needs in concise words. Alice yanked at the buttons on her shirt and wrenched them from the buttonholes, baring her plain white bra. She tugged her bra cup aside. "Now. Touch me now." The harsh note in her voice gave her pause but she didn't stop.

Weird. The inheritance focused her on sex, her needs and everything she'd missed in the past. Some people might think her a good girl but they'd be wrong. In truth, she'd lacked opportunity, too busy with study and work to experiment. It was time to investigate now since this dovetailed with her inheritance. She inhaled, cocked her head and beamed with encouragement.

"You're a bossy little thing." Laughter underscored his words and echoed in his expression. "God, you have the most beautiful breasts I've ever seen." He brushed a delicate finger across the upper curve of her breast.

Alice shivered. His touch helped assuage the need coursing through her, but she wanted more. "Your mouth."

"Your wish is my command." James bent to nuzzle her breast.

She cradled his head, savoring the moist magic his mouth worked as he kissed the pale globe. Her sex clenched and pulsed when his mouth moved nearer to her taut nipple. She shivered, her legs rubbery. Alice clutched his upper arms, holding her breath, eager for his hot mouth to close over her flesh.

James paused, raised his head, and she wanted to commit murder.

"Don't stop!" Her heart thudded in time with her pussy.

"I was about to say—"

"Don't talk," she said, forcibly returning his head to her breast. Thankfully, he took the hint because finally, finally his mouth connected with her nipple. Or at least his tongue did. It seemed the bad boy wasn't good at taking orders. He had to do things his way. His tongue circled her areola in tantalizing licks. James used his fingers to massage while he teased and drove her to distraction with his tongue.

Alice stopped issuing orders. Her eyes drifted closed to concentrate on the sensations coursing the length of her body. Each rasp of his tongue sent a darting sword of pleasure downward. Her feminine folds moistened, and she ached for fulfillment, something to fill the emptiness. James shifted a fraction and his hot mouth closed over her entire nipple. Alice shivered with delight. He drew lightly and a shooting star of sensation rippled through her. Her pussy clenched again.

"Harder," she whispered.

Thankfully, he didn't argue or try to torture her. He sucked her breast and the pleasure spilled over to intense ripples in her pussy.

"Here they are." Rodney burst into the boardroom, laden down with a cardboard box and two clipboards. "Oh sorry. Were you warming up for the trials? Don't let me stop you. Carry on as you will." He glanced at Alice, clearly curious, but James tugged her blouse over her naked breast and angled in front of her.

"Tell us what we need to do and tell me how the new condom should perform," James said.

Mortified didn't begin to cover her thoughts as she struggled to put herself to rights. In the middle of the boardroom. What was she thinking? One taste of an orgasm and her hormones acted as if they were on steroids, clamoring more, more, more.

She was vaguely aware of James and Rodney discussing the technical side of condom testing and knew she should listen but her concentration suffered. The second episode with James and still no penetration. Surely the third time would be the charm?

Her mouth firmed as she forced the final button home. After a deep breath, she peeked from behind James.

Rodney gaped, his hazel gaze going from her to James and back again before dropping to stare at her breasts. "Ah, I could come back later." His eyes remained glued to her chest.

Alice looked down and gasped. She'd buttoned her blouse all wrong! She slapped her hand over the gap that broadcast her abundant curves and glared at Rodney.

James wanted to laugh but held it back. Alice looked disheveled and male pride roared with satisfaction. Damn, he liked this woman. Her bravery, her courage, her commonsense and the curvy body beneath her one-size-fits-all suits. Normally he went for the obvious when it came to women, because they knew the score and didn't push for more than he wanted to give.

Alice might be an exception.

"Thanks, Rodney. Is there anything you want me to look for?"

"I've used a different latex, a recent experiment. I want to make sure the condom fits and doesn't come off with vigorous thrusts. Don't want people to have accidents and sue us."

"Shit!" James turned to Alice. "I don't suppose you're on the Pill?"

Her cheeks reddened as she shook her head.

"Make an appointment with the doctor today. No, wait. I'll do it and come with you." "We can discuss our plan of attack while we wait."

"The Vibration comes in gold, silver and bronze. Each model differs in the amount of vibration and the features are different.

71

Gold is lubricated and strong. Silver is flavored. Bronze has surface adaptations designed to hit a lady's sweet spot." Rodney pumped his hips to emphasize, and James grinned at the distaste on Alice's face. Prudish might be a new turn-on for him.

He hid a grimace. "Sounds good, Rodney."

"If you can think of any new variations, we can add platinum or jewel categories."

"That's a fantastic idea," Alice said. "The packaging can match the model inside."

"Early stages yet," Rodney reminded them. "This model might not pass the tests."

Alice frowned. "What about a special promotion? Maybe we can shift more units at a lower price. Undercut the competition."

James picked up the box of condoms. "Rita and I will work on costings when we go over the budgets this afternoon. Anything else, Rodney?"

"Make sure you read my notes first. I've tried to think of everything. Ring me if you have problems with use. I can come over and help."

James shook his head. He had no intention of inviting Rodney to ogle Alice. Alice was personal business, for his eyes only.

An hour later, James ushered Alice into the doctor's surgery. It was full, although not surprising given that James had needed to twist the receptionist's arm to squeeze in a visit. She'd granted an appointment after he'd lied and implied an emergency. Every adult in the waiting room turned to watch them enter. The visit to the doctor was meant to protect Alice from an unwanted pregnancy. Instead, he'd opened the door for gossip.

Too late now.

Suppressing a sigh at the predictability of Sloan's residents, James headed for the reception desk. "Hi, Joanna. Alice and I are here for our appointment."

"Take a seat. Shouldn't take long since the doctor's on time today." She cast a curious glance at Alice before turning back to him. It wasn't difficult to see she wrote off Alice straight away, judging by appearances.

James knew better.

"I don't care what you say," an elderly woman said to a younger one. "The Children of Nature cult is up to no good. I bet there's drugs involved." She nodded. "There's always drugs involved where there is a cult."

"They're good parents and care for their kids," the young woman replied. "They can't be that bad."

"They have a lot of children," the elderly woman agreed.

James scowled. They had kids all right. No way could anyone accuse them of using Fancy Free's products.

"There are two free seats down the end." Alice squeezed past a blue pram and a toddler scooting between chairs and legs. He followed and stepped over the kid.

"James, what are you doing here?"

He hesitated. His sister. Just great. He inclined his head and kept his expression neutral. "Melissa."

Melissa's gaze wandered to Alice and dismissed her. The narrowing of her eyes and the nose lift, a fraction higher in the air, gave it away. "You don't look sick."

James knew his sister. She'd push until he satisfied her curiosity. "It's a work matter."

"I don't know why you call what you do work. It's peddling sex. You could do so much more with your life and work with the family law practice. But no. Instead you waste your chances and your training." Melissa's perfect nose rose even higher.

"I love you too, sis." Old news. Nothing changed—not the words or the subject. He threaded his way through the crowded room until he reached the spare chair next to Alice. He dropped into it, trying to ignore the flash of hurt. Why couldn't his mother and sister accept that he chose to walk a different path? Their way wasn't the only one.

Alice cast a curious glance at Melissa. She leaned closer. "How do we go about testing? What do we do first? Where will we do it?"

Good point. They needed to find a place to do the tests without creation of gossip, which was difficult in a small town where everyone knew everyone else's business.

"I guess we'd better go to my place."

Not that he was sure about that either. He didn't want Alice to get the wrong idea because he intended to leave soon. He'd promised Alicia he'd stay for six months. Although he loved his job at Fancy Free, he wouldn't stay longer. Besides, it was difficult to ignore his mother and sister and pretend their attitudes didn't hurt. A man could only take so much. There was nothing to hold him in Sloan.

"How many...um..." Alice blushed. "I don't know a ladylike way to ask this. How many times do we need to test the models? I know it's important to get the product on the market quickly, but how many...uh...times do we do it each night?"

James smirked. "Who said we have to do it at night? Sex isn't a nighttime-only activity."

"But sex isn't work," she retorted, her voice rose enough for the woman sitting next to them to hear. "It's meant to be fun."

The room seemed quieter than it had been seconds before, as if everyone waited with bated breath for the next words in their conversation.

"Oh sweetheart. The sex will be fun. I have special toys for us to try and massage oil. It will make your breasts gleam in the light." James glowered at his sister, the rise of his eyebrows a silent dare. Let her chew on that.

The receptionist appeared from behind the counter. "James, the doctor will see you now."

"Thanks." He stood, gesturing for Alice to walk in front of him. Her brandy-colored eyes glinted with heightened emotion. Anger combined with acute humiliation.

"Did you have to embarrass me like that?" she whispered when she brushed past him.

Well, hell. He'd managed to piss off Alice too.

Alice attempted cool dignity, but it was difficult while maneuvering around children and toys. When she'd agreed to help test the condoms, her thoughts had centered on making love.

What she hadn't considered was the embarrassment factor. Jeesh, she'd never been so mortified. She marched past the inquisitive men and women in the doctor's room with her head held high while praying she didn't fall flat on her face.

She understood James had been teasing. Unfortunately, she'd attracted attention, but the casual way he'd spoken of them making love had riled her. It made her realize she wanted more—the experiences she'd missed in the past. She wanted romance along with the hot, down and dirty sex. She wanted flowers and walks under the stars. She wanted chocolate and cozy candlelit dinners. All the discussions about where to do the tests and how to do it made the situation work like, taking away the spontaneity factor.

Alice stepped into the room indicated by the receptionist and sat. James followed and dropped onto the seat beside her.

A young woman entered the office and closed the door.

75

"Hi, James. I haven't seen you for ages."

"Carol, this is Alice Beasley. We need a prescription for the Pill."

Alice was glad of James' presence. Their reasons sounded so mercenary, but an unwanted pregnancy would be worse.

"Have you used this method of contraception before?" the doctor asked.

"No." Alice glanced at James. Okay for him to jump in any time now.

"Alice and I are about to conduct tests on a new condom. We want to make sure she's covered in case there are problems with the tests."

The doctor glanced at her. "Let me ask you about your general health and check your blood pressure. You realize the prescription needs to be taken for several weeks before conception is prevented?"

"What can we do meantime if one of the condoms rips?" James asked.

Alice released a shuddery breath only half listening while the doctor mentioned the Morning After Pill, should there be a problem, and suggested the use of spermicide if it didn't react with the latex. None of this had occurred to her before her agreement to go ahead with the scheme. At least one of them was thinking with their head.

Ten minutes later they left, prescription in hand. James paid for the visit and they stepped outside into the sunshine. Baskets of flowers hung from the lampposts all the way down the main street. Brilliant pink petunias and bright blue pansies drooped over the edges of wire baskets in colorful balls of floral magnificence. A crocodile line of school children ambled down the footpath, heading for the local swimming pool with their teacher bringing up the rear. Alice smiled at their mischievous faces. A nice town in which to settle down. Alice wondered if the town had any accountants with vacancies.

After they stopped at the chemist to have the prescription filled, James halted outside the busy cafe opposite the police station. "How about lunch? We can discuss our plan of attack." He cupped her face in his warm hands, smoothing a thumb across her mouth.

"Okay." She melted under his gaze, shivering when he traced her lips with his thumb.

"Don't worry," he whispered. "Everything will work out fine."

James had noticed how jumpy Alice became after the interaction with his sister. Hardly surprising. Meetings with Melissa always spoiled his mood too.

The casual lunch in the cafe relaxed her noticeably. This was the key, James decided. To take things slow and easy so he didn't scare her. The last thing he wanted was for Alice to change her mind. If they tested the condoms instead of outside testers, it cut down on the security measures they'd require. The future of the company depended on positive tests for the new condom. And, dammit, he wanted to get to know Alice in the carnal sense. Tonight. He'd cook her dinner. They'd have a few drinks. Relax together. A little music. Candles. Yeah, sounded like a plan.

"What will you have today, James?" the waitress asked.

After scanning the menu and the special's board, he decided on a chicken and cranberry panini while Alice ordered a salad.

The waitress jotted their orders down before flashing a grin at him. "Where are your followers? Your entourage of protesters?"

"Hopefully they didn't notice us slipping in here," James said. "The last time they protested outside the café, Ruby threatened to bar me. Ruby owns the cafe," he added to Alice.

"Do you think they…" she trailed off to study the waitress.

James appreciated her reticence in front of strangers, although Alicia had told him her goddaughter bore a wide streak of integrity. "Nah, all their protests are peaceful. They've never done anything except shout."

"That's true," the waitress confirmed. "Word is they settled in Sloan because of the mystical forces present in the town. Evidently it's conductive to rearing extra-intelligent children. They're not violent people. They're family orientated." She giggled. "It's just that condoms are against their beliefs."

"Lucky for us not everyone thinks the same way." James gave a careless shrug. "The company would go broke in no time."

"Yeah, the safe sex message must help sales." With a cheeky grin the waitress hurried off to deliver the order to the kitchens.

"Do you think the cult members have anything to do with our problems?" Alice asked in an undertone after a quick glance behind her and to each side.

James had difficulty controlling his amusement. He leaned closer, savoring her floral scent. "My gut says no, but I thought I'd mention it to Richard. We need to check out our newer employees."

Her eyes widened. "Me?"

"No. Alicia trusted you to look after the company. Besides, our problems started before you arrived."

Alice nodded, her forehead puckered in a frown. "I hope we can sort this out. The company can't afford to lose money."

"Don't worry. We have a dedicated team." She was mentioning money again. James reminded himself he intended to complete his contract because Alicia had asked him to and not for any other reason.

The tables were close together, making it difficult to talk in specifics. The elderly woman and her companion from the doctor's surgery came in and sat at the table next to them. They whispered a lot and Alice became so self-conscious he took pity on her and confined their discussions to the mundane.

After a quick lunch, they left the cafe and walked down the main street of Sloan, their reflections displayed in the windows. When they passed the Children of Nature shop, several robed women poured outside and shouted anti-condom slogans.

"Just ignore them. That's what I do." He slipped his arm around Alice's waist and drew her against his side.

She stiffened then relaxed when the women ceased their commotion and returned inside their shop. "Apart from the cult, this is a nice town. Did you grow up here?"

"Yeah. My parents and grandparents grew up in Sloan. The family business is here." James didn't want to talk about his childhood and how out of place he felt—a round peg in a square hole. "I'd better get started on those budgets. Rita and I need to finish them today."

Alice nodded, a sense of anticipation bubbling through her. Dinner at James' house. She'd be on his territory. A grown-up date with sex as dessert. Yum. She sure liked dessert. The eagerness spiked into a physical reaction, her nipples tight and lower, moisture flooded her sex. Alice's gaze drifted to his butt. Tight. Muscular. Very attractive. She sighed and followed him into his office.

James stepped behind his desk and pivoted, catching her stare. He winked. "Wanna help me with the budgets for the bank?"

"Sure." Untrue. What she had in mind didn't come close to banking, not unless deposits in the sperm bank counted. "I'm a trained accountant. Budgets are my thing."

"Let's get to work then," he said. "The sooner the budgets are completed, the quicker we'll get to the tests of Rodney's latest invention."

As incentives went, Alice thought it was an excellent one.

# Chapter 7

A lice refused James' offer to pick her up from the bed and breakfast. She preferred to walk and wanted to explore her new hometown. It wasn't a long walk to the house he rented on the outskirts of the town—half an hour according to James.

Dressed in a black and white floral skirt, a baggy black blouse and a black cardigan, Alice wandered down the main street, past the cafe where they'd eaten lunch. They did an evening meal and diners occupied most of the outside tables.

She checked out the mannequins in the window of Kellie Anne's Ladies Wear. Lots of fashionable dresses in pastel pink, turquoise and white. A longing to purchase new clothes crept into her mind—a foreign concept. Something in this season's colors to enliven her predominantly black and white wardrobe. But the expense... She glanced at her scruffy black sandals, old, in need of replacement. Maybe not. She couldn't afford to dip into her savings, not when things were shaky at Fancy Free.

After checking her watch, Alice hustled, past the hall where the lawyer had read the will. The town clock struck six as she turned onto River Road. The water appeared more of a stream than a river. A group of boys fished from the bridge that crossed the stream. They didn't have any fish, but their youthful laughter made her grin.

The startled quack of ducks filled the air. Alice slowed to watch the argumentative water birds, took the time to appreciate the musical tinkle of the rushing water and the rustle of the breeze through the totara trees that edged the stream. Aware of the passage of time, she continued to walk. The road curled around the base of a hill gradually rising until Alice could see across the valley. Winded by the unaccustomed exertion, she paused at the top to study the view. Wheat and corn grew in the paddocks, the gold and green colors of the crops like a patchwork quilt on the hillside.

An out-of-place metallic grinding interrupted the peace. She whirled around, her hand pressed to her heart. A bright lime green van chugged up the hill and pulled up beside her with a screech of brakes. The window wound down on the passenger side.

"You're the condom heiress." It sounded like an accusation.

Alice gaped at the van occupants. The passenger wore full clown makeup while the driver sported a tan and white dog suit.

Just like the business cards she'd received. Talk about peculiar.

Instinct had her backing away. She glanced left and right, praying for other traffic. The hairs at the back of her neck prickled. Why were they in disguise? Had they followed her?

"Are you lost? Do you need directions?" Alice regretted the tremor of her voice, but despite the red painted smile on the clown's face, she sensed a swirl of anger.

"Stop this madness. Condoms are the modern man's plague. Man should beget children. The woman who founded Fancy Free has brainwashed the public."

"I don't know what you mean." Alice backed farther away and prepared to run. Condoms promoted the safe sex message—a good thing for everyone concerned given the modern crop of sexual diseases—but she didn't intend to argue the point.

"That's right." The driver's voice emerged low and whispery. Alice couldn't decide on the dog's gender, but the clown sounded masculine. She shuddered at the creepy tone, her skin breaking out in goose bumps.

When the clown opened the door, Alice's self-preservation kicked into gear, and she broke into a lope.

"You can run, but you can't hide," the clown shouted.

To Alice's relief, the van didn't follow. She didn't care what anyone said. The cult members were peculiar, and she wouldn't be surprised if they had something to do with the sabotage at Fancy Free. She hastened her footsteps until she sprinted, aware of her vulnerability on the quiet road.

Over the crest of the hill, the road forked to the right. A group of four houses sat halfway along a gravel track. She searched for the red mailbox James had mentioned and found it a few meters past a yellow weatherboard bungalow, the last in the cluster of houses. At the red mailbox, she darted past and ran up the dirt road, each breath a gasp that sounded like the set of bellows her father used to blow the fire to life.

James' one-level house was white. After another glance over her shoulder, she saw the van hadn't followed and her steps slowed. The paint peeled and flaked in places but it had potential. It was the type of home she'd pictured in her mind a thousand times, the sort she hoped to own one day. She walked up the cobblestone path and paused to catch her breath before knocking on the bright blue door.

James opened the door almost straight away, a grin on his lips that brought his dimple into prominence. "Hi."

"Hi," Alice parroted, and a sense of shyness struck her. With his dark hair damp from a shower, he stole her breath. The faded blue denims and the white T-shirt set off his body, attracted attention and let her know that here was indeed a rascal who knew about sex. His sensual grin reinforced the impression.

He studied her closely, his smile slowly fading. "Are you all right? You look flushed."

"I saw a dog and a clown in a lime-green van," she blurted. "They stopped and lectured me about condoms." She wiped her clammy hands on her skirt. "They gave me a heck of a fright."

"I can't see anyone." James leaned down and kissed her, nibbling at her lips with his teeth before tasting her more fully. When he pulled away, all she could think about was having dessert before the main course. Talk about flustered. "Nope, you haven't had too many drinks."

Indignant, she opened her mouth to hotly dispute the claim, but he forestalled her piqued words with another kiss. This time he used tongue. Alice stood passively, allowing him to seduce her. He probed the seam of her lips, right at the corner of her mouth, entering and withdrawing in slow, steady moves that left her breathless. When they drew apart, her knees shook.

"Who drove the van? The dog or the clown?" James stroked her cheek with his forefinger. "Any flying saucers or little green men?"

Alice drew up, her eyes narrowing on him. "The dog, and you're right. I haven't had a single alcoholic beverage."

"Shh, I'm teasing." He tucked a lock of hair behind her ear. "According to Luke Morgan—he's one of the local cops and a close friend—several Sloan residents have seen the dog and clown but from a distance. With the rest of the locals I would have called it a bad batch of beer at the pub, but I know you haven't had time to drink anything stronger than coffee today." His eyes gleamed with laughter and lazy sexual heat. "It's probably nothing to worry about. A publicity stunt or for kids' birthday parties. Come inside."

"I don't think they had anything to do with children's parties. They mentioned condoms."

James frowned. "They did? Tell Richard when you see him."

"I will." They'd scared her more than she'd acknowledged, especially with the business cards and her surprise package. She definitely intended to speak with Richard.

After kicking off her sandals, she followed James down a tiled passage into the kitchen. That clown and dog... She made a mental note to pay attention to local gossip and to read Ms. Knowall's column for more information. James might consider them harmless, but he hadn't encountered them yet. They'd acted creepy, and she hoped to avoid them in the future.

The rich scent of a tomato sauce filled the kitchen. Curiosity made her scan the room, eager to learn more about James. She hadn't known what to expect. Maybe clothes tossed around the room and lots of clutter. Sort of like her parents' house. James' tidy home with everything in its place took her by surprise.

The kitchen wasn't huge, but the breakfast bar would receive the morning sun. Modern stainless-steel appliances and a gas cooker stood against the walls. A plain white clock hung on the wall, clacking merrily while it counted off the seconds. A blackboard, near the fridge, bore the start of a scrawled shopping list. The mottled gray countertop held two empty white bowls. A cutting board sat beside them, a tomato ready to slice.

"I'm in the middle of making salads," he said. "Would you like a glass of wine while I finish off?"

Alice thought about her flirtation with alcohol yesterday and decided to risk a drink. "Yes, please." Yep, no doubt about it—next stop hell. Alcohol. Sex. Who knew what would come next? A private grin curled across her lips.

James pulled a bottle of white wine from the fridge, poured a glass and handed it to her. "Why don't you sit at the counter?" He lifted her onto one of the wooden barstools that sat on the other side of the breakfast bar and calmly went back to salad preparations.

Alice sipped her wine, hoping to still her pounding heart. The man had lifted her without a pause. She wasn't the lightest female. Well, she wasn't overweight but she wasn't slim either. His heady citrus aftershave tickled her nose and she had the absurd desire to lick him. Her hand tightened on her glass as her gaze skirted his shoulders and face. With competent moves, he sliced the tomato, shredded some fancy lettuce and added olives, croutons and slivers of Parmesan cheese.

Alice sighed, mesmerized by his hands. She imagined them roving her body, strumming sensitive nipples as they had this morning and sighed again. It'd be difficult to choke down food when she wanted to rip off his clothes and explore his gorgeous muscles. Yep, maybe she should add brazen and sluttish to her list of sins.

She sent a glance heavenward and hoped Santa wasn't checking his list, because she liked Christmas presents.

Suddenly James set down the knife. He prowled around the counter, heading straight for her. Alice gulped. He still resembled a bad boy with danger lacing the enticing package.

He took the glass from her tense hands and placed it out of reach. His arms went around her, and he drew her close until their chests touched. Softness met hard muscle.

"Spread your legs," he growled low and gritty.

When she was slow to obey, he slid her skirt up her legs and forcibly parted her legs. He stepped into the space created and folded her into his arms more completely. His body burned through her clothes, igniting an answering warmth that skipped across her skin. She inhaled. Lemon. Warm spices. She'd never look at her mother's spice cookies again without thoughts of sex invading her mind.

Instead of a kiss, he nuzzled the tendons where neck and shoulder met. His groin brushed her inner thigh. Fully aroused, his erection shoved against the faded denim. On the plus side, at least he wanted her. Alice hoped he wasn't disappointed.

James' entire body hummed with lust fueled by this woman. He nuzzled her neck and pressed an open-mouthed kiss to an erratic pulse point. She smelled of old-fashioned flowers, of simplicity and lazy days spent in the country.

Not his normal type.

He wondered for an instant about mistakes then his shaft lengthened and reared, silently protesting confinement in his jeans. He had to have Alice now. After his restraint this morning and the afternoon appetizer, he might explode if he didn't have her soon.

He lifted his head, buzzing a kiss across plump pink lips. With purposeful moves that left no doubt as to his intentions, James undid the top two pearl buttons of her black blouse, and when she did nothing except inhale sharply, he continued, revealing creamy skin for his personal pleasure. He peeled the black cotton fabric off her shoulders and tossed it aside to reveal her ugly bra. No getting away from it. He reached behind her and twisted his wrist. The bra loosened with a satisfactory twang. James grinned while he removed the hideous under garment and tossed it on top of her blouse.

Talk about hidden treasure. God, she was beautiful, and all his. He stroked the underside of one breast and gradually widened the circles, fascinated by the way the areola darkened. He puffed his warm breath over her nipple, loving her body's reaction to his caress. But James wanted more. He wanted her naked and open to his touch, her legs spread for him to taste. *Moving right along...*

87

He stepped back and lifted her off the barstool, setting her on her feet. With quick, competent moves, he made short work of the zipper on her skirt. He pushed the skirt over her hips and silently encouraged her to step out of it.

Finally she stood before him clad only in her white cotton panties. They were as plain and ugly as her matching bra and covered too much. James made a mental note to purchase silk and lace lingerie for her. He'd get a kick knowing she wore sexy lace beneath her conservative clothes. He slid the cotton panties down her hips, taking a moment to fondle her bare arse before he stood.

Better. Much better.

Time to move this to the bedroom.

James pressed a long, drawn-out kiss to her lips, despite the urgency prodding him to action. He tasted tart wine with its hint of peaches and sunshine. His cock pulsed and James quit thoughts of delayed gratification. He swung Alice into his arms and strode to his bedroom.

He dropped her in the center of his double bed. "Pick a condom," he ordered, indicating the wooden trio of drawers on the far side of the bed. "They're in the top one." James stripped off his T-shirt, his gaze on Alice. She looked superb spread out on his navy-blue quilt cover. As he watched, she turned her back to him, rolling onto her side with a flash of rounded buttocks. It was done so unselfconsciously he knew the talk of condoms had distracted her. Her clear curiosity brought a grin. Best he educate her about condoms soon. Lack of knowledge wasn't good for a Fancy Free executive.

"These aren't the new test condoms." Alice turned back to James and caught him ogling her butt. Her face reddened, and she rearranged her body to restrict his outstanding view. "Where are the Vibration samples we're meant to test?"

"Not this first time." Given his desperation, James wanted a fast fuck without the worry of a faulty condom. He prayed he didn't mess up and make her first genuine experience something she'd want to forget. He didn't want to hear her blurt out her almost-virgin speech to other people. Pride bade he did his best work. He wanted to use her throughout the night so she had no doubt of her sexual status.

He laughed at himself. Never had he become so hot and desperate for plain cotton and prudish. His old school mate Luke would laugh himself stupid when he realized. James would never hear the end of it, but he couldn't find it in himself to care.

"Pick a condom. Any condom. They're all Fancy Free products."

"Any one?" Alice peered into the open drawer, flashing her butt at him again. James craved a bite. He stepped out of his jeans and briefs while Alice studied the condoms selection.

"Hurry up." He sat on the bed and moved close enough to touch Alice's creamy skin. He ran his hand down her bare back until his hand rested on her buttocks. His cock pulsed insistently, and he shifted nearer still, unable to resist full-body contact. James nuzzled her ear as he pulled her flush, her back against his chest, her backside teasing his erection. "Alice."

"I've picked one," she whispered, a breathless rush.

James chuckled at her quick glance at his groin. "It's obvious I'm ready for action, but I want to explore you again like I did this morning."

"Um, all right."

James chuckled and turned her in his arms to smile down at her. He dropped a light kiss on her lips before moving down her body. This time he skipped her breasts, prepared to hurry things along. He rimmed her belly button with his tongue and moved lower still. Parting her legs, he blew the length of her slit. Alice issued a sexy as hell mewl.

"Let me take care of you first," he responded when it seemed she might protest.

Alice propped up on her elbows, her eyes wide with a trace of anxiety. "We will do things properly, this time? Go all the way?"

"I've done this before. I know what to do."

"I know the mechanics. I believe you need to put your cock here." She gestured at her entrance. "It's the bells and whistles I require."

James smothered a chuckle but couldn't control the amused roll of his eyes. "Quiet. Let me do my thing. I don't want another word out of you for the next five minutes." He hoped five minutes was enough because his balls ached. She hadn't touched him or studied his privates, but she turned him inside out. Impatient much? Hell yeah, frustration bubbled through him. "Follow my directions."

Her eyes twinkled with mischief. "Yes, sir."

An invisible salute. He concealed his amusement again and returned to the task at hand, determined to wipe that humor from her face. He settled his body between her parted legs and lifted her hips by placing his hands beneath her bottom.

Alice tensed since it was difficult to remain unconcerned when a man peered so closely at her intimate parts. But his touch and intent expression held her in thrall. Half apprehensive and half excited, she couldn't have moved if she tried. The puff of warm air on her most private flesh felt blissful, but after this morning, greed reared its head. She wanted more and she wanted it now before he changed his mind or something else went wrong.

Nothing less than full penetration would do.

A quiver sped through her when his fingers drifted across the same path as the burst of warm air. Awareness peaked her nipples. Her belly danced with anticipation. He parted her folds and stroked a gentle finger across her clit. Oh yeah, she knew the names of the body parts. It was the practical application she lacked. He moved closer until he had an excellent view. Up close and personal, she was sure he could tell her a few things. Alice wondered about the smell and frowned, her muscles tensing.

James looked up her body, across the curls guarding her sex and over her breasts, meeting her gaze with a smile. "This will be good. I promise."

Without another word, he used his mouth.

The sensation was incredible. Soft. Arousing—just as it had been this morning. His tongue glided across her clit before he moved lower. A tingle sprang to life, shimmering through her with enticing promise. He slid a finger into her tight channel, an unhurried push while his tongue teased her clit.

"James," she murmured.

On hearing her voice, he stopped the tongue movements and she almost cried. That would teach her to interrupt before the allocated five minutes. "Don't stop!"

He smirked. "I thought I wasn't doing it right."

"Back to work. Right now," she said in her best school-teacher-type voice.

"Yes, miss." He spoiled his moment of obedience with laughter but returned to his task, stoking her desire with each subtle lick. Her legs fell apart and without volition, her hips rose. She shook, the intensity of the pleasure almost unbearable.

This wasn't a condom test, but too bad. It was an experience, one she wanted to remember in detail since it felt *sooooo* good.

His tongue did this little wiggle thing, delicate like a butterfly's wing over her swollen nub. A repeat of the move shot sweet agony through her flesh. Unsure of whether she wanted him to continue or not, she tensed, her teeth sinking into her bottom lip. The sweet assault continued with tiny flickers of touch with his tongue. Alice gasped. She opened her mouth to beg him to do something, to stop this decadent agony.

"James." Her body soared higher and higher, and suddenly it became too much. She shattered, the waves of pleasure going on and on until finally she slumped back to the mattress with a satisfied sigh.

"Good for you?" James asked.

Too replete to grouch at his smart-arse remark, she murmured a nothing sound. An orgasm was an amazing thing. She opened her eyes when James moved. His blue eyes blazed full of heat and the sensual tension in her ratcheted sharply upward again.

"My turn now." He bent and kissed her, a prolonged caress where he teased the contours of her mouth.

Alice's pulse jumped. Oh boy. She could get used to this.

He pulled away to smile down at her. "Where's that condom?"

Alice shook her head to get with the program and control her choppy breaths. "Here." She fumbled for the foil package. She held it in front of her face and made a surprised sound. "It's called the Adventurer."

"Ah, the pearl gray condom with special warming lubrication." His eyes twinkled in a naughty fashion. "You'll like this one. Most of the girls do."

Alice wasn't sure she liked being grouped with the rest of the girls. She handed him the gray foil packet and tried to avoid thoughts of his other women. Jealousy, an emotion that had rarely touched her, hovered like a raincloud when it came to James. She pushed the thought aside to pull out later and watched him unwrap the condom. After tossing the foil packaging aside, he pinched the tip and rolled it onto his erect penis with an expertise she admired. When the condom sat in place, she saw it had sexy blue stripes.

Her laugh of delight filled the bedroom. "Cool. Very chic."

"Come here." James tugged her into his arms and rolled her until she lay flat on her back. The cotton duvet cover was cool on her spine as she stared up at him.

"Spread your legs for me," he whispered. "This chic little model wants an adventure."

Alice bit her lip to stem her laughter. Sex was a serious business. She took a deep breath. "Come check out the uncharted territory." Her mouth quivered but she managed not to laugh as she opened for him. Jolts of pleasurable excitement gathered in her pelvic region as he studied her with his slumberous gaze.

He took his erection in hand and dragged it along her cleft. Alice whimpered even though there wasn't a scrap of pain involved.

"Things a little serious in the uncharted territories?"

"Misbehavior is punished with torture," Alice fired back.

"Sweet torture." James repeated the move, dragging his cock against tender flesh.

"Yes." Very sweet. If only he would hurry up because the suspense might kill her.

As if he read her urgency, he positioned his cock.

Alice wriggled, instinct wanting him deeper now. She'd absolutely die if he stopped this time.

James didn't move.

"This isn't meant to be a battle or a punishment," she murmured, the addition of a chiding *tsk* designed to foster guilt in him for mean behavior.

He pushed until his erection rested inside her, embedded around an inch.

"Is that all you've got?" *Why wouldn't he hurry?*

James forged deeper, gritting his teeth the entire time. "I don't want to hurt you. You're tight."

Alarm surfaced. "Please, don't stop." If he stopped, she'd kill him.

He withdrew until only his tip rested inside then he thrust, gliding smoothly. Deep.

"Oh." Her eyelashes fluttered while she breathed deeply. She sighed. This was more like it.

James repeated the move, his strokes even and regular. Warmth bloomed inside her. Alice gripped his shoulders while she reached blindly for his lips. Their mouths mated, duplicating the slow withdrawal and invasion of his penis. Each stroke intensified the heat inside until she simmered once again with enjoyment.

He increased the pace, shoving harder with greater vigor. The bed creaked. Each of his drives moved her up the mattress until she felt the headboard through the pillow. James ripped his mouth from hers and kissed a trail toward her breasts with unhurried rocking strokes. He drew a nipple deep into his mouth and alternatively sucked and nipped.

The jolt of pain from his bite lashed like a whip on her clit. Alice gasped and bucked against him, nerve endings vibrating with a quick punch of heat. A surge of wetness met his next stroke. He bit her nipple again and she shattered, ripples of pleasure coursing the length of her body. James slammed deep, his cock swelling, filling her sheath and prolonging the pleasure. He stilled, his grip tight, while deep inside her, his cock pulsed.

"Holy shit." He pressed a whisper-soft kiss on her lips and rolled so she lay sprawled on top of him. He inhaled and grinned at her. "What did you think of the Adventurer?"

"If the Vibration is anywhere near as good as the Adventurer, then we have a winner." Her stomach rumbled.

"Hungry?"

"Yeah."

"Stay there and I'll bring in something to eat."

Alice stared as he stood. Totally at ease with his nakedness, he removed the Adventurer and disposed of it. Aware of potential rudeness from her end, she spoke quickly. "Will we conduct tests tonight?"

Desire flared in his eyes. "If you're up for it." His voice held a seductive, smoky quality that set a tremor of awareness burning inside her again.

"I don't need to worry about a rise to the occasion. That's your department."

James snorted and swaggered to the door.

"Aren't you going to get dressed?" All that bronzed, muscled body. How could she concentrate on food with temptation on parade in front of her? "Do you want any help?"

He slanted her a look of challenge. "Talk to me while I serve our meals."

"I'll get dressed."

"Why? We're not expecting any visitors."

What? Parade around butt naked with her breasts lunging toward the floor every time she moved? Alice reached for her underwear. The armor of clothes made her comfortable.

"I dare you."

"No, I'll grab my blouse."

James strode back to the bed. The mattress depressed as he settled by her side. "I love your body, your breasts. You don't need to hide from me because I would never make fun of you." James cupped one weighty globe in his palm, bent his head and took her nipple into his warm mouth. His dark hair contrasted starkly with her creamy skin. Alice stared, mesmerized. The sight was erotic. Sexy. Watching his cheeks hollow as he sucked stole her breath. He wasn't repulsed. The hot glow in his eyes when he glanced up at her confirmed the thought.

"Okay," she whispered. "You've convinced me." If he didn't have any unannounced visitors, she could do this.

"Good girl. We need to be comfortable together especially since we're the test team." He stood and stretched out his hand. "Come on. We'll have you at a nudist camp soon."

"Don't think so." Alice's tone sounded very dry. "This is as adventurous as I get."

# Chapter 8

R eplete and relaxed from a tasty meal and excellent company, James dragged the pillow from behind him and punched it twice to reposition for comfort. He appeared at ease with his naked state, which was more than she could say for herself. Alice watched him, hardly able to believe she sat naked on a bed beside this hunky man.

"Come here," he murmured.

Willingly, she scooted closer until their bodies touched from shoulder to hip. "Will we test the Vibration now?"

"Soon. Talk about impatient." He toyed with a brown curl, twirling it around his finger.

"It's important to do a decent job. I want the company to succeed or I won't receive my inheritance." Success meant security. Simple.

James stopped playing with her hair to study her intently. "Is that why you agreed to sleep with me and help test the condoms? For money? Money isn't everything."

Alice frowned at the edge to his voice. He removed his fingers from her hair and she regretted the loss, wanting desperately to direct his hand back. Something in his manner halted the impulse.

"I don't understand." They both worked for Fancy Free. Surely they had a common goal to ensure the success of the company, to ensure the success of the Vibration condom to maximize profits?

"We'll test now and get it over and done with." He grabbed a condom from the box Rodney had given them. They were packaged in sealed plastic bags with a large black number on the outside of the bag. Eight in all. James had chosen number five. He wrapped his fist around his semi-erect penis and pumped vigorously. Under her startled gaze, his cock lengthened. He stopped, grunted and opened the bag. He pulled out the condom and rolled it over his erection.

"Grab the clipboard, will you? Feels okay. This is thinner latex; a new patent is pending. Rodney said it's super thin yet still strong with no loss of sensitivity."

Alice picked up the clipboard that held the questionnaire and handed it to James.

He scanned it and handed the clipboard back. "You can fill out Rodney's forms. The first questions are in relation to feel and appearance of the condom. Here's a pen." He plucked the pen off his bedside cabinet and switched on the bedside lamp for extra illumination.

She'd upset him but couldn't explain how. He was acting like a stranger. Indifferent and uncaring. Alice accepted the pen and read the first question aloud after deciding to pretend nothing was wrong. The ostrich approach. Sometimes it worked.

"How does the condom fit?" With pen paused, she waited for his answer.

"It feels tight, clasps the penis firmly and doesn't feel in danger of sliding off. The reservoir at the end looks a bit on the small side. The latex is smooth and comfortable. Make a note for Rodney that added lubricant won't be necessary if we decide to go with this grade of latex."

Alice scribbled down the points he made, fascinated despite herself. "How does Rodney do his initial tests?"

"Alicia imported a special machine for him to use. It tests the latex to make sure it's strong and durable for the purpose. Things like thrust and force."

Oh. That didn't sound romantic. "The next question is about taste. Um...how do we do that?"

"You open your mouth and I insert my penis. You lick and give a verdict."

Alice set the clipboard and pen aside ready to do her duty. James stopped her by taking her face between his hands.

"Are you sure you want to do this? Is the money enough for you to want to suck my cock?"

Yes, something she'd said had changed everything between them, but the cause remained a mystery. "Rodney needs us to do the tests." She scrutinized his stormy expression. "Besides, you didn't have any problems with my taste."

Frustrated anger seared James. He sure knew how to pick them. He'd known part of the reason she remained in Sloan was because of her inheritance, but he hadn't realized money held such importance to her. Alice Beasley reminded him of his mother and sister. Appearances and money meant everything to them and they stopped at nothing to achieve their goals. The important things disappeared in the frenzy to grab more money than the next person. Critical things like friends and family, admiring a sunset or the view down the valley.

James shrugged. Who was he to stand in the way of progress? He'd promised Alicia he'd continue to run the company for six months, train the replacement she'd selected and help ensure the board remained involved. *Take them out of their humdrum existence,* Alicia had ordered. *They're all intelligent but they'll stagnate if they're not careful. I want them to have a good reason to get up in the mornings.*

He sighed at the memory. He'd promised Alicia, and he never went back on his promises—a point of pride. This man had principles.

"Way you go then." As Alice crawled down the bed to a better position, his cock stirred despite his dark thoughts. Wisps of hair curled around her face, her lips swollen from his kisses, her eyes heavy-lidded. She looked as if she'd spent a few hours in bed engaged in vigorous sex.

Her hair tickled his lap. Timid hands reached for his shaft before she glanced up with uncertainty. James stared back unable to voice the words of betrayal that whizzed like an unleashed balloon inside his head. He hadn't known her long but this woman with her innocence and smiles had bypassed his usual emotional barricades. He didn't know how to react and that brought irritation. Her tongue darted out to moisten her lips before she bent over him again.

He felt the cautious kisses along his length even through the latex. A curious finger smoothed over his blunt tip with dangerous precision. James sucked in a hasty breath, his heart thundering. Slowly she leaned over his lap, her features hidden by the fall of brown hair. Her warm mouth closed around his cock and her tongue swirled across him, tasting him like an exotic sweet with languorous licks. Alice explored his genitals while she teased his cock with her mouth. Her fingers feathered over his balls then her tentative touch firmed and she massaged the tight sac. The combination of mouth and hands forced anger from his mind. Another firm sweep of her tongue over the sensitized head dragged a groan from deep in his chest.

"That's enough," he said, with a gentle push against her shoulders. "I won't last through the rest of the questions if you keep this up."

Thankfully, Alice heeded his plea and pulled back but not without a final crafty lick that sent heat searing through his balls. James cleared his throat. "Taste? Write your comments on the chart."

"Actually, it tasted of spearmint. I expected a chemical flavor, but I liked that. It tasted refreshing." Alice's eyes glowed golden and mysterious. She licked her lips in a seductive move that made him want to grab her and forge into her with one powerful stroke.

James shook away the image and gave the chart a pointed stare. "Better write down your impressions before you forget something."

She reached over to pick up the pen and scribbled several sentences. "Next question is fit inside the vagina with and without the vibration sensor activated." Alice peered at his groin, and predictably, his cock hardened to a point shy of pain. "Where is the vibration sensor?"

After clearing his throat, he glanced at his condom-encased dick. "It's this tiny tab here. You pull it when you want the vibrator in motion."

She nodded. "How do you want to do this?"

"You wanna go on top? I'll go much deeper that way and it will be a better test for the condom." *Liar, liar.* After his first sight and touch of her breasts, a fantasy had filled his mind. He wanted to see her breasts bobbing and swaying above him. He wanted to touch and taste and watch her expression while she rode him hard.

Intrigue filled her face. "Okay."

James lay back on the deep blue and cream sheets, to all purposes sprawled comfortably. He was anything but relaxed. His heart pounded, his cock throbbed hard and heavy and it pissed him off that his body reacted this way when he'd been mistaken about her character. Another money-hungry woman...

Through narrowed eyes, he watched her. She cautiously straddled his hips, darting worried frowns in his direction. Her expression betrayed her unease and told him she flailed out of her depth so he decided to help her. "That's it. Move up a little. Take my cock and guide it to your entrance. Wait. You are aroused enough to take me, right?" James combed a finger through the triangle of hair between her thighs. His finger glided with little difficulty, her cream smoothing the way. "You'll do," he said, his voice rough around the edges. "Okay. Yep, that's it. Guide me in so I don't hurt you then when you're ready, sink down and take me inside. Yeah, that's it. Just like that." God, it felt incredible as he pierced her flesh and tunneled deeper. Tight muscles clutched his shaft, massaging his rigid length.

"Is that right?"

"Yeah. How does the condom feel inside you?"

"*Goood*." She dragged the sound out so he knew it wasn't a lie. Alice pushed down farther until fully seated. Her vagina pulsed, gripping him in velvet sensation. "Um, there's a lumpy bit and it's right... Oh my god," she muttered.

He grinned inwardly. Rodney had lined up the massager correctly. It had obviously hit in the region of her clitoris. "Move up and down, Alice. Have you ridden a horse before?"

She bit her bottom lip, her face delicately flushed. At the back of his mind, he noted the color had spread down her neck to her chest. Her nipples pouted, swollen with arousal. "Yes, I've ridden horses before."

"Move up and down on my dick like you'd rise to the trot."

Alice's eyes widened and a small grin burst forth. "I'll never think about horse riding the same way again." She obeyed his instructions, rising before sinking down. "Ooh, that feels fantastic."

She wasn't wrong. It felt bloody good on his end as well. Time to activate the vibrator feature. He reached down to tug at the tag pull, noting the time on his watch. He was sure he remembered length of vibration time as one of the questions on Rodney's list.

The tag pull changed the sensations rippling through his body. Made them more intense and powerful.

Alice swayed above him, moving in her own rhythm, her eyes screwed shut.

"Open your eyes." James wanted to see everything. The swirl of gold colors in her brandy eyes, the moment her climax hit and she shattered. Yeah, he wanted everything and that accounted for his earlier anger. He couldn't have it all.

Alice rose and unhurriedly went back down, taking him deep. The vibration was like a series of small pulses that rippled the length of his cock. While it didn't feel as though the vibrations would push him into orgasm, the sensation intensified the powerful currents rampaging through his body. "Howzit feel?"

"The tiny pulses feel amazing but it's that little lump thing I hit every time I go down that makes me hot."

"Go faster." An order, but he thought this slow pace might kill him.

"I'll forget to take mental notes if I go faster."

Ah, yeah. Good point. They were meant to take notes for Rodney so he could finesse the product into a top money-spinner. Too bad. They'd just have to repeat the experiment. They had another seven condoms to test. James gripped her hips and set up a faster rhythm. His gaze caressed her breasts, and once he was sure she'd keep up the pace he'd set, he released her hips to cup her breasts. He took one nipple into his mouth and rolled it across his tongue. Alice moaned at the back of her throat, a sexy cry that sent an answering surge through his body. She rose and fell, rocking their bodies together, burying him deep in her wet core. On the downward stroke, Alice hit her clit against the lump. Her startled gasp of pleasure gave it away. A ripple sped through her pussy, triggering a return spasm in him. James gripped her hips again and pumped with rapid strokes. Her vaginal muscles clung, squeezing him tight. She gasped and her body convulsed with the force of her release. James followed seconds later, the exquisite clamp of her pussy wringing him out.

Long moments later, she fell forward, her breasts squashed against his sweaty chest. James didn't complain. He wrapped his arms around her shoulders and drew her against him. The Vibration continued to pulse, setting off aftershocks in Alice.

"Enough," she murmured. "Any more vibration and I won't be able to sit for a week."

He rolled her off him and after a thorough check for rips or tears in the condom, disposed of it before tugging Alice back into his arms.

Outside, darkness had fallen and a faint sliver of moonlight pierced the filmy curtains. She sighed and relaxed against him in the boneless manner of one who'd fallen asleep. James yawned but his mind remained too busy for sleep. Her preoccupation with her inheritance bothered him. He liked her. They were compatible in bed and out, but their differences regarding money...

He couldn't get past greediness for wealth.

Alice woke slowly, the chatter of birds outside the window informing her daylight had arrived. She stretched, the pull of sore muscles a reminder of the previous night's activities. Turning her head, she saw James. His eyes were closed, his jaw dark with morning stubble. As she watched, his blue eyes opened.

"Morning, James." His cock dug into her hip and suddenly her mind was on sex and condoms. It dwelled there a lot these days, but then the prod of an erection against a hipbone would do that.

"How do you feel?" He cupped her jaw in a gentle gesture and rubbed the back of his hand across her jaw. "Up to another condom test?"

In truth, she felt a bit sore, but the idea of more of the same rapture she'd experienced last night was too tempting. "Should I pick a number?"

"Why not?" he said with a lazy chuckle.

Alice picked number two. She plucked the condom out of the bag and handed it to him.

He rolled it on with a competent move. This version was a pale pink and although it had the vibration apparatus, it differed with a rash of raised dots all over the condom. She supposed the final products would be in theme and either gold, silver or bronze but this sample looked like a condom with measles especially with the reddish pink spots.

"Feel?" Alice asked, reaching for the clipboard. She spotted the pen on the floor and rolled off the bed to pick it up. After crawling back into bed, she arched a brow. "Well?"

"The latex on this one is different. It feels much thicker. Maybe too thick. It might cause sensitivity loss." He leaned toward her and kissed her neck, nibbling across her collarbone. Alice tilted her head to give him better access. "It will be interesting to see how you find the latex when it's inside you."

Alice quivered. His hands wandered her rib cage then rose to cup and lift both breasts. Squashing them together, he took both nipples deep into his mouth and sucked. Her heart lurched painfully, the tug to her feminine parts immediate. She hadn't realized a man's mouth would feel so intimate, so right.

James let one nipple pop from his mouth. Her freed nipple shone in the early morning light. Still sucking strongly, he made a brief foray with his free hand and probed her delicate nether lips. She widened her legs to give him better access, letting her eyelids drop to half-mast to concentrate on his soft, butterfly stroke across her nub. The hard ridge of his cock prodded her lower belly while he continued his delicious assault. The beginnings of climax shimmered through her.

"I need you inside me," she whispered. "Please."

"What about the taste test?"

"Oh okay." She pulled away and shoved him to the bed.

"I do like a pushy, demonstrative woman," he drawled, laughter deepening his dimple.

Alice decided to explore, perhaps a little teasing first. Since she liked her nipples suckled, perhaps he would enjoy the same attentions. Alice teased him with tiny kisses, tantalizingly brief. She scraped her fingernails across the flat discs and watched his reaction with interest. His muscular chest was smooth and sculpted and tempted her to bite.

"I do like a well-built man," she murmured. "It's very sexy."

"You find me sexy?"

"Oh yeah." She kissed down his chest, then across his ribs to his groin. With her hand, she guided his arousal to her mouth. Her tongue darted out and she licked the underside of his cock.

"Do that again," he said. "Please."

She repeated the move and he shuddered. "This one tastes more minty," she said, "but I have to agree on the feel of the latex. There are too many raised dots. It's like kissing the bristles of a harsh brush."

James snorted. "Good simile."

"Do you want me on top again?"

"Not this time. Hard and fast. Let's put this baby through its paces." He grabbed her and flipped her on her back before she could utter a word. Seconds later, he impaled her with one seamless stroke. Reaching between them, he pulled the vibration tab.

The pulsation commenced, strong and intense, kindling an instant fire in her. James kissed her, feasting on her mouth while maintaining an even pace with his strokes. The combined vibration and the friction of the raised dots dragged against her sensitive skin. She gasped and arched into him.

*So good. So, so decadent and delicious.*

James continued to thrust and angled his strokes until the tiny knot on the condom struck her clitoris. Hot pleasure spilled through Alice, and the blissful vibration within her sex intensified, making her cry out. James plunged into her, then he stiffened and remained planted deep inside her. His arms tightened, and he embraced her for an instant longer before pulling away.

James pulled out of her and disposed of the condom. He flopped back onto the mattress at her side, turning his head to glance at her. "What did you think of number two?"

"Ah, the vibration felt more intense with this model. I didn't like the dots. They felt weird."

"Yeah, I thought it had reduced sensation because of the thick latex. Mark that one down for redesign and improvement."

Alice reached for the clipboard. That made one maybe and one dud in need of improvement. She'd seen the budgets yesterday and they hadn't reassured her much. If they didn't get the Vibration model out on the market soon, she wouldn't have an inheritance. The thought brought horror. She remembered the dark years of her childhood when her father had declared bankruptcy, and she never, ever wanted to go through a situation like that again.

# Chapter 9

James drove to work with Alice, dropping her off at the bed and breakfast so she could change clothes before heading to Fancy Free. Deep in thought, James wandered into his office. Loud chatter from the boardroom made him put off his mail and messages in favor of investigation.

He halted in the doorway. The entire board was present, and it looked as though one of them had shouted morning tea.

"I thought we weren't meeting until later in the day."

"Ah, James." Harriet paused in her knitting. "You're here in time for the banana cake."

"I checked the security angle," Richard said. "The references and backgrounds for all the recent employees have checked out. Maybe our problems are related to the cult."

"Get to the good stuff," Katarina muttered, cutting her hand through the air. "How did the tests go?"

As one, they peered at him, anticipation and curiosity on their faces, the silence in the boardroom very telling. They expected to hear the sordid details.

Nonplussed, he went for evasion. "I'm not the kiss and tell kind of guy. What's up with the security?" No way would they get intimate details. It was personal, dammit.

"Stuff and nonsense," Katarina counteracted, a gleam in her pale blue eyes. "We have a right to know about the condom trials since we're on the board. We own a slice of this company and we need full disclosure to make informed decisions."

Damn, why couldn't she take up knitting or crochet to keep her busy like Harriet? Then maybe she wouldn't pick on him quite as much. "Why don't you knit a scarf for your granddaughter?"

"Stop the prevarication," Joseph said. "How did you go?"

He and Alice had tried some of the condoms, with number five the best model to date. They'd made love, and the vibrations had lasted longer than they had. It had been bloody good. James shook himself from memories. They worked well together but their personal philosophies were miles apart. He wouldn't sacrifice his principles for a woman who chased the almighty dollar. This couldn't be anything other than a fling.

Aware the oldies wanted details he spoke in technicalities. "The vibrating feature is different. I don't know if you'd want to use it every time—"

"Did Alice enjoy it? Will I like it?" Harriet asked.

"Why don't some of you assess them?" James hoped to disconcert the oldies. "I know you won't be security risks." Only yesterday, they'd quoted their age as a reason for him to test the Vibration with Alice. He'd see how they liked it when he reversed their strategy on them.

Richard Morgan stretched. "That's actually a good idea," he said. "Should I get Rodney to come up with some more samples?"

Everyone shifted their attention to Richard.

Ben spoke for them all. "Just who do you intend to use the Vibration with? The rest of us are married but you're a bachelor."

Richard spluttered while James grinned, glad he'd managed to deflect attention from himself.

"I bet it's the mystery woman," Joseph said. "Ted Edwards reckoned you had a woman. Said he couldn't get you to talk either."

"And here we thought you were a confirmed bachelor." Ben's left eye closed in a sly wink.

"I'll get Rodney to bring up samples and questionnaires," James said, deciding to rescue Richard from persecution. He strode from the boardroom, down the short, carpeted passage to his office. Rita sat at her desk, fine-tuning the budgets they'd prepared for the bank.

He paused by her chair, noting the mess of computer printouts. "How's it look?"

"It looks pretty good to me, especially after Alice studied the budgets. She's a whiz with money. I think the bank manager will like what he sees. Did the tests go well?"

There was no mistaking the undertone of humor. James ignored it just as he discounted the tidbit about Alice and money. He didn't want to know.

"We were pleased with one of the models. The other wasn't so impressive. Did you know the oldies want to run tests?"

Rita's brows rose to a well-defined arch. "Keeps the security problem under wraps. I wish Alicia were here. We had a bet about how long it would take them to get curious. She wins."

"I wish they'd spoken up yesterday." Then he wouldn't be craving another go-round with Alice.

"Problems?"

"Alice and I don't have much in common." Hell, they stood at opposite ends of the spectrum.

"You don't need anything in common to have great sex," Rita countered.

She spoke the truth so he nodded. But if they hadn't slept together, he wouldn't know how generous she was in bed, how she loved new experiences. James suppressed a shiver. They still had a few variations to trial.

"Are you going to let the board members help?"

"What do you think? Can they do it?"

"They have a hell of a lot more experience than you do, young man. And a vested interest."

James grinned, trying not to let his mind drift down that path. It was like imagining his parents and sex in the same sentence. That thought wiped the smirk clean off his face. His mother... Ugh!

"Do you want to check the budgets one last time before I drop them off at the bank?"

He darted a look through the door at the pile of mail on his desk. It balanced delicately, threatening to topple at the slightest touch. He needed to scan the urgent stuff then grab Alice and do more tests since they were on a timeline. His lips twisted in irony. No matter how pissed he felt about her attitude to money, he still wanted her physically. There was a double standard there somewhere. "No, the sales forecast figures looked okay to me and you said Alice had checked them. It was just the repairs and maintenance and a few of the other running costs that needed a tweak."

Rita frowned. The crease between her brows brought a worried expression to her face. "I hope the bank goes for this. We're up to our overdraft limits already this month. The cost of latex has gone through the roof and we had that breakdown on the production line."

"Roger will approve it. He knows the company is solid. We're just going through a slight downswing. We'll turn it around." James reached for the phone and contacted Rodney about more supplies.

After a brief chat with their inventor, James returned to the boardroom. "Rodney will be up soon. Who wants to test the Vibration?"

Each of the board members raised their hands. A pregnant silence ruled as he inspected their individual expressions. Looks of innocence shone in every single one. "You didn't think to mention your willingness to test condoms yesterday?" His question hovered a shade away from tetchy. He wasn't sure whether he should shout or subject them to icy silence. Bloody hell. The oldies acted worse than a pack of teenagers. If only Alicia were here to manage them. Lord, he missed that woman. She'd had a way of cutting through the crap.

"Right," he muttered, after glaring at them. "Telling me you wanted to help with the tests would have spoiled your fun. I'll expect full results by the end of the week. Remember you are to swear your partners to secrecy. If we have any leaks about the Vibration and the competition gets wind of our new product, we're in trouble. It's imperative to get our product on the market first. If we don't, we'll lose everything. Do you understand?"

"We do," Joseph snapped. "We're old not stupid."

"That's right." Ben rubbed his hands together. "I'm looking forward to helping with the tests."

James scowled at his feet. No, they weren't stupid. They were wily and cunning and yanked his strings as if he were a damn puppet.

The door flew open and Rita strode in to the boardroom with several copies of the local paper tucked under her arm. "Today's paper has arrived. Some interesting reading. Check the gossip column." The significant glance she directed at James sent swirls of alarm through his gut.

Richard grabbed a paper from Rita, placed it on the table and skimmed the headlines. "Scurrilous muck," he muttered.

"They're running a story about condoms—from the cult's point of view."

James winked at Rita. "Free publicity for our products."

"Huh!" Richard turned the page and James watched the color slide from his face, leaving him chalky white. "Who the bloody hell writes this garbage?" Richard spluttered after a moment's silence.

James peered over his shoulder, scanning the page the older man had read. "Fuck."

"Language, young man," Harriet barked, rapping him over the knuckles with a knitting needle.

"Sorry." He rubbed the sting from the back of his hand.

Ben, who had picked up another copy of the *Sloan Gazette*, read aloud. "A local businessman, who we'll call Mr. X was seen entering the bed and breakfast with Miss A late at night. Witnesses state he didn't leave until the next morning. Let's hope Mr. X availed himself of Fancy Free products! Local policeman R was seen in the company of a mystery woman several times during the past week and they're looking mighty cozy. Maybe another customer for Fancy Free? Watch this space for more news on the identity of the mystery woman."

"Ooh, care to give us the inside scoop?" Katarina asked, tongue in cheek.

"Don't look at me," James said. "I don't kiss and tell. I've told you that before." His mother would have a cow when she saw the latest gossip column. It didn't matter if they didn't talk to each other these days. She would still find a way to make her views known. At least Ms. Knowall hadn't picked on him exclusively. Richard Morgan had a few secrets as well.

"And I'm not a tattle either," Richard snapped. "So don't look at me."

"Morning everyone." Alice breezed into the boardroom in a wave of delicate floral perfume.

"Well," Harriet said, pausing in her knitting. "Don't you look nice today. That's a beautiful glow in your cheeks. It's very flattering." Her sly gaze hit James as she commented and one eye closed in a saucy wink.

"I have work to do." A man could only take so much. James stomped back to his office, irritation dogging his heels. If the oldies had spoken up yesterday, they wouldn't have spent the night together and his gut wouldn't churn like a bloody cement mixer. He came to a decision because he sensed the oldies would back track on their announcements to help test if he stopped doing the wild thing with Alice. They were in full matchmaker mode and he'd stepped right into their trap.

"What's wrong with James?" Alice stared after him, her heart engaging in a pitiful pitter-patter. Maybe they would know why he'd turned moody last night. She plonked on the nearest chair.

"The local gossip columnist has written about him," Joseph said. "It's put him in a bad mood."

"Oh." Something in their expressions told her there was more. "Is that the paper there?"

"He's under pressure because of the company too. Because we're fairly new, our finances sometimes run a little tight. This business of having our new product stolen from under us has put even more strain on James," Harriet said.

Richard stood and paced the length of the boardroom, each step a betrayal of his agitation. "Dammit, is nothing sacred around here? If I discover the identity of that gossip columnist, I will kick their scabby butt from here to jail and back."

"It's just words." Joseph clapped Richard across the shoulder. "Remember, sticks and stones, man. Sticks and stones."

Richard snorted. "I don't see your name in that column."

"I'm not going around town with a mystery woman," Joseph fired back. He straightened abruptly, his gaze on the door.

"Richard, do you know, if I weren't married, I think I'd run away with your woman. She's one hot potato."

"Keep your damned mitts off," Richard snarled.

"Language!" Harriet's knitting needle whistled as it snapped through the air.

Alice scowled at the column in the paper. Just as well her employer and fellow employees weren't here to read the gossip. It was easy to imagine their slack-jawed reaction. No wonder James looked so grumpy when Ms. Knowall scrutinized his private life so closely.

"What about young Alice? A bit of a dark horse." Ben's grin held cheeky slyness. "There was something between the two of you before the condom tests commenced. Did you know James has agreed to let us help? We're starting today."

"That's right," Katarina said. "We're all helping with the tests."

"Was there something going on with James before the tests?" Ben demanded, returning to his original subject.

Alice blinked, felt heat crawl into her cheeks. A pity they hadn't mentioned their willingness yesterday. She looked left and right. No hope of rescue anywhere. She jumped to her feet. "I...ah...have work to do."

"We'll take that as a no comment," Harriet said.

The oldies cackled as if Harriet had said something witty and stared so hard Alice started to feel like a museum curiosity.

"Yes, I have work to do. Very busy." Definitely time to escape! Still carrying the paper, she fled, feminine titters and masculine chuckles following her out the boardroom door. Alice wasn't about to fence words with the oldies since she'd lose. They had age and experience on their side.

She scuttled into her office and closed the door before hurrying over to her desk and dropping into her chair. No sooner had her butt hit the seat than someone rapped on her door.

"I'm not here," Alice shouted. She was a good person. Her taxes were always paid on time, she was kind to children and the elderly, although the elderly might be heading for trouble if they didn't stop giving her a tough time. She didn't deserve this drama in her life.

The door cracked open. "Alice, it's me." Rita's head poked around the corner. "A delivery for you."

The door opened fully, and Rita walked inside wearing a broad grin and a bouquet of balloons in her right hand. She handed them over. "Aren't they lovely? Who do you think sent them?" She offered a small white envelope to Alice. "Go on. Open it. Did James send them? Or is there someone else?" Her light gray eyes twinkled with humor and curiosity.

Alice accepted the card and smiled until she studied the balloons more closely. They were covered with pictures of clowns and dogs. With a loud gasp, she let the balloons go. They rose until they hit the ceiling, bobbing gently.

"Are you all right?" Rita asked. "Is something wrong?"

Yes, someone kept sending her clown-and-dog-themed messages, and they were scaring her half to death. It was time to have a quiet chat with Richard. When she'd attempted to discuss the matter with James, he'd laughed and treated it as a joke. He'd obviously thought she had exaggerated the situation.

"Someone keeps sending me...ah...presents," she said to Rita, forcing a light laugh that came off as strained. Alice glanced at the nearest balloon. Bright green, it sported the grinning face of a clown. It seemed to smirk at her in a snide manner. She shuddered and hurriedly stared at her desk.

"You mean you have a secret admirer?" Rita's eyes widened and she snapped her fingers. "I bet it's that boyfriend of yours. The one who attended the reading of the will with you."

Alice forced a smile while inside she remained frozen with fear slithering up and down her spine. Steven had never bought her an impulsive gift during their entire time together. It would be out of character for him to start now. "Maybe." She tried to hide her unease to avoid further questions.

"Anyhow, no matter who it is, they have a sense of style. Balloons are such a fun gift."

"Yes." If only they weren't covered with dogs and clowns.

"Open the card."

Rita didn't intend to leave until she opened it. That was as clear as the freckles on Alice's face. With trembling fingers, she ripped the envelope. A clown card. She stared at it for an instant before opening it to read the message. "It says it's from Bozo the clown and his dog Fido."

Rita wrinkled her long nose and tossed her head, setting her tight dark curls into springy movement. "Is that it?" She sounded disappointed.

"Yes."

"Oh. Interesting. No, exciting," Rita amended. "I wish I had an anonymous admirer."

"Hmmm." Alice remained noncommittal. She could have told Rita that it scared the bejeezus out of her but enough gossip floated around the office. Alice didn't intend to add to the craziness because who knew when or if Ms. Knowall might hear and publish it in her column. Oh no, she intended to keep this to herself but made a mental note to mention her fears to Richard.

# Chapter 10

Two weeks later, Alice leaned back in her office chair and let tiredness flow through her. Her gaze skimmed across the bouquet of balloons in the far corner of her office. A repeat gift from the clown and dog. They gave her the willies, so she focused on her paperwork instead. This condom business was exhausting. It seemed that every spare moment they tested the Vibration or James taught her how to run Fancy Free. A small smile curved her lips. Exhausting but very satisfying. The phone rang at her elbow and she straightened, letting the front legs of the chair hit the wooden floor. The latex supplier. About time.

"Hello. Alice Beasley speaking."

"I've rung half of Sloan searching for you." Not the latex salesman. *Steven.*

"Hello, Steven. Now you've found me." Alice scowled at the phone. She had no idea why he had contacted her. Surely he didn't want to reinstate their relationship or something equally stupid? The last time they'd spoken he'd told her she was an idiot. The upshot had been silence between them.

Until today.

"When are you coming back?"

She rolled her eyes and picked up a pen. They'd discussed this during their last call and argued. The pen tapped impatiently on the desktop. "I'm on temporary leave. I'm not coming back this year."

"It's not too late to change your mind," he said.

The urgency in his voice raised alarm bells. The tone contained wheedling. He'd been certain of his needs last time they'd spoken. "What's changed?"

"Nothing. I hadn't realized how much I'd miss you when you weren't here."

"I'm sorry, but under the terms of the will, I'm committed to stay in Sloan for a few more months." And besides, she didn't want to return to Steven.

"But I'm up for promotion."

"Congratulations." She had no difficulty infusing her voice with warmth. An excellent and conscientious lawyer, he deserved the promotion. "You've worked hard."

"But it means we can get married just like you wanted. We don't have to wait."

Talk about romantic. Alice dragged in a breath and fought to contain crazed laughter. A man wanted to marry her and she was turning him down. Her life careened way out of control. It had to be something to do with this stupid rabbit hole. "I don't want to get married," she said when she had her amusement under control. Not quite true. She'd love to get married, but since her shift to Sloan, she'd discovered Steven was the wrong man.

James was the right man.

Ironic since he didn't feel the same way. Oh, they were compatible in bed and they had fun testing the condoms, but James didn't seem interested in anything more than business. Such was her life in chaotic Wonderland.

"But I—"

"I have to go. I have an appointment." She hung up without giving him an opportunity to speak. A quick glance at the clock told her it was time to meet with James. Acute anticipation filled her as she stood and stretched. Her body moistened and butterflies commenced fluttering inside her belly. Today they'd arranged to meet by the river, leaving separately to avoid more gossip or another mention in Ms. Knowall's column. She grimaced. The author of the column had eyes everywhere. No one was safe from having their private lives splashed across the pages of the *Sloan Gazette*.

On impulse, she stopped by the cafe and picked up two deli sandwiches and a mixed berry tart to follow for dessert. She added a bottle of sparkling water since they both needed to keep their wits about them for the tests and packed everything in her lemon straw basket.

On the way out, she nodded to Richard Morgan who sat with a younger man. His son perhaps? They bore a faint resemblance. Richard waved her over.

Good, the perfect opportunity to have a casual word about her problem with the dog and clown. Every time she'd tried to talk at the office someone had interrupted, and then when the incidents had tailed off, she'd let things slide. This morning a postcard had arrived in the mail and more stupid balloons.

"Hi, Richard." Alice liked the older man with his old-fashioned manners and no-nonsense attitude. It wasn't difficult to like any of the board members. They reminded her of her parents since they all lived life to the full.

"This is my son Luke," he said. "He went to school with James. The pair was always up to no good." Richard tugged a lock of his hair at the same time a rueful grin twisted his lips. "Made me gray before my time."

Luke's gaze appeared friendly and direct. "Ah, the condom heiress. Welcome to Sloan. I've heard a lot about you since I returned from leave. I've been meaning to drop by Fancy Free to say hello. It's been busy lately and we've been short-staffed. Haven't managed the time."

Alice squirmed inwardly even though she knew he was teasing. Her eyes narrowed as a thought occurred. At least she hoped he meant it as a joke. James remained touchy when it came to discussions of her inheritance. The only time she felt as though they communicated was during the Vibration tests. When they made love, he seemed more relaxed, apart from the bits that needed tension and tautness of course.

"Ah, the cop who was always up to mischief in his younger days," she returned, grinning when surprise flickered across his handsome face. If James hadn't already claimed her attention, she'd pursue a friendship with this man.

"Touché." Luke's eyes twinkled.

"I wish I knew the identity of that gossip columnist. I'd wring their bloody neck," Richard growled.

"Oh? I didn't think cops could do that," Alice said. "Bodily harm and all that. Aren't there rules against that sort of thing?"

"Mouthy," Richard chided.

"Yeah, we might have to arrest her." Luke smirked.

"Actually, Richard, I wanted to have a private word," Alice said.

"Have a seat." Luke grinned at his father before turning back to her. "Should I leave?"

She shook her head. "No, you can stay, but I don't want anyone else to know. Heck, I might even be overreacting."

"Only one way to find out," Richard said.

"I keep receiving gifts. Anonymous ones." She paused to inhale. "I've received a clown jack-in-a-box, a bunch of clown and dog balloons and two cult members handed me a clown and a dog business card when I left the reading of the will. I haven't received anything for almost a week, but this morning I received a postcard and another bouquet of balloons."

"Someone thinks Fancy Free should go in for theme parties." Luke chuckled.

"Luke, she's frightened." Richard's gruff kindness brought a rush of moisture to her eyes. It was true. She was scared and constantly looked over her shoulder, jumping at shadows.

"Sorry." Luke picked up her hand and held it in a very personal manner. His brown eyes gleamed. "Carry on."

She tugged furtively, trying to regain possession of her hand but he didn't release it. She swallowed, warmth surging up her arm. Her cheeks flushed and she swallowed again, unable to meet his twinkling gaze. "Once when I visited James, a van pulled up beside me. A dog drove or rather a person dressed in a dog costume and a clown sat in the passenger seat. They gave me an earful about the evils of condoms."

"Don't they know about sexually transmitted diseases?" Richard snapped. "Sounds like cult members to me. Natural birth control is their philosophy. It's a religion to them."

"Was the van green?" Luke suddenly donned his professional hat and moved into cop-mode.

"Yes."

"I had a few reports about a green van. Witnesses reportedly saw it up at Lovers' Point. We think they were selling happy cookies to the teenagers," Luke said in an undertone. "I don't suppose you managed to get the registration number?"

Alice shook her head, remembering back. "Sorry. They scared me half to death. I ran."

"Have you seen them again?" Richard asked.

"No. I just keep receiving the gifts."

"Do you still have them?" Luke asked.

"The card is in my rubbish bin and the balloons are in my office. I threw the other gifts away."

"Dad, do you want to check them out? If you receive anything else, call. I'll come straight over." Luke produced a business card from his pocket. "What did James say?"

"He laughed and said they were probably going to a kid's birthday party."

"Maybe," Richard said. "Or maybe not. Make sure you don't wander off on your own. If you walk anywhere, make sure you have someone with you."

The town clock struck one.

"Whoops, look at the time. I'd better go. Work to do." Alice rose, lifted a hand in farewell and rushed from the cafe. An elderly woman entered at the same time Alice tried to leave.

"You're the woman." She glared at Alice. "The condom woman."

The woman wore normal clothes—a skirt and lightweight blouse with smart leather sandals. No robe to indicate she belonged to the cult. The residents of Sloan slotted in one of two camps when it came to Fancy Free. Judging by her condemnation and sour expression, this woman belonged to the sex-is-disgusting team.

"I'm pleased to meet you," Alice said politely.

"If you hadn't sunk your claws into James, he'd be heading the family law firm." The woman shoved past without another word, leaving Alice staring after her in shock. James? A lawyer? First time she'd heard that. Ms. Knowall, the gossip columnist was falling down on her job.

"Wait, Alice!"

Alice turned to see Luke prowl toward her. "Where are you off to?"

"I have to meet James down by the river."

Luke's brows rose and he ran a hand through his curly dark hair. "Oh?"

Heat collected in her cheeks and she silently cursed her propensity for blushing. "We have work to discuss."

"I'll walk with you," Luke said, his firm tone brooking no refusal.

"I...um...okay," she said finally. With Luke at her side, she hurried past the flower shop, the cult shop, the town hall and down the road toward the river, arriving red-faced and out of breath ten minutes later. Luke teased her unmercifully the whole time.

When they arrived at the river, James waited on a blanket spread out on the ground, concentrating on paperwork.

"Hi."

"You're late." He packed up a folder of reports and glared at Luke for an instant before his expression blanked.

"My fault," Luke said, a lazy grin curling across his sensual lips.

Confused, Alice ripped her gaze away from the sexy sight. How could two men attract her at the same time?

"Dad and I waylaid her at the cafe. Nice meeting you, Alice. James, we have to catch up for that drink. How about later in the week?"

James stood. "Sure. Ring me when you can make it."

"Have fun." Luke grinned and wandered off, whistling a tune.

"Sorry. Richard and Luke stopped me to chat in the cafe. I bought some lunch for us."

"Great." James nodded, although he still didn't appear happy. "I thought we'd go to a picnic spot that only Luke and I know about. It's private. We can eat and do our tests there without fear of interruption."

"Make love outside?" Alice wasn't so sure about that. Exposing her breasts in broad daylight...

"We don't have time for you to turn prudish now," James said sharply.

She studied him. Faint circles shaded under his eyes. Worry clouded blue eyes that normally danced with fun and life.

"Is something wrong?"

"The bank manager phoned. They've decided to call in our overdraft."

*Money*. Fear kicked her in the gut. Memories of a childhood with no money and little food came back to haunt her. "But why? I thought they'd agreed to extend it."

"For some reason they've lost confidence in us. It means we won't have enough money to keep paying the staff. Probably another three weeks and we'll have to start with redundancies."

"Can't we try another bank?" She'd recheck the budgets when she returned to the office. There must be something they could do, some way they could cut corners.

"Rita and I have rung around every bank and financial institute this morning. Someone has spread rumors about Fancy Free and no one is jumping at the chance to finance an ailing condom company."

Alice swallowed painfully, her chest suddenly tight and aching. If the company failed, she'd lose everything. "What will we do?" Her dreams...

"I'll call a board meeting. Once we've met and pooled our ideas, we'll take it from there."

She'd taken leave from her job for the rest of the year. They'd already organized a replacement. It wouldn't be easy to find another job that paid the same wage, which would force her to dip into her precious savings—her security blanket. She frowned, sick to the pit of her stomach. After all the time and energies they'd expended she couldn't get past the idea that they might fail and lose everything.

"No point worrying about it until we know the worst." James picked up the chocolate brown rug he'd been sitting on, grabbed her basket and led her toward an overgrown path.

They brushed past floppy ferns and skirted prickly blackberry bushes. The bubble of the stream followed them as they made their way deeper into the cool bush. Alice tried not to worry but it wasn't easy. They walked past several punga tree ferns, karaka and totara trees. Moss grew on fallen tree logs and she spotted colorful red and white toadstools. The scent of moist foliage filled the air along with the faint drift of citrus from James.

A bird flitted from a low hanging branch and Alice's heart almost jumped out her mouth. A nervous laugh escaped. It was the clown and the dog. They had turned her into a nervous wreck.

"It's not far now."

Alice trailed him, her gaze stealing to his butt. Sex. At least that was one way to keep worry at bay. He had a truly splendid rear end. Despite his managerial position, he always dressed casually in jeans and a shirt. Denim suited him, cupping his buttocks and drawing every feminine eye in the vicinity. Alice had noticed Harriet and Katarina give him the once over when they thought no one would catch them. It gave her a thrill to know she could not only look but touch.

Up ahead, the sky lightened and sunshine crept through the bush canopy. James kept walking and turned down a hidden path she hadn't noticed. After another ten minutes, climbing over a fallen log and crossing a tiny stream, they exited the shade into the warm sunshine. A waterfall flowed into a pool before the water ran through the clearing, disappearing in the direction they'd walked from. He stopped by a grassy area and spread out the blanket.

"Feel like a swim before we get to work?" He started to unbutton his shirt before she'd answered, flinging it down onto the rug. He made short work of shucking the rest of his clothes then strode to the edge of the waterhole.

Alice sighed with pure appreciation. She'd never tire of studying his masculine form. Muscles that rippled beneath the surface but weren't too bulky. Long legs. Slim hips. A butt worthy of photos. And she had the freedom to use his body as a playground. A slow grin crawled across her mouth. Yep, a tough job but someone had to do it.

James waded into the water without hesitation and ducked beneath the surface, kicking strongly enough to churn up white water before disappearing.

She waited for him to surface. When he didn't, fear rippled through her. Apprehensive, she stripped off her white shirt and black trousers then sprinted into the water still dressed in her panties and bra. She squeaked as the chill washed over her calves and thighs, halting abruptly. Water surged around her legs while she searched frantically for him. It was bloody freezing.

Something brushed against her legs and she peered through the water, her mind dwelling on all sorts of dangerous creatures.

"James?" Her voice wavered with uncertainty and a trace of worry. She thought she heard a voice and listened intently. "James?"

"I went behind the waterfall," he called over the rush of water.

Alice exhaled with a whoosh, concern giving way to irritation. "Don't do that again. I was worried."

He swam up to her and plucked her bra strap when he reached her side. "Your underwear is wet."

"No thanks to you." Shivering, she turned to head for the grassy bank. He held her fast, gripping her gently but firmly.

"I'm sorry. I didn't mean to frighten you. Since you're wet now, why don't you stay in? Let me show you the waterfall." He reached behind her and flicked open the clasp of her sodden cotton bra. He had it off before she had time to blink, and while she thought about the expertise he'd shown and jealousy reared its head, her bra floated away on the current.

"My bra!" Alice splashed through the water after it but he held her in place.

"Good riddance. It's not sexy enough for your beautiful breasts. I'll buy you a new one."

The money-conscious Alice was taken aback, horrified at discarding a perfectly good garment. "But I can't afford—"

"Is money all you think about?"

The sharp note in his voice brought a frown. Angry James had returned.

"No. I think about you and sex a lot," she retorted.

As quick as the delete key removed words from a computer screen, his bad mood faded. A grin crawled across his face, highlighting his gorgeous blue eyes and spiky eyelashes.

"You won't miss these then."

Once again, he took her by surprise, ripping her panties with an ease that shocked the heck out of her. They drifted away on the current too. Alice stared after them hoping with a kind of morbid fascination that the kids of Sloan didn't choose this particular day to fish.

"Come on." He tugged her hand and led her toward the waterfall. "Take a deep breath and duck under the screen of water." He disappeared.

Alice puffed out her cheeks with oxygen and followed his instructions. She came up with a gasp, her hair hanging in wet strands, obscuring her vision. After wiping it away, she spied him on a small rock ledge. The water rushed over their heads.

"Cool, huh? Luke and I discovered this when we were boys." The glee in his voice reminded Alice of a kid.

Shivering with the chilled water, she slid up on the ledge beside him. "It's cool, all right. I'm freezing." She spoke a little louder than normal but didn't have any difficulty hearing him.

"Come here." He patted the spot beside him. "I'll warm you up."

"We can't test condoms here. It's dangerous."

"Don't you think about anything but those damned condom tests?" The sharp edge of his tone made her stare. What had she said now? Wasn't that what they were here for? She didn't understand his mood swings. And they said women acted temperamental.

# Chapter 11

A fter a calming breath, she said, "I thought we were on a timeline."

"We are. But that doesn't mean we can't enjoy the sex. Savor it instead of bonking ourselves stupid until we're tired and sore." James sighed suddenly. "Hell, you're right. We'd better get the latest samples tested and the results back to Rodney." He jumped off the ledge, vanished behind the rushing water and left her staring after him in confusion.

Scowling, she jumped into the water to follow. Yep, unpredictable. She'd obviously done something to offend him. In the past, she might have backed away, but she liked James. Really liked him.

She held her breath and bobbed under the screen of tumbling spray. Gasping at the icy cold despite the sun overhead, she waded to the riverbank where James waited. She strode from the water, about to demand he tell her what she'd done when the play of his muscles distracted her.

"You're beautiful," she whispered. And it was true. His dark hair lay flat against his head while his face glowed with good health and a golden tan from the sunshine. Dark stubble shaded his jaw, giving him a rakish air. A droplet of water escaped the attention of his towel and traveled slowly down his chest, across his belly toward his lean hip. Alice had the sudden desire to duplicate the travel path of the water and stepped closer, almost as the idea formed. Grasping his shoulders, she leaned over and licked across his collarbone, dragging the tip of her tongue leisurely over his skin. He tasted clean and fresh, his flesh cool to the touch after the swim. She glanced up through lowered lashes to gauge his reaction.

He stood still as if waiting for her next move. A test. Alice froze, her heart thundering. She felt way over her head, on the verge of traveling into uncharted territory, especially since he seemed so moody.

"Go on," he said when she hesitated.

Alice shivered again, but this time it had nothing to do with the cold and everything to do with the sensual heat coiling in her pussy. With a deep breath, she licked down toward a masculine nipple. She dragged her tongue over the disc before teasing it. He growled deep in his chest, his hands coming up to tangle in her hair so Alice figured she was doing something right. Continuing by instinct, she scraped her teeth across his nipple and bit lightly. A groan slipped from him. Alice explored lower, stroking his skin with her hands. She licked and laved with her tongue. Her hands fluttered the length of his erection.

"Take my cock in your mouth."

Alice hesitated, tipping her head back to stare at him.

"I want your mouth on me." His gaze held steady and contained a hint of challenge. She considered remarking on their tests, but she held back. Mention of their task seemed to make him angry. "Alice?"

She wanted that too. Holding his gaze, she knelt in front of him. She grasped his muscular legs for balance, taking his shaft in her hands, and licked across the bulbous head before a glance up to check his expression. Encouraged when she saw nothing but pleasure etched on his face and desire glowing in his blue eyes, she explored further. She licked across the tiny slit at the end, tasting him before growing adventurous and taking him fully into her mouth. Alice sucked and ran her tongue over the flared head of his shaft. Her reward was a groan, and his hands laced in her hair while their gazes held.

She smiled around his cock, enjoying this power over him. She sucked again and hollowed her cheeks until another groan rumbled deep in his chest.

"Damn, that is awesome."

Alice gripped his thighs and played the seductress, licking and sucking, hoping to drive him to lose control. He rocked, thrusting deeper into her mouth before he pulled from her without warning.

"What's wrong?" she demanded, confusion roiling through her. She didn't pretend to understand him. Originally she'd suspected the bad boy was all about lovin' and leavin' women, good times and no responsibility. Alice realized she'd made assumptions and assigned him a label.

"You'd better grab a condom."

Resignation swiftly followed disappointment. Condoms. She was sick of testing the stupid things. Since they'd started with the trial, things had gone wrong between them. He'd changed, behaving differently. Not with everyone, only with her.

Reconciled to more tests, she reached for her bag. "Any particular number?"

"How about number one?" He sat and sprawled on the blanket, casual and at ease with his nakedness. "We should have probably gone through the samples in number order. It would have made it easier."

Alice shuffled through the bags in lieu of staring at his sun-kissed body. Number one wasn't there. With a frown, she went through the numbered bags again. She grabbed the clipboard from her straw basket and flipped through the pages.

"What's wrong?"

She glanced over at him. His eyes were closed while he reclined at ease, waiting for her to find the condom.

"It's not in my bag. I've checked our copies of the results. This is the third batch of condoms Rodney has given us."

He sat up, his scrutiny intense. "Would one of the other board members have received it in their test lots?"

Alice shook her head. "Rodney delivered the box of samples to me. We checked them together before I divided them between us and the board members."

"What did you do with the samples after that?"

His sharp tone and rapid-fired questions annoyed her. She wanted the company to succeed. Her future security depended on it. Surely he didn't think she had something to do with the problems the company faced? "I locked them in my office and rang the board members concerned. Everyone except Richard Morgan came in to pick up their test samples, and I handed them over in person. I locked Richard's samples away until he picks them up, probably this afternoon."

James nodded. "What about our samples?"

"I put them in my handbag until I met you for lunch."

"Did anyone come into your office this morning?"

"Rodney. Several of the board members—they came to pick up their condoms. I had a meeting with a sales rep from one of the latex companies this morning. Rita showed him in for me."

"What about the other sales rep from Plastiques Incorporated?"

"I talked to him via phone. He couldn't fit in a visit this week."

"Did you leave anyone alone in your office?"

Alice narrowed her gaze at his sharp tone. "No, I didn't."

"I'm not accusing you."

"It sounded like it."

He grunted and scrubbed his hands over his face. "Grab one of the other samples and come here. Please," he added when she glared at him.

"Aren't we going to go to investigate? Isn't that more important?"

"As soon as we get back to the office," he said. "Half an hour won't make much of a difference."

Alice scowled, not feeling like sex in the slightest. He'd practically blamed her when she had more to lose than anyone.

James moved closer and tugged her tense body against his side. "I'm sorry. I have a lot on my mind." Such as feeling more for Alice than he wanted to. They were so different and had opposing points of view when it came to money. James had fought with his family all his adult life about money—he didn't want it to drift over to his social life. "I'm not blaming you. So much is at stake. Although Rodney has worked on the design for months and we're doing the final product tests, release on the market is still a few months away. At the moment we're existing day to day. If someone has stolen that sample..." He trailed off. "You're right. I won't be able to concentrate until I know if there has been an error or something more sinister is afoot. We can do the rest of the tests tonight." He stood and tugged Alice to her feet. "Get dressed and we'll go back to the office now."

"But I don't have underwear." Accusation shaded her voice and she glanced in the direction of the stream.

James grinned, the change of subject lightening his mood. Good riddance to them. "You'll have to make do." He made a mental note to purchase replacements, something sexy and enticing, and he knew the woman to help him with that chore. While James dressed, he watched Alice don her clothes. Although he knew she worried about her size, he thought she was perfect.

"Are you sure this doesn't look indecent?"

He restrained his amusement. Her wet hair had dripped on her blouse, making it cling to her full breasts. Bedraggled and breathless from hurrying to dress, she looked so enticing he found it difficult to breathe. Hell, he had it bad. Only a few months to go...

They started their walk back to the office, retracing the path to the road.

Halfway along River road, a small white car slowed before it passed them. The two female occupants stared before the driver sped up and drove off.

Great. Just bloody great. His mother and sister possessed an inbuilt antenna where he was concerned. No doubt he'd hear about his Lothario tendencies and his bad reputation next time they met.

Back in the office, he waited for Alice to check the paperwork.

"Ben has numbers one, two and three. Harriet has numbers four and five. Joseph has three, four and five. Katarina has one and two. And we were meant to have one of each."

James nodded. "I'll ring them to confirm they have the correct numbers. Where did the balloons come from?"

"Someone delivered them to the office earlier. I don't know how they got up there. They were in the corner of the room when I arrived this morning."

James' eyes narrowed. He grabbed a chair and stood on it to reach one of the colorful helium balloons floating on the ceiling. "This one is covered with clowns. And this one has dogs on it."

"Yes."

He studied her in a thoughtful manner before he gathered up the rest of the balloons and clambered down. "You said you saw a clown and a dog driving a van."

"Yes."

"I don't like it. It's time to let the police know." A twinge of unease rippled down his backbone. It was easy to see the gifts made her uncomfortable. Why hadn't she mentioned them earlier?

Alice grimaced. "That's part of the reason I was late for our lunch date. I stopped to have a word with Richard and Luke."

"So that's why Luke escorted you." Relief hit James. Until then he hadn't realized jealousy had played such a big part in his reaction. It made him look at her with new eyes. Sure, they were compatible in bed, but they had nothing in common apart from their interest in Fancy Free. They were too different for him to consider anything more than a fling.

"Luke said I shouldn't go anywhere alone, to be on the safe side. I'll go and check with Rodney about the samples," she said, "although we both checked the numbers together. I don't see how we could have both made a mistake."

"Wait." He grasped her forearm to halt her departure. "Has anything else happened that I should know about?" He gestured at the balloons he'd rescued and tied to the chair.

"A couple of things."

"Why didn't you tell me?" he demanded. "Such as what?"

"Some business cards, a jack-in-a-box at the bed and breakfast. More balloons."

James didn't like the sound of it, even though taken on their own they seemed harmless. "Be careful. Don't go anywhere on your own."

"I won't," she promised. "I won't leave the premises."

He gave a clipped nod. "Straight there and back."

Half an hour later, she returned and he finished his last phone call. "Everyone has the correct model numbers." He grinned without warning. "Good results, by the sound of it. They're having fun doing the tests."

"That's fantastic." She frowned. "Rodney is as sure as I am about the correct condom numbers. I've checked my handbag again in case I missed it but the sample isn't there."

"It's not in the office. I checked in case it had dropped out."

Alice's brows drew together, and he had to admit, it didn't look good. "That leaves Rita and the latex salesman."

"I can't believe either of them had anything to do with it." James leaped to his feet. "Rita has been here since the start, and we've dealt with the same salesmen for ages. Burt Williams, our normal guy, right?" At Alice's nod, he added, "Besides, you said he wasn't alone."

"He wasn't." Her voice was sharp and her nose lifted in an imperious manner. "I didn't do it either."

"I never said you did. But we'll have to tighten security again. We can't afford to take risks."

"I'll take care of it," she snapped. "I'll liaise with Richard."

A taut silence hummed between them before James gave a curt nod. "I intend to work on the new campaign and do some cold calling to try to shift Fancy Free products. I'll see you tonight."

"At your place? Around six?"

"Make sure you grab a cab or call me. Don't walk."

"I won't. Believe me, I don't want to come face-to-face with the clown or the dog again. I want to go back to the bed and breakfast to change and chase up the bank about the overdraft. I can't believe the bank manager is being so pedantic. There must be some way out of this mess."

James left Alice to continue with her day and headed back to his office, troubled by the missing condom. After dropping into his swivel chair, he pulled a pad out of the drawer on his right. He studied the list of names—every one of Fancy Free's staff along with the board members. It was obvious someone didn't want the company to succeed. But not Alice. He knew that automatically. Besides, she'd made it clear she wanted her inheritance, and in all fairness, she pulled her weight, working hard to make sure the company succeeded. He crossed off Alice's name. He crossed off several other names since they had nothing to do with production or had entry to the offices. That left about ten names—all friends and known to him for years.

He grunted. It was obvious they harbored a viper in their bosom, one they'd have to weed out before the company failed.

And the problems Alice had with the clown and dog harassing her. He wondered if this was something to do with Fancy Free or completely unconnected. James made a mental note to talk to Richard and Luke to get their feedback.

Knowing there was nothing else he could do at present, he started his cold calls. Not his favorite task but a necessary one if they wanted to boost sales.

Three hours later, he reached the end of his list. He picked up the orders he'd taken, deciding to deliver them to dispatch in person. After letting Rita know he'd finished for the day, he strode from the offices and turned toward the warehouse that housed both production and dispatch. He waved to Rodney, who as usual seemed in a world of his own and didn't register his presence. The man obsessed about his work, living and breathing condoms and sexual aids.

James didn't suspect their inventor was responsible for their problems either and mentally crossed the man off his list. He pushed open the door to dispatch and entered.

"Hi, Tim. I have some orders for you to send out to new customers."

"Great." The teenager accepted the orders and scanned them. "It's been slow."

"What about the order for McEntee and Jerry? That was due out today."

"Canceled," Tim said. "I had it ready to go and a woman rang up from the company saying the order wasn't needed."

"Did she say why? It's the first I've heard of it." Alarm filled James. They couldn't afford to lose orders. "Let me check while you start on these. I'd like them to go tonight."

Tim nodded and began to box the new orders while James rang Rita to discover why McEntee & Jerry had cancelled their order.

"Rita, Tim says today's orders were canceled."

"When? Why?" Rita's surprise carried down the phone.

"Exactly what I'd like to know." Hell, not again. This was starting to piss him off. He'd discover the culprit's identity if it were the last thing he did before his contract ended.

"Should I ring McEntees?"

"No, I'll do it." He disconnected his cell phone and dialed McEntees. A three-minute conversation revealed the saboteur had hit again. James hung up and checked his watch. The courier truck should arrive in half an hour. "Where are the orders?"

"On the spike. Do they still want them?"

"Yeah."

"I'm sorry," Tim said. "I unpacked all the boxes since I didn't think they were required."

"Not your fault. I'll help box them." James went to work, pulling boxes from the stack, scanning, checking and addressing them, cursing under his breath all the while. Dammit, heads would roll over this. He would find the damn culprit. Working as quickly as possible, they packed the orders. Unfortunately, the large order took time to package and the courier arrived before they'd finished. "Damn." He scowled down at the current order. There were several more to complete after this one. "Can you wait?"

"No time, man." The courier puffed on his cigarette and blew three perfect smoke rings. "Have a schedule to keep. Do ya have anything for me to take or not?"

James came to a quick decision. "Yeah." He indicated the pile of three boxes he'd packed along with the three that Tim had completed for the extra orders. Once the courier left, he'd pack the rest and deliver them himself. No way did he intend to let the saboteur win. The courier loaded the boxes in the back of his truck and took off in a cloud of dust, revving his engine until it roared in protest.

"Do you need a hand?" Rita hurried up, gasping her words out between puffs.

"Yeah, thanks." James yanked another carton of condoms off the shelf and slit the tape fastening with a sharp knife. A pity the orders weren't straight boxes of the same condom. Instead, they had to hand pack each order individually. Still, it was the offer of a mixture of condoms that had nailed the huge order. He could hardly complain now.

Between them, they packed the other fifteen boxes. "Rita, would you ring Ben and Joseph and see if they can help deliver this order. I think with the three of us we'll have enough vehicles to deliver the rest of the order in time to catch the flight to Wellington."

When Rita headed for the phone, he checked his watch. Almost seven. He grabbed his cell phone and rang his home number. Engaged. He shoved the phone in his pocket and loped to his SUV. It was going to be a long night.

141

A lice glared at the phone when it rang yet again. No way did she intend to pick that phone up for a third time. First, Mrs. Bates, James' mother, had rung and blasted her for the despicable behavior with her son. Then James' sister had rung and taken the next shot, lambasting her for walking down the street without underwear. Alice had told James everyone would notice. Her mouth drew to a thin line when she recalled the biting words that had poured down the phone. According to Melissa, if it weren't for her, James would toe the line and work in the family business as a lawyer. She'd tried to tell them he was an adult and did as he pleased but both women had refused to let her get a word into the conversation. Finally, tired of the abuse, she'd hung up.

When the phone rang for a third time, she turned it off while she prepared dinner. Stress roiled in her stomach. Her afternoon had been a traumatic one, and it dismayed her each time she thought about it. She'd arrived at the bed and breakfast to find Lindy distraught. Someone had broken in while she'd visited the supermarket in the neighboring town.

They'd rung the police and Luke had arrived at the house quarter of an hour later.

"Have you touched anything?" he'd demanded.

"No, I arrived home after Lindy. We rang you straight away." Alice wrapped her arm around Lindy's trembling shoulders. "The front door was wide open, and we could see someone had been inside."

"I locked the door," Lindy said. "I know I did. I wasn't even gone for long. All I wanted were some extra supplies to finish cookies for the school fete tomorrow."

Luke slipped past them in full cop-mode, his brown eyes narrowed in concentration. His face set in harsh lines, his normal heart-stopping smile absent. "Wait here while I check to see that the intruder has gone." In seconds he prowled from sight, and although Alice strained to listen, she couldn't hear a single footstep despite the creaky floorboards in the old Victorian house.

"I feel violated." Lindy swiped the traces of tears from her eyes. "I'm sorry to be such a watering pot but I've never been in this situation before. This is a good town, a safe town. That's why we chose to settle here." She cupped a hand over her stomach in a protective manner, and Alice suddenly clicked. Lindy was expecting a baby.

Luke returned. "It's safe to come inside. There's no one here. It looks as though they came in via the laundry window and left through the front door after opening it from inside. I'll call the guys who check for fingerprints."

"Have they...they done much damage?" Lindy asked in a timid voice.

"I think you need a cup of tea," Alice said. "Can we use the kitchen?"

"The kitchen is clear. I don't think they went in there." Luke stood aside and let Alice guide Lindy toward the kitchen. She heard him speak quietly into his cell phone while she took care of Lindy. Alice pushed her into a chair before bustling about to make the tea. "I'll ring Jake for you."

"No, I can do it. I'm pregnant not injured. Arriving home to a break-in was a shock." She stood abruptly, walked over to the counter where the phone sat and picked up the handpiece.

While Lindy spoke to Jake, Luke strode over to her. Something in his expression brought a wave of tension, her stomach tight with nerves. "Problem?"

"They've trashed a couple of rooms. There's not much damage, but they've been creative in your room. At least I'm assuming it's yours."

"They?"

143

Luke hesitated before saying, "Looks like the clown and the dog."

When Alice took several steps toward the doorway, he stopped her with a hand to her shoulder. "Wait until the fingerprint guys arrive. I presume Jake is coming home?"

"I think so." A shudder worked down her backbone.

Without speaking, he wrapped his arm around her shoulders and squeezed. "We'll catch them."

"This has something to do with Fancy Free," Alice whispered. "I'm not sure how or why but someone is trying to scare me so I won't keep to the terms of the will."

"But practically everyone in town knows about the six-month stipulation in Alicia's will."

"Then you have a tough job, don't you?"

Luke snorted his amusement. "Oh yeah?" The mirth faded leaving latent sensuality—enough to cause a hitch in her breathing. "What's up with you and James? Would I tread on his toes if I asked you out?"

Alice hesitated before deciding on honesty, or as much as she was prepared to give. "James and I are testing condoms. We're spending quite a bit of time together but we don't have a commitment between us. It wouldn't feel right going out with another man while I'm working with James so...uh...closely."

Luke smoothed the back of his hand over her cheekbone. "It's not just work for you."

A sigh whispered between her lips and regretfully she shook her head. "No."

Smiling, Luke lowered his head and brushed a soft kiss on her lips. He drew back to study her intently. "We can be friends."

Alice nodded, understanding he'd give more if she wanted, if she gave the slightest indication. "Friends," she agreed. He hugged her briefly, reminding her she wasn't wearing any underwear. Her gaze flew to his and his slow, sexy grin told her he had noticed her lack of bra. Oh dear. Here's hoping she didn't have a sudden attack of clumsiness because that really would give the show away. All of a sudden she was aware of cool air around her upper thighs and buttocks, the swish of her skirt over naked skin. She prayed she didn't trip.

Luke chuckled, humor shining in his eyes. "James is a lucky man. Is he still going traveling once his contract is up?"

"Yes." Pain sliced her heart at the knowledge. She didn't understand James sometimes. He confused her.

They heard the front door open and hurried footsteps.

"Lindy?"

"In the kitchen, Jake," Luke called.

Jake burst through the door seconds later, the panic on his face only clearing when he saw his wife, safe and unharmed. A trace of envy struck Alice hard. James held her heart but he never looked at her like that. Mostly he snapped at her these days.

"Jake, Alice and I are going to check out her room. There's a bit of damage in there and I want to know if anything is missing."

Jake nodded. Alice followed Luke from the room, and when she glanced back, Jake had Lindy in a tight embrace. Security. Friendship. Love. That's what they had together. They had each other and were a team. Gosh, she envied them.

"Sometimes James doesn't know what he wants or needs," Luke said. "His parents have been hard on him because he refused to follow the path they wanted. It's colored the way he sees things."

"Hmmm." She followed Luke up the curved flight of stairs to the first floor. Her room, the Sunflower room, was halfway along the passage.

The door stood open and Luke stopped her on the threshold. Suddenly, she was glad of his solid presence. The intruders had tipped out all her drawers and emptied the contents of her wardrobe, tossing her clothes all over the floor. She gasped in shock and clapped a hand to her mouth to still the sound. Her plain white panties looked like giant stepping stones fording a stream. Heat crawled into her face and seeped down her neck. Oh dear. They looked enormous. Maybe there was some merit in owning tinier pairs of panties instead of the sort that helped suck in a stubborn tummy. When she looked more closely, she saw that clown stickers had been slapped on her bras and they were arranged neatly on the bed to display this fact. They also looked large—they had to be to hold her breasts—and plain. Alice closed her eyes briefly, trying to stifle her embarrassment and the sense of violation.

"Alice?"

Her eyes flickered open and she inhaled, desperately seeking calm. Her gaze took in the rest of the room. When she stepped closer to the bed, calm deserted her. A stuffed toy leaned against her pillows—a dog—and it had a spear through its heart. "That..." her words trailed off when she noticed the clown doll. It had toppled off the bed and lay in two parts, the head separated from the body. "Do you think that's a message?"

"There's a note. *Down with condoms. Save a life. Don't use a condom.*"

"That's all very well not using a condom but what about STDs and the other nasties out there?"

A smirk danced across Luke's handsome face. He held his hands in front of his face in a gesture of surrender. "Don't preach to the converted. James told me I should always be prepared."

Alice wondered who had told James.

"Dad told both of us," Luke added, almost as if he could read her mind.

"Well someone should let the cult members know it's not illegal to use or manufacture condoms." She reached out to grab the note Luke had indicated.

"No, don't touch it. I want it checked for fingerprints."

Alice toed her black skirt with the tip of her sandal. She wrinkled her nose, trying not to think about the foreign yellow substance on the fabric. "I'll need to buy new clothes. No way am I wearing these."

"Is that going to include a bra?"

Alice frowned and folded her arms across her chest. "Yes."

"Shame," he said, devilry lurking in his eyes.

She gave an indignant sniff. "Do you need anything else or can I return to work?" Throughout her life she'd hated her breasts, their size and the way they attracted male attention. Funny how both James and Luke made her feel secure in her femininity rather than self-conscious.

His eyes gleamed. "I know where you are if I need you."

After a clipped nod, she left the room, her smile blooming once she knew Luke couldn't see. If it weren't for James, she'd accept his offer in a shot. Alice flapped her hand in front of her face. Yep, a very sexy man.

Downstairs, Lindy seemed calmer. "I'll stay with James tonight and drop by tomorrow to clean up my room. Luke said the fingerprint guys need to go through everything first." Alice tried not to think about the display of underwear, but Sloan was a small town. She had no doubt that details of the burglary would appear in the *Gazette*, maybe even in Ms. Knowall's column. Gee, wouldn't that be fine and dandy. Her reputation was already in shreds.

Alice made an emergency stop at Kellie Ann's to purchase a bra and panties before visiting the bank, once again fully dressed in battle armor—or her breasts at any rate. Luckily, the bank manager could see her. He remained adamant about his position regarding their overdraft. Fancy Free was not a viable risk now and the most recent budgets backed up that fact.

"Alicia's stipulation in her will has placed the company in a difficult position. The money invested to pay for your inheritance cannot be touched, which means Fancy Free is seriously short of working capital."

"But I don't understand. Why won't you approve the overdraft? The money is still there. Surely the company can use this money as security over the loan?"

"The recent budgets show the company will make a substantial loss during the next six months. Your shortage of cash for day-to-day expenses will only compound the problem. And although the inheritance has been set aside, there is nothing to stop you taking the money and walking away once you've complied with the terms of the will."

Alice scowled, not understanding his comments about the projected losses. "I helped with the budgets. They showed a respectable profit." His other comment, she tried her best to ignore even as guilt gave her a swift kick. She had intended to take the money and walk away without looking back. She'd slowly come to understand how many people relied on Fancy Free for employment and as a focal point in their lives.

The elderly bank manager shrugged and indicated a pile of folders on the corner of his desk. "The set of budgets I have predict a loss."

Huh? They'd been fine the last time she'd seem them. "It's obvious there has been a mistake. Somehow you've ended up with an incorrect version of the budgets."

The bank manager steepled his hands and regarded her gravely. "That is not very reassuring, Ms. Beasley."

Traces of panic unfurled in Alice. He had to change his mind. They depended on the bank coming through for them.

Her most of all. "Is there any way that the overdraft could be extended?"

"There is one thing—is there someone who would act as guarantor?"

"Guarantor?" Alice knew what he meant but wanted to stall him while she thought. An idea had popped into her head, but it made her hesitate because of the high stakes. Her stomach roiled uneasily at the risk and the resulting lack of security.

"Yes, someone to guarantee the company's debt."

"How much are we talking about?"

"The bank would require a one hundred-thousand-dollar guarantee."

Alice attempted a smile. A hundred thousand. She had her savings, almost thirty thousand dollars. "What would happen if we managed to reduce the overdraft to within acceptable levels?"

"There wouldn't be a problem if that were the case," the bank manager had said.

Although it had made her heart ache and every bad childhood memory return to haunt her, she had gone ahead and transferred most of her savings to clear a portion of the overdraft. She hoped she'd done the right thing. One thing was for sure. Alice needed to talk to James, about the overdraft and about the budgets that had gone to the bank. She couldn't believe Rita would make a mistake of that magnitude, not with her years of administration experience. She peered out the window and saw nothing but trees and grass. Perhaps a glass of wine would take the edge off her trepidation and help calm the sense of panic that gripped her so tightly.

Along with the anxiety about the company finances, the dog and clown figured high in her thoughts.

An hour later James still hadn't arrived. Where the heck was he?

Darkness fell and the stars twinkled to prominence. Alice gazed out the window again, trying to decide whether to brave the dark and walk back to the bed and breakfast or not. The moon offered the only illumination. Alice picked up her handbag and stepped outside. She walked to the end of the footpath and stopped by the wooden letterbox. A pukeko screeched in alarm, the flap of wings as the ungainly black bird flew to safety compounding her anxiety. She whirled and marched back into James' house. No way would she leave without an escort. Alice shut the door and reentered the kitchen, uncomfortable about being in James' house when he hadn't turned up as planned. After an attempt to watch television, she gave up and prepared for bed.

Not one light showed when James drove up to his house and parked out front. Alice had probably gone home when he didn't show up as arranged. He'd tried to ring a couple of times but the line remained engaged. A bit weird if Alice wasn't at his house. Must be a fault. At least the order had made the plane in time and Fancy Free had fulfilled its obligations.

He let himself into his house, noting the locked door. Sometimes he locked it and sometimes he didn't—the beauty of living in the small country town. He noticed an envelope on the floor just inside and stooped to pick it up. It was addressed to Alice. He dropped by the kitchen and set it on the counter. The phone was off the hook. No wonder he hadn't managed to get a call through. He replaced the handpiece and walked down the hall to his bedroom without bothering to turn on the lights.

The moon shone through the windows of his bedroom, highlighting Alice's sleeping form in the middle of his bed. She lay curled up on her side, dressed in one of his T-shirts with a sheet covering her feet and not much else. James smiled, his tiredness dropping away. Rapidly, he shucked his clothes and joined her on the bed, curling his arms around her and nuzzling her neck. She stretched, her body undulating against him and drawing a startled hiss when her bottom brushed his groin. Aware, but not fully awake. He slipped one hand beneath the hem of her T-shirt to cup a weighty breast. Lord, she felt so soft, so unconsciously sexy. His dick agreed with the assessment, rising against Alice's curved buttocks.

James kissed across her collarbone, taking delight in her sleepy sighs as she slowly woke. The delicate scent of flowers wafted up from her silky skin.

She tensed, coming to full alertness. "James?"

"Who else did you expect in your bed?"

"Maybe an alien. According to the news on the television there's a lot around."

"I don't believe in UFOs," James growled. "There are lots of other things I'd prefer to think about." He grasped her nipple between finger and thumb and twisted it, giving her a physical demonstration of what he'd rather do.

She turned toward him, her breasts squashing against his chest when she drew closer. "Your mother rang."

Hell. "I don't want to talk about my mother or my sister."

"She rang too."

Both his mother and sister ganging up on Alice. No wonder he hadn't been able to get through with his phone ringing hot. "Did you take it off the hook?"

"Yes."

He could hardly blame her when he'd do the same thing. "Sorry."

"Not your fault."

"I don't want to discuss my family." James edged up the T-shirt until her breasts were no longer covered. Dipping his head, he licked around one nipple before sucking it into his mouth. She slipped a hand into his hair, threading her fingers through the strands and pressing him more firmly to her breast. Not that he needed much encouragement. He'd thought about making love to her the entire drive home from the city. He'd imagined French kisses, thrusting his tongue deep, the taste of her mouth and of teasing them both to distraction. He released her nipple and reached up to kiss her just as he'd imagined.

She parted her lips and their mouths and tongues mated in a slow tango. He gripped her shoulders a tad tighter and fit their bodies together until they were in perfect alignment. When he pulled out of the kiss and pressed a playful one to her upturned nose, she breathed heavily.

"Lift your arms." He whisked his T-shirt over her head the second she obeyed. Tossing it aside, he ran his hands over her naked body, stroking, shaping, plucking. "That's much better."

Before she could move, he caged her in place with his arms and kissed her again.

Slow. Thorough. Deep.

Alice clutched his shoulders, her response letting him know she enjoyed their interaction. He kissed her mouth, the tender place where shoulder met neck and the slopes of her breasts. Despite his mind and his aching dick encouraging him to hurry, James kept the pace slow and easy, building the heat between them until she trembled and each of her breaths turned ragged. Her skin glowed in the moonlight that crept into the room. His nostrils flared, the perfume of flowers and sexy musk along with a hint of his aftershave filling each breath.

James stroked the flare of her hips before he slipped his hand between her parted thighs. Warm liquid heat met the delicate brush of his questing fingers. His shaft jerked in reaction when he massaged drenched folds, blood crowding his cock along with clawing tension. He slipped one finger into her heat. A moan fell from her lips, the knowledge of her pleasure a strong intoxicant.

He kissed her again, dancing finger and tongue in rhythm. Unable to resist a second longer, he moved over her, feeling the desperation etched in his face. He pushed deep into her hot, wet core. She felt so good, her flesh clinging to his cock, her hips cradling his body while her lips returned his kisses. Her fingernails dug into his back and the pain made him hotter. The sensation spiraled through his body, making a familiar low pressure gather in his balls. He set up a steady pace of thrust and withdrawal until his heartbeat became a loud tempo in his ears. Using one finger, he teased her swollen nub. Alice moaned, arching against him. He felt the tremors deep in her pussy, the clench of her inner muscles. Clawing tension tightened his balls.

"James." A moan spilled from her lips and her inner walls convulsed with the force of her orgasm.

He stroked hard and fast, no longer trying to hold back. Once. Twice. He plunged into her one final time, exploding, hot spurts of his cum flooding her core.

For a moment, he lay motionless to let his heartbeat recover while a truth beat him over the head. He hadn't used a condom. For the first time in his adult life he'd had unprotected sex.

Confusion filled him even as he withdrew and tugged her into his arms. He arranged the covers over them and didn't utter a word. He couldn't because for the life of him he didn't know what to say. He knew the danger of pregnancy remained low since Alice took the Pill. But, dammit, that was the whole point. They were having sex together to test the condoms and ensure the company survived.

This wasn't about fun. He scowled into the darkness, her even breathing telling him she'd fallen asleep. Their sleeping together wasn't about anything except money. Having sex was all about the condoms.

It wasn't about making love.

# Chapter 12

J ames separated their bodies and flopped onto his back. After a brief pause, he held his left wrist in front of his face to check the time. "It's almost eight. We'd better move."

Alice stretched, enjoying the sensual aches in her body before curling into his side. "Do we have to?" She sighed and pressed a kiss to his chest. They'd had a slow start since they'd taken the time to test two of their condom samples. A tingling sensation shot from her breasts, landing in her nether region at the memory. Making love with James was fun. Excitement plus. Her thoughts drifted to the previous evening when she had woken to find him in bed with her. They'd made love without a condom in sight.

Alice had no idea whether this rated as good or bad. Oh, she knew about sexually transmitted diseases, but after getting to know James, she knew his reputation was pure exaggeration.

"Things to do." James pulled away from her and rolled out of bed, taking the covers with him. She shivered at the chill on her skin, wanting nothing more than to curl up and go back to sleep. After a quick ogle of his backside, she dragged the covers over her naked body and lay there deep in thought.

Each time they made love he distanced himself. Sometimes she felt like a commodity, like a...a used condom. She'd fallen for him and would jump at the chance to make their relationship permanent, but it was obvious he wanted nothing to do with her. The sting of tears made her blink. Maybe security wasn't in her future. Despite the problems, she enjoyed learning to run Fancy Free. James was a good teacher. Perhaps she was meant to be a business tycoon.

The shower shut off and he returned to the bedroom, dressing rapidly. "I'll make coffee. I want to leave in half an hour."

Alice watched until he disappeared before climbing from bed. Luckily, she kept some of her clothes here or else she'd have nothing to wear. Now that she'd used her savings to prop up Fancy Free she couldn't afford frivolous expenditure. Lord, she hadn't even mentioned the break-in to James. They'd have to take better security measures here.

Fifteen minutes later, she entered the kitchen. The scent of coffee welcomed her, and she noticed James had also made toast and put out her favorite marmalade. It gave her a warm, cozy shimmer in her tummy.

"There's a letter for you." He handed her a white envelope. Immediately her arms prickled. She didn't want to take it but reached out anyway, her hand trembling.

"Someone broke into the bed and breakfast yesterday. The intruders trashed some of the rooms and left messages in mine. It was the clown and dog. We called Luke."

"Hell." James ran his hand through his damp hair. "I thought that was a stupid prank by students or one of the cult members. I mean, I know they don't agree with condoms but they've never resorted to violence."

"You saw the balloons in my office." Alice stared at the envelope again. "I think this is another note."

"Do you want me to open it?"

"Maybe we should call Luke."

"It might be something totally innocent."

Alice studied the neat writing on the outside of the envelope, handwriting rather than the childish block printing she'd seen on television shows whenever a star had attracted a stalker. "Maybe you're right and I'm paranoid." Before she could second-guess herself and panic too much, she opened the envelope and extracted the single sheet of white paper inside. The unease in her gut intensified when she unfolded it.

"Hell," James said, after reading over her shoulder. "I'll call Luke."

She placed the sheet of paper on the table and stared at it with horror. It contained the obligatory clown and dog signature in the form of two shiny stickers, one with a grinning clown and the other a dog sitting on its haunches. The message, composed from chopped up words from magazines, carried more sinister overtones.

***You have been warned. Ignore the warning at your peril. Leave Sloan now or suffer the consequences.***

A piece of red and white floral fabric, taken from one of her blouses was pinned to the corner of the letter. Alice shivered, unable to look away from the letter.

"Luke will be here in ten minutes." James tugged Alice to her feet and wrapped his arms around her, holding her tight. Although he felt warm and smelled good, his touch did nothing to ease the chill that curled around her heart.

She couldn't leave Sloan, even if she wanted to. All her savings had gone, sucked away by Fancy Free's overdraft. If she ran away, she'd end up with zilch. She snorted at her previous naivety. After getting to know the people of Sloan and those involved in Fancy Free, she couldn't walk away at the end of six months. A soft sigh resounded in the kitchen. No going back. Fancy Free was her future now, no matter what dangers lay ahead.

On hearing the strident thump on the front door, James released her. He raked a hand through his hair, reminding her of a devilish angel. Sexy and so attractive. The thought of losing him made her chest ache. "That was a quick ten minutes." He stalked off to answer the summons.

Luke prowled into the kitchen, dressed in his uniform. Alice took one look at his set face and felt instantly safer. James stopped beside him, equally tough and impressive. Alice's mouth quirked upward in a slight smile despite the seriousness of the situation. With these two warriors on her side, the clown and dog didn't stand a chance.

"Where's the letter?"

"On the table," Alice said.

Luke bent over to read the message. "James said he picked it up off the floor when he arrived home late last night. You didn't hear anything?"

"Not a thing. I received several calls last night and in the end I took the phone off the hook."

"Who rang?"

"My mother and sister," James said. "I know they don't like the way I live but I can't believe they'd threaten Alice."

His friend let out a bark of amused laughter. "Hell, no. I can't imagine your sister dirtying her hands, but I'll speak with them both, ask a few questions in my official capacity. Did anyone else ring?"

"There was a third phone call. I didn't answer it. I just picked up the phone and left it off the hook," Alice said. "I thought it would be Mrs. Bates or her daughter again, and I didn't want to speak to them."

"I don't blame you, sweetheart." James wrapped his arm around her waist in a possessive manner. She let him, his touch calming her jittery nerves. "I hang up on them all the time."

Luke produced a plastic bag from his pocket. "I'll take this note and have it checked for prints. James, look after her. Don't let her go anywhere on her own."

"I won't." James' deep voice sent her heart into a vigorous pitter-patter until she remembered he intended to leave. Despite everything they had going for them as a couple, he was still departing Sloan.

Luke left and shortly afterward, James and she locked the house and drove to work.

"I visited the bank manager yesterday. I think everything is okay now. There was a problem with the budgets, and I told him I would take another look at them. I—"

"Good."

A man of few words. Alice noted his set face and clamped jaw and decided to tell him about how she'd sorted out the predicament another time. His mind was obviously elsewhere. Even when they'd tested the condoms this morning, he'd remained silent. Maybe it was something to do with his family. She shuddered, remembering the venom in Mrs. Bates' voice. For all their faults, her parents and brothers and sisters would help her in the blink of an eyelid. No matter what their differences, she could ask for their help at any time. Apart from monetary aid since they were all hopeless with money.

"I intend to collect the test results from the board members and work out which sample numbers we need to delete from the test," she said. "Do you want me to check with you before I go to see Rodney?"

"No, I'm visiting some of our customers today."

"Will I see you tonight?" The moment she said the words she wanted to recall them. James didn't want permanent. He'd never made a secret of the fact yet she sounded like a...a girlfriend.

"I'll ring you this afternoon and let you know." He glanced across at her. "Make sure you don't leave Fancy Free on your own. Luke's right. It's obvious this bloody clown and dog friend have kangaroos in the top paddock. Take care, huh?"

Alice nodded, relief flooding her at his concern. Maybe she hadn't sounded as possessive as she'd thought. She offered a cautious smile before climbing from the SUV and heading for her office. He didn't return her smile and that hurt.

Voices from the boardroom grabbed her attention as she neared her office.

"Hi, Rita. Joseph. Ben." She noticed Joseph and Ben had their clipboards with them. "Oh good. Are those for me?"

Rita grinned. "They've been telling me about their preferences. Oh good news. The bank seems to have changed their mind and given us a little slack. I'm not sure why they've had such a change of heart, but I wasn't about to argue."

Alice smiled back, hiding her worry and suspicions about Rita. Maybe she had made an honest mistake with the budgets. "Yes, I went to see the manager yesterday." The board members and James might trust Rita implicitly, but Alice remained open to possibilities especially since speaking to the bank manager. Friendship didn't blind her the same way. She decided to have a quiet word with everyone testing the condoms, ask them to give the results directly to her and not to discuss them with anyone, not even each other. This morning, she'd scrutinize the budgets again. If it meant she hurt feelings, then so be it.

The company must succeed. Her future security depended on it. "Would you like to come to my office, so we can discuss the results?"

"We can do it here," Ben said.

Alice shook her head. "I have the paperwork locked in my office. It would be easier if we went through everything with all the information."

"All right," Joseph said.

"You know." Alice strove for normalcy, so no one took offence or became alert to her suspicions. "Lindy made me some chocolate chip cookies. She was baking for the school fete. I have a tin in my office."

"You have a stash?" Ben asked, cocking his head. He stared at Alice for a fraction longer before turning to Joseph. "Damn, the woman has Lindy's cookies. I intend to buy some at the fete tomorrow, but hell, I'm set to eat cookies now. Let's go."

"Lindy made dozens for the fete. You can buy more tomorrow." With a laugh, she led the way to her office. "Rita, would you be able to make us a pot of coffee?"

"As long as you save a cookie for me."

Alice nodded in relief. Rita hadn't suspected a thing or read her request as a slight. "No problem."

They discussed Sloan and Ms. Knowall's column, due out later in the day, until the coffee arrived. Alice handed over two of the homemade cookies to Rita and waited until the woman left, shutting the door after her before bringing up the test results.

"Do you have any favorites?" she asked, picking up a pen and grabbing a pad so she could jot notes.

"I like number three—the one with the golden tattoo pattern. It's easy to put on and fits firmly. Vera liked it," Ben said.

Joseph nodded vehemently. "That's the one Maggie liked best. I like the striped one as well. Number four, I think. It vibrates a bit faster."

"I found that distracting." Inwardly, she marveled at the discussion, the use and features of a condom, with scarcely a blush on her part. "I liked number three best as well."

A tap sounded on the door. After a brief pause it opened and Rodney stuck his head inside. "How are the latest tests?" He entered the office and shut the door behind him.

"We're discussing our findings now."

"Which one is the favorite?" Rodney's gaze landed on the tin of cookies. "Can I have one of those?"

Alice shunted the tin in his direction. "Grab a coffee. Number three is a clear favorite."

"Ah, yes. I like that one. The latex is thin so it feels natural but it's still strong enough to cope with just about anything."

"What about that anal sex?" Ben demanded. "Is the condom all right for that?"

As one, all the men turned to her. Bother, she'd thought she'd become blasé about sex, but it appeared there were still things that threw her. "Don't ask me," she huffed. "I'm strictly a vanilla girl."

Ben turned his attention to their inventor. "Rodney?"

"That particular version is very good for anal sex. The vibrations work well in both alternative and traditional positions." The man didn't even crack a grin. When it came to his work, their inventor was very serious.

"How do you know? Have you tested it?" Ben asked.

"Yes," Rodney confirmed.

Alice would have liked to ask questions. It looked as if Ben wanted more information too.

"When can we start marketing?" Joseph glanced at Alice. "It's not your fault, but when your prospective inheritance was taken out of the coffers and slapped in that investment, it ran us short."

"I know." Alice bit her bottom lip, distracted from thoughts of anal sex. She tried not to think about the will stipulation and her discussion with the bank manager. If the company failed...

Unease slithered through her mind. Fancy Free was vulnerable and the fault belonged to her.

"I've already done most of the machine tests. The human trials are the last step in the process. Shouldn't be much longer before we can finalize packaging and start our advertising campaign."

Ben nodded. "Good. Good." He eyed the tin of cookies with such blatant desire that Alice shunted it toward him.

She sighed, glad the tests were almost completed, but it meant she didn't need to spend personal time with James. Their sexual relationship would turn into a business one again. No fringe benefits. She swallowed and stopped that thought right there. She didn't want to think about being alone again.

J ames whistled as he strode into the offices of Fancy Free with a package under his arm. His visits had gone well—very well—and he'd scored several more orders, which he'd already dropped off for dispatch. Alice's door was closed but he tapped on it and entered when he saw she sat behind her desk. She had papers strewn everywhere and a laptop computer in front of her. Glasses gave her a serious air while the pucker on her brow made him want to kiss away her worry.

"Hi." His gaze drifted across her face before moving lower. She still insisted on the bulky clothes even though they were ill fitting and did nothing for her. He'd had a private word with Luke before coming back to the office. From what his friend said, the intruders had hacked up most of Alice's clothes, although he knew she kept some at his house. Luke didn't like the situation, especially since the escapades had increased in frequency. Between them they'd agreed to keep an eye on her. "I bought you something."

A shy smile curled her lips, making him want to lean over the desk and kiss her until desire brought a sparkle to her eyes and color to her cheeks. "What?"

"Open it and see." He handed over the parcel and attempted to clear a space to perch on the corner of her desk. After sliding several pages aside, his mouth tightened. Budgets. Alice was working on the damn budgets again. Irritation swelled up in a crashing wave. Didn't she ever stop thinking about money, profit and the bottom line? There were more important things in life than money.

Alice opened the parcel carefully, peeling away tape and lifting aside tissue paper. Her hands hovered over the lingerie he'd purchased for her. She stared before she raised her head. "You shouldn't have. They're too expensive."

"I said I'd replace the ones lost in the river," he gritted out, his anger growing.

Her eyes widened. "But these are expensive. You didn't need to pay so much. I would—"

James gave an irritable shrug, pretending unconcern when fury gripped him hard. Why the fuck did people get so hung up on money? It didn't make them any happier. "They're a present. Take them or throw them away. It's all the same to me."

"Oh, I couldn't do that." Shock colored her voice. "That would be a terrible waste of money."

"Is that all you think of?" he demanded, springing off the desk to put distance between them. Hell, he sure knew how to pick them. He should have learned by now that most women put money and material possessions in front of the things that mattered. Yeah, he'd watch over her and keep her safe, but at the end of the six months, he'd walk away without regrets.

"What?" Confusion marred her smooth brow.

Hell, she didn't get it. "There are more important things than money," James snapped.

She straightened abruptly, her chair creaking with the force of her weight, and they glared at each other. "Money is pretty important."

"No. It's not."

Alice's eyes narrowed, her chin lifting in a stubborn manner. "Money gives security. It might not matter to you, but I need the security that comes with having money. I can't do it again. I just can't."

The hint of panic in her voice gave him pause. He studied her carefully and noticed the sheen of tears in her eyes. "Can't do what, Alice?"

"When I was twelve my father declared bankruptcy. It ch-changed everything. We had to move from our home." She sniffed and a tear spilled over and ran down her cheek. "I had to sell my pony Holly and we...we couldn't afford to keep our dog any more. We had to adopt him out." She rubbed away another tear with the back of her hand. "All I want is the security a little money brings. What's wrong with that?"

Aw, damn. Her confession explained so much. The anger in him seeped away. James stepped around the corner of the desk and tugged Alice to her feet. He pressed her to his chest and smoothed his hand down her back. Her entire body was stiff, and guilt whacked him over the head. Hell, he'd practically accused her of being a gold digger, desperate for money. "I'm sorry."

"You weren't to know," Alice whispered.

Yeah, but he'd judged her without the facts. "What happened?"

Alice swallowed and avoided his gaze. James gripped her chin firmly but gently and tilted her head so their gazes met. "Everything changed after my father..." She winced and appeared to marshal her emotions. "We had to move to a new house and change schools. The other kids laughed and teased my brothers and sisters and me because of our clothes and where we lived. I hated school. I made a promise to myself I would never be in that position again. I worked an after-school job, went to university and studied hard. I never wanted to be dependent on anyone else again."

Which was why she took such care with her money and remained set on obtaining her inheritance. It wasn't greed. Alice craved security. Now that he knew, her behavior made sense.

Hell, he could understand her attitude, but he could also see that Alice was taking things to the extreme to compensate for her need. He cupped her face with his hands, smoothing her hair out of her eyes. "Are you ready to leave?"

"I wanted to finish my run through the budgets. There's something wrong with them, and I wanted to go through the figures again."

James brushed a kiss across her pink lips, keeping it light and platonic when what he wanted was to distract her from everything except the idea of making love. "It can wait until tomorrow. Come home and model the lingerie for me. Please." He'd imagined her in the silky lace and satin panties and bra, envisioned the way the fabric would enhance her luscious curves. Unable to make up his mind on color, he'd purchased several sets and styles in different shades. Kellie Anne had helped him with sizes and color choices. "Do we have more condoms to test?"

Alice's eyes closed for an instant and he cursed inwardly. Damn, he shouldn't have mentioned the condoms. That brought them right back to money and the necessity of finishing the tests.

"Yes, I have them packed away in my handbag. It's the last lot according to Rodney."

"Good. Alice, would you like to go out to dinner with me?"

She inhaled rapidly, drawing his attention to her breasts. "Dinner?"

"Yeah." *A date*. Shit, what the hell was he doing? Even though he knew now she wasn't the money-hungry woman he'd accused her of, he still intended to leave Sloan. They had no future together. They were too different and had diverse goals and takes on life.

Alice cast him a shy glance. "That would be nice."

Without giving her a chance to change her mind, he ushered Alice from her office, and after scooping up her handbag and the lingerie, locked the door. They drove to the Red Fox Tavern, a bar and restaurant on the far side of town.

"I haven't been here before," Alice said when they walked into the entrance of the English-themed bar. "It's very nice."

James gave the dark wood panels and hunting prints a cursory glance. Already Alice had relaxed, her expression no longer set in lines of tension. He knew then he'd made a wise decision bringing her to neutral territory. Just inside, they paused at a desk to speak to the hostess.

"Hi, James. A table for two?" It was Katarina's granddaughter. James remembered Katarina had said she wanted to save money to purchase a car.

"Hi, Tina. Have you met Alice Beasley?"

"No, but Nana talks about the two of you all the time." Tina lowered her voice. "My father doesn't approve of Nana spending time at Fancy Free, but I think it's wonderful. My grandparents seem young again. They go out more and have fun together."

"Katarina and the gang keep us on our toes." Alice's wry tone and the cute wrinkle of her nose brought a smile to James. Alice fit in perfectly, handling the oldies with tact and good humor. Even though the two of them were often the butt of the oldies' sly humor, Alice never raised her voice, treating them with indulgence and listening carefully to their opinions. He could see why Alicia had insisted on leaving most of the company to her goddaughter. Even though they hadn't known each other well, Alicia had monitored her goddaughter's progress once she'd left school. James wondered why she hadn't helped the family when they'd obviously needed the money. He guessed he'd never know since Alice hadn't seen her godmother often. She hadn't even known Alicia ran a condom company.

Tina showed them to a private table overlooking the cottage garden at the back of the building. Still relatively early, the restaurant was quiet with only two of the tables occupied.

James turned to Alice. "Would you like a drink first?"

"A glass of white wine sounds lovely."

"House Chardonnay?" Tina asked.

Alice nodded.

"I'll have a Speights dark," James said.

Tina hurried off, leaving an uncomfortable silence between them. His fault, and he badly wanted to fix the tension between them. He snorted inwardly, amused at himself. Women always flocked to him—he didn't usually need to put himself out, but with Alice, he wanted to make the effort. And that scared him. To divert his thoughts, he picked up one of the menus Tina had left with them. "The roast beef is my favorite and anything on the specials board is an excellent choice."

"I might order the hot lamb salad. James, I'm sorry about the lingerie. No one has given me a present like that before. It threw me."

"What about the boyfriend?" James liked to buy small gifts for the women in his life. "Surely he's bought you flowers?"

"Steven isn't my boyfriend," Alice said. "I wouldn't make...er...sleep with you if we were still together." She glanced away, pretending interest in the menu even though she'd made her choice.

*Make love.* She'd been going to say make love. "I wasn't sure. I knew he'd rung you a few times. Rita told me."

"Steven isn't big on romance."

James made a silent promise that he would give Alice the romance she'd missed out on in the past. Although he intended to leave, there was no reason he couldn't depart leaving her feeling good about herself.

"He...Steven is ambitious and that didn't leave room for anything else."

"Ambition doesn't keep a person warm at night." Not like Alice curled up beside him. James loved her pillowy curves pressed against him. A perk of the job.

Alice smiled and a delightful blush stole across her face. "Do you think things will come right at Fancy Free?"

"Yes. By the time your inheritance comes due, you'll be an expert in company affairs. It will be smooth sailing after that. Alicia would've been proud of you."

"What about you? You talk as if you intend to leave Sloan permanently."

"I'm heading overseas. I'm not sure where yet or if I'll come back here. Haven't decided."

Alice's mouth dropped open, her eyes widening in surprise. "Don't you have a plan? What about money? How will you live?"

"I'll pick up work here and there. I've done it before." The look of horror on her face raised a smile. He reached across the table to claim her hand. "Honestly, it's fun. Haven't you ever wanted to travel, to see the world?"

"I've dreamed about it, but that's all. I've never had the money to travel, especially since I have my student loans to pay off."

"But you've been working for a while."

"I want to buy my own house."

Ah, Alice wanted a sanctuary along with the security. James forced a smile while he thought about her almost-virgin status and her boyfriend. Alice Beasley wanted happy ever after. What the hell had he done?

# Chapter 13

A lice enjoyed every mouthful of the lamb, but the time spent with James was even better. Chatting. Just being together. It was different from when she'd gone out with Steven. With Steven, work dominated most of their outings and that became boring and tedious. All that good behavior.

The locals stopped by to chat and they included her in their discussions. All the time James held her hand or touched her in some way. And he didn't seem to mind that his friends and neighbors noticed, just tightening his grasp when she tried to extract her hand. Finally, she gave up and enjoyed the intimacy, her pulse jumping every time he grinned or winked at her.

She learned that James mowed elderly Mrs. McGregor's lawn every fortnight and helped one of his neighbors with their garden while with each unsteady inhalation she breathed in the citrus tang of his aftershave. The rich timbre of his voice sent shudders of awareness through her as they talked about music and movies, favorite foods and hobbies. Alice was intensely aware of the fabric of her clothes, of the teasing, sensual rub of his thumb over the back of her hand.

Work or condoms didn't enter the conversation.

"Are you ready to go?" He squeezed her hand while beneath the table his foot ran up and down her calf.

"Yes," she whispered.

Oh yes. So ready. Arousal soaked her panties and she throbbed deep in her core. She nodded, excitement pulsing inside her when she imagined where the night might lead. Lots more touching but of a more intimate nature, she hoped.

James signaled Tina and handed her his credit card when she arrived with the bill.

"Let me pay my share," Alice said, even though she needed to take care with her money. There was none to spare for luxuries, but in this case, she wanted to make the offer.

"Not this time. This one is on me." His stare held challenge as if he expected an argument.

"Thank you. I enjoyed tonight." She gave in gracefully.

James leaned close and kissed her, holding her head still with his large hands. Not that she wanted to avoid his skillful lips. When he finally pulled away, her heart sang with joy.

"My pleasure." His grin held a dollop of sin and set off a reaction inside her. Sweet anticipation.

He took care of the bill and they walked from the restaurant hand in hand. The minute they stepped outside, he tugged her to a stop and kissed her again.

This kiss was different.

One full of sexual intent and promise. A brush of mouths. A nibble of her bottom lip, the nip soothed with a swipe of his tongue. Their lips sipped and tasted, tormenting and gently biting. James drew her close and slipped his hands low to cup her butt. He squeezed gently, pulling her against his erection and gradually deepening the kiss. The erotic duel of tongues brought a flutter to her womb. She moaned at the back of her throat, feeling the thunder of his heart and his obvious desire. When they finally pulled apart, her legs shook and she teetered unsteadily.

"Wow."

"You should get a room." The tart voice came from behind them.

James' sister. The woman haunted them. Alice started to apologize because his sister was right, but James pressed a forefinger to her lips.

"We have a room, Melissa. We're off to use it right now."

"Mother is right. You're a disgrace to the Bates name."

When he opened his mouth, the flash of anger indicating the approach of a verbal zinger, Alice copied his action and placed a finger across his lips. Family was important, no matter what they did or how they acted. James wasn't responsible for his mother's and sister's behavior, just as she wasn't responsible for her parents. Each person had their own path to tread, their own way to make in the world.

"Let's go home." She gave him a sultry smile. Her gaze shifted to James' sister. "Goodbye, Melissa. It was nice to see you again."

"Humph!" His sister stuck her nose so high it was a wonder she didn't suffer from frostbite. Melissa stomped into the Red Fox, letting the door slam after her.

"Don't let her bother you." She kissed his cheek before slipping into the passenger seat, ready for the drive home.

The drive to James' house was a silent one, each deep in thought. Alice wondered whether she should move in permanently but didn't like to presume. The situation between them might change once the tests on the Vibration were completed. And that would be soon according to what Rodney had told her today.

James pulled up outside his house and turned to her. In the dim light, she caught the glitter of his eyes, the stark lines of passion on his face, and answering desire kicked through her.

"James."

Their gazes held for a fraction longer.

"Inside," he ordered. "I want you, and I want you now."

173

"Yes." Alice grabbed her handbag and fumbled for the door handle, desperate for the throbbing hardness of his erection and the frantic slide of their bodies as they ground together.

They met in front of the car. James grabbed her and kissed her hard, his hands busily undoing the buttons of her cotton shirt while he pushed her back against the hood. "Not fast enough," he muttered in a guttural voice.

Her handbag dropped to the ground while he wrestled with her bra. Finally he gave up and scooped her breasts from the cotton cups. His mouth fastened around a nipple and he sucked hard. Alice shuddered in helpless pleasure. When he lifted his head, she whispered a protest.

"Shh," he murmured. "Take off your panties. Let me take away the ache."

She squirmed against the hood of the car and attempted to obey his orders. A sob built because her fingers had turned into thumbs and there wasn't much leverage room since James busily kissed and sucked her breasts again.

"Not fast enough," he repeated. "Let me." He grasped the hem of her skirt and dragged it upward. With two hands, he ripped the seam of her plain cotton panties and tugged them aside. James roughly parted her legs and ran a finger through her drenched folds. As he pumped a finger into her moist center, the wet sound of arousal brought a cry of surrender from her. She quaked, desperate for more. An intense burst of heat exploded from the delicious assault of his fingers.

"James. Please." Alice fumbled, attempting to undo the stud fastening of his jeans. When her fingers failed to cooperate, a groan of disappointment echoed in the darkness. She cupped the bulge in his jeans, marveling at the heat of him. "I want to touch too. I don't want to come alone." The truth. She desperately needed the smooth plunge of his cock, the solid reassurance of his body as he pumped into her.

With a strangled laugh, he managed to unbutton the stud. The whine of the zipper sounded loud but full of promise. Alice burrowed her hand into the briefs he wore beneath and lifted out his erection. Ignoring his hiss, she curled her hand around the hard shaft and gave an experimental pump.

"Alice." Her name emerged disguised as a primeval groan. "No more. I can't hold back."

Alice agreed. She couldn't take much more of the slide of his fingers across her slippery folds either, but the siren lure to taunt and tease took over. She explored the flared head of his cock, unsurprised by the pre-cum that smoothed the massage of her fingers.

Their lips met in an explosive kiss. No gentleness, just a carnal mating of mouths. Desperation. Urgency. Pure need.

"Enough." He dragged his mouth away and lifted her. Seconds later, he plunged deep into her tight, aching sheath. A unified groan of pleasure pierced the night air. Leaning over her, he took her mouth again while he slammed into her receptive body.

Alice clutched his shoulders and held tight. Jolts of pleasurable excitement went off inside her like solar flares, each one hotter and brighter than the previous. He stroked quicker, pushing deep. The pleasure coursed through her body, hot and molten, building hard and fast until her climax broke over her in long waves. Basking in the aftershocks, she was dimly aware of his guttural groan, the harsh sound of animal enjoyment and the flood of dampness when he came.

James squeezed her briefly before brushing a gentle kiss on her parted lips. "We should shift this to the bedroom before we get side-tracked again." He pulled away from her, his cock slipping from her pussy. James helped her off the hood of the car. When she straightened, her skirt fell into place. She groped for her handbag and finally located it along with the remnants of her panties. She scooped up both and on unsteady legs, moved up the path to the front door. Behind her, the rasp of a zipper and rustle of fabric signaled James righting his clothing. His footsteps sounded soon afterward. A shaky laugh sounded. She couldn't believe they'd done that, even though she'd repeat it again in a heartbeat.

James reached past her to flick on the hall light. He squeezed her shoulder. "I'll be with you in a minute. Don't start without me."

Alice chuckled and continued to his bedroom. After turning on one of the bedside lamps, she sat on the corner of the plain navy cover and unbuckled the straps that held her black shoes in place. Once she'd unfastened the buttons on her shirt, she shrugged out of it, unsnapped her bra and tossed it aside. She grabbed Rodney's condom samples from her handbag and placed them on the bedside table where they were readily accessible.

He entered with a package under his arm. "I thought we might play and work at the same time. Are you game?"

The glint of naughtiness in his blue eyes melted her heart. His expression reminded her of a mischievous boy, but the fundamental heat beneath gave away adult intentions. "Sounds interesting." She stood to unfasten her skirt. The black material slithered to her feet and she stepped out of it.

"Much better."

"Tell me more," she invited.

"Do you trust me?"

"Yes." Unreservedly.

James didn't react, but she thought her reply pleased him. "Lie on the bed. Place your arms above your head. Spread your legs."

Her limbs trembled enough that she gladly followed his instructions. Where in the past she might have felt scared and apprehensive, now curiosity and eagerness came to the fore. Alice lay in the middle of the double mattress and lifted her hands above her head.

"Perfect." He set his package aside and opened one of the bedside cabinet drawers. He pulled out two cream scarves constructed of silky material. James fastened one scarf around each of her wrists and tied them to the bedhead. "Good girl."

"I feel as though I should waggle my butt."

"A very nice backside it is too. Part your legs for me. Excellent. Don't move."

Amused, Alice asked, "What about if I get cramp?"

"You won't have time to think about cramps."

The positive note in his husky voice made her believe. "What do you intend to do with me?"

"Oh, I thought we might test a few condoms." His gaze lingered on the engorged and wet folds between her legs.

"And?" She moved restlessly, the hot intent in his face bringing a flood of moisture, making her heart jump in awareness.

"Have you checked any of the merchandize in our store?"

"I haven't had a chance. We've been so busy with the tests and the associated problems."

His sensual lips curved. "Pity. You're missing out. We have some excellent products that complement our condoms. The board members suggested the idea and it has paid off. Profitable."

"When do I get to see more skin?" she asked. "Your skin?"

"Soon." James paused to remove his boots and socks but that was all. He reached for the package and peeled away the brown paper that covered it.

She lifted her head. "What is it?"

He leaned over to kiss the tip of her nose. "Curiosity killed the cat. You should take that as a sign."

"Humph." She tried not to laugh and failed. The sly humor in his expression was difficult to resist. "Will I enjoy whatever you intend to do to me?"

"Maybe."

Alice narrowed her eyes. "That doesn't sound promising."

"Another scarf, I think."

"What for?" she demanded, a whip of erotic fear skipping through her. She wasn't sure she wanted anything too adventurous. "I'm tied up like a trussed turkey."

He paused to stroke her arm in a gentle motion. "I thought you trusted me?"

"Yes." Without hesitation.

"I'm going to put a blindfold over your eyes. It will enhance your other senses. It might even stop your questions." He winked at her, his amusement captivating. Alice couldn't help a return smile. He opened his bedside drawer again and pulled out a midnight blue scarf. She watched the silky fabric ripple across his hands and the way he rubbed the soft scarf between his fingers. Her heart skipped a beat, as she recalled his caress on her skin. She stared at the scarf with a hint of jealousy before snorting. Jealous of a scarf. Well, heck.

James let the end of the scarf drift across her breasts. He held both ends and slid it back and forth through her cleavage creating a sensual friction. "Can I cover your eyes with the scarf?"

She exhaled and inhaled again, her heart racing in anticipation. Something new. Arousing. And nothing to do with condom tests. "Yes." Her response emerged scarcely louder than whisper.

"I'm going to tie your legs as well."

Alice paused then gave an abrupt nod. "Okay." A quick punch of heat zipped straight to her sex at the thought of being at his mercy. Gently, he lifted her head and smoothed her hair away from her face. He slipped the scarf over her eyes and tied it, blotting out all sight. She inhaled the lemon tang of his aftershave, a hint of laundry powder from his shirt and the underlying hot male scent she'd come to associate with him.

The mattress moved when he stood. A rustle indicated his search for more scarves. He was lucky he had so many available. Then the truth hit her—he'd done this before with another woman or women. Anguish wrapped around her heart and made her acknowledge the truth. She'd fallen in love with James even though he intended to leave.

Alice swallowed to dislodge the lump of emotion that clogged her throat.

Tears stung the back of her eyes when another realization hit her over the head. Once he left, she might have her inheritance and a house, she might have security, but she'd be alone.

She flinched at the irony. All this time she'd equated money and a home with security but without anyone to share her life with it would be a lonely one.

It was clear to her now.

Loneliness didn't equate with security. Alice finally understood what her parents had tried to tell her all those years ago when she'd told them she would never, ever follow their example. She squeezed her eyes tightly shut, willing herself not to cry.

Her parents had each other and were secure in their mutual love. No matter what happened, in the past or the future, they faced it together. A scary thought, one she shied from because it made her want to rail and sob at the unfairness of it all. All this time, and she'd never known.

"Comfortable?"

"Y-Yes," she said, glad of the interruption. Too much thinking. It wasn't good for her mental health. Time for that later, once she was alone. The cool silk of a scarf slithered around one ankle and then the other. James stood and she tested the bonds, finding he'd tied them securely. She wasn't going anywhere without his permission.

"Good." The faint rustling of paper told her James was opening the mystery package. "Do you like chocolate?"

Alice chuckled. "Did you hear about the man who asked a genie to make him irresistible to women?"

"No." His tone sounded cautious.

"Poof! The genie turned him into a box of chocolates."

James gave a bark of laughter. "So the moral of that story is that if I have chocolate, you'll find me irresistible?"

"I love chocolate. Can't you tell?" She possessed generous curves. Too generous, according to Steven yet James didn't seem to have a problem with her ample shape. And yes, the man was too dashing and dangerous for her peace of mind. Irresistible.

"Alice?"

A smile kicked up her lips. "Yes."

"I have chocolate."

"Oh." Her pulse raced a tad faster and a heavy pulsating sensation burst into life at the juncture of her thighs. She stirred restlessly, the tension from the scarf bindings driving her desire higher. Being bound was an incredible turn-on. If it weren't for James, she'd never have known.

"Part your legs as far as you can."

It was as if he read her mind, knew how arousing she found the situation he'd placed her in, how provocative. But she was learning how to tease back. Taking her sweet time, she followed his instructions until the scarves stopped her from moving any more. Cool air brushed across her moist folds. She wondered what he saw and what he'd do next.

Her imagination ran wild, thinking up all sorts of sexual scenarios. Maybe he'd crept from the bedroom and had left her there, tied and helpless. Her womb spasmed at the thought, a spike of awareness hitting her like a mellow wave.

"Are you ready to play?"

He was still in the bedroom. Her breasts prickled on hearing his husky voice. "I think so. What...what are you going to do with me?"

"Give you pleasure," he whispered.

She sucked in a wildly excited breath. Her very own sexual pleasure slave. The texture of his voice, rough and smoky, plus her imagination brought a flood of arousal. A tickle of sensation whispered across her breasts, her nipples pulling tight in reaction. Alice couldn't tell if it was because of her sexual thoughts or caused by James. A brush of warm air wafted across one taut nipple.

"James?"

"Yes?" When he spoke another puff of warm air feathered across her sensitive flesh.

Alice nibbled her bottom lip. She wasn't sure she enjoyed the helpless sensation. "Could you talk to me while you're doing whatever it is you're going to do? My imagination is running rampant."

"A lot of people enjoy bondage," he whispered near her ear. The brush of lips tickled her neck. A nibble of teeth scraped across the delicate flesh. "I know you're aroused. I can smell your juices."

Heaven help her, it was true. Although the feelings coursing through her were tinged with a trace of unease, she could hardly deny the erotic pleasure that moistened her pussy and pulled her body taut. It was official. She'd edged into kinky. "I need you to make me come," she said in a firm voice. Not only kinky but determined. Her initial hesitation had faded.

James laughed, his fingertips feathering across the curve of one breast. "Ah, sweetheart. We've barely begun. The payoff will be better if we wait. But I can take away some of the mystery. I'm going to tease your body until you don't think you can take any more. I'll lick, nibble and suck your breasts until your pussy is flooded with honey. With my tongue, I intend to lap up your juices and tease your clit until it's a hard little nub. My fingers will stroke you, thrusting inside. I'll find the sweet spot that makes your climax even more explosive than normal. And then…"

"And then what?" Breathless with anticipation, she prompted him. What would he do next?

"And then I'm going to do it all over again."

Well, she could hardly argue with that. "That sounds okay. For starters."

"Excellent. I'd better move on to the teasing part. I'm going to apply chocolate body paint in a tribal tattoo pattern. Your breasts first."

"How will you apply the paint?" Her mind conjured up several possibilities. His tongue. His fingers. Heck, she'd even heard of a man who painted pictures using his penis as a brush. That sounded like a lot of fun and she'd get to clean the paintbrush later. Sudden heat filled her face. Good lord! What was she thinking? Inheriting a condom company had affected her thought processes, and it wasn't necessarily in a good way.

Alice considered that for a moment longer before shaking her head. Nah, that wasn't it—she'd caught it from the elderly board members. They'd corrupted her! After all, they'd had more years to learn than she had.

"A combination of methods," he answered, languid and lazy. His fingers trailed across her breast again and squeezed lightly.

Oh heck. He really was going to use his cock. A shudder of excitement swept her. The mattress shifted as James moved. She sensed he leaned over her. A wheezing groan made her jump. Seconds later cool liquid dripped between her breasts. The chill came as a shock when her skin tingled so warmly, when she felt so aroused. Wow. Alice suppressed a giggle. No cock this time. He was using a squeezy bottle. The decadent scent of chocolate drifted on the air and a hint of mint if she wasn't mistaken.

James moved again and she felt the liquid chocolate trickle across her belly and lower between her legs. It ran between her folds, feeling curiously erotic.

Arousing. Amazing.

The mattress moved again. She heard the thud of the bottle when James set it aside. The rustle of cloth indicated James was finally undressing. A pity she couldn't appreciate the sight of the broad, muscular chest and hard thighs. He straddled her body, his knees cozying up to each side of her waist. A delicate, almost ticklish sensation made her start.

"Steady," he said.

"It's all right for you."

"Think of pleasure." Dark promise laced his voice, and an instant later his mouth closed around one nipple. She sighed when the feeling jumped from her breast and ended in her pussy. He drew sharply with a strong pull of his mouth. A moan escaped. The man knew exactly which buttons to push, the things that gave her enjoyment.

*Pleasure.* Yes, she could do that. With James stroking and laving her breasts, it was easy. He pinched her other nipple between forefinger and thumb and tugged.

Alice bucked her hips upward and collided against him. He grunted so she did it again, rolling her hips in a teasing move.

"Enough of that," he growled.

"You're not going fast enough."

"Lie still or I won't touch you."

An ominous threat. She stilled unsure if he joked or not.

"Good girl." His legs flexed. Alice felt a brush—she was sure it was a brush—feather over her rib cage. It wasn't ticklish exactly, but the brush made her ultra aware and the progress of it across her skin. She inhaled deeply. James would have an intent expression on his face, his blue eyes darkening while he watched her reaction. He moved again and the brush movements went lower. He circled her belly button, gradually moving downward. James painted her thighs and legs. His fingers slipped into her drenched folds. She panted, even more moisture pooling between her thighs. He parted her folds and she felt the brush again, this time spreading chocolate syrup across her clitoris. He stroked her clit but not enough before moving again. This time he paid attention to her nipples. Alice heard the bottle hiss air and syrup again before he painted her nipples.

Without warning he moved and whisked the scarf off her eyes. She blinked and took a sharp inhalation at the supreme male satisfaction she saw on his face. His sensual lips curled upward while his eyes glowed.

"What do you think?" His head jerked, indicating her lower body.

"Um...interesting," she said. "You're very arty."

"I'm also good at pleasure."

"Promises. Promises." Alice held her breath waiting for him to respond to her flirtation.

"I want to try out the rest of my paint set," he said. "I haven't tested this product before."

Ah, back to business. She bit back her disappointment and forced a smile. Testing Fancy Free's products was the reason for them sleeping together after all. She hadn't meant to fall for James. No, that hadn't been part of the agreement.

"Where else are you going to paint?"

"I'll show you now." James picked up the brush and dabbed it into a small tub of red paint. "Keep your legs parted for me. I'll paint your pussy lips." He settled between her legs and carefully painted her outer labia. "Blue paint next." With deft strokes he painted her intimate flesh. A tingle simmered, converging low into an ache. "Some green. And black." A few brush strokes later, he sat back to admire his handiwork. "Very pretty," he said in approval.

"I'll take your word for it."

James frowned then the lines on his forehead evened out. "I have just the thing." He wandered from the bedroom leaving her alone. When he didn't return straight away, she started to worry. Alice tested the bindings, but to her frustration, she couldn't free herself. Just as she panicked, footsteps approached the bedroom and made her still, her anxiety subside.

"I knew I had a mirror." James wandered back to the side of the bed, unconcerned with his nakedness. His cock bobbed up and down with each step, drawing her attention. Alice licked her lips, wishing she could touch, lick, suck.

"I won't be able to see if you don't untie me."

James grinned and set the mirror aside. He untied both her hands and helped her sit up. After picking up the mirror again, he set it between her legs.

A splutter of laughter shook Alice. "I look like a very strange dart board!"

"Katarina and Harriet reckoned X marked the spot."

"I bet the boys liked that," Alice said, her tone dry.

"There was some good-natured banter."

"I'm glad I wasn't there and dragged into the conversation." Alice shuddered. "The oldies have no shame."

"I don't want to talk about them. I have more important things in mind."

"Tell me," she said.

A rough growl vibrated in his chest. "Lie down and let me show you." He removed the scarves from around her ankles.

Anything. She just wanted him, wanted to soothe the ache between her legs. Alice maintained eye contact while she reclined on the mattress.

James moved between her legs and placed his hands beneath her bottom, lifting her to his mouth. He licked the length of her cleft, stopping just short of her clit to glance up at her. His mouth bore traces of red and green while his eyes held plain mischief. His tongue darted out to lick his lips. "Chocolate." He didn't give her time to comment but licked again before grabbing a condom. James rolled it over his erection and turned to her full of leashed power. A muscle jumped in his jaw and the humor left his eyes. This was a man intent on pleasure.

Their lips met. Mated. He plundered her mouth, and when they pulled apart, they both breathed harshly.

"Turn over." James flipped her on her stomach before she had a chance to question him. He covered her from behind while Alice waited breathlessly to see what he'd do next. James lifted her up on all fours and pushed deep into her pussy in one hard stroke. Once fully impaled, he stilled. The fire he'd kindled flared brighter. James gripped her hips then pulled back until his cock was poised at her entrance. He reached between them to activate the vibrating feature on the condom and stroked back into her pussy. He cupped her breasts and squeezed, teasing her nipples to hard points.

Her belly quivered. The vibrating condom set off a series of tingles inside her. She gasped when he licked a path along her spine and buried himself in her hot, wet core again. It always felt so good when he pushed into her channel. His cock slid over her swollen clit and massaged the walls of her pussy. James moved faster, pumped harder. He tugged her nipples, driving her higher with the tiny pinches of pain.

Alice pushed her butt back against his groin. He stroked again with delicate precision. Tiny flutters grew. Flesh slapped against flesh. A shiver speared through her body. This man...he was so damned sexy. He played her like a musical instrument, heat stabbing her when he rubbed a finger across her clit.

"James." She scarcely recognized her own voice. It was a groan, an indication of the way he made her feel. The condom continued vibrating. She cried out with raw need, desperation. Another thrust and a pass of his fingers and she shattered, exploding for long seconds afterward.

James' hips jerked. He pumped into her in short, hard strokes before freezing fully seated, his cock convulsing. Long seconds later, he kissed her shoulder and separated their bodies. After removing the condom, he lay on his side and pulled her into his arms.

She smiled, relaxed and boneless after their loving. They'd made a mess of the sheets with the chocolate paint but it had been worth it.

# Chapter 14

"James, we need to talk. I've put it off but it's been nagging me." Alice gave an unhappy sigh while she waited for him to navigate the herd of cows on the road during their drive to work. "I'm worried."

He took his attention off the road to glance at her. "Sounds serious. Are you going to tell me you're not wearing panties?"

"No!" Laughter escaped as she shook her head. "I'm wearing one of the pairs you bought for me."

"Which ones? Show me."

"No! You're driving. I want to make work in one piece. I want to attend this school fete that everyone is so excited about." She paused to take a deep breath, her good humor fading. Anxiety crept into her instead.

"Well, spit it out." His tone sounded light and full of encouragement. "I won't bite." His swift peek at her face and breasts told her he'd like to snatch a nibble or two.

"I think Rita is responsible for the bad luck Fancy Free has encountered recently."

"Rita? I don't think so. Rita has worked for Fancy Free from the start. She was Alicia's best friend. They…" James trailed off to glance at her again.

"What?"

"Not many people knew but it doesn't matter if I tell you the truth. Alicia and Rita lived together."

Alice frowned, her mind tripping ahead of the conversation. Surely not? "As housemates? Or something else?"

"Lovers," he said, quashing her hastily erected illusions. "People knew they shared a house, but most thought they were just friends. They were very circumspect when out in public."

"Oh."

"I thought you'd have known since Alicia was family."

"No," said Alice faintly. "I didn't really know my godmother. Heck, the condom company was a shock."

"It's a wonder someone didn't tell you. Sloan is a small town."

Her parents must have known her godmother had a female lover. Alice attempted to untangle the mess of thoughts flooding her mind. Lovers. That didn't make sense. Rita was the only person with opportunity. If not Rita, then who had done it? "The budgets were changed before they went to the bank. I didn't do it and I'm pretty sure you didn't either. That leaves Rita. I'll show you when we get to work. I suspect where the problem is now. It came to me this morning."

"While we made love?" he asked, with a conspiratorial grin.

"While I was in the shower."

"We made love in the shower."

"Yes." Her tone sounded prim and a little proper. "And in the kitchen and outside against the car last night." She squirmed on her seat, the twinge of overused muscles directing her mind to the previous night of loving.

He pulled into the car park behind Fancy Free and parked in his usual space near the door. He switched off the ignition. "But you had fun."

"Yes." An understatement. The heat of her skin intensified. Even though sensual aches accompanied her today, she'd didn't regret a second.

189

"Excellent." He leaned across to brush a kiss on her cheek. "Why don't you check out of the bed and breakfast and move in with me? There's a spare bedroom you can use. Besides it will save you money."

He climbed from the car without waiting for her reply. With her heart thudding erratically, she grabbed her handbag and clipboard and hurried after him. "James, wait."

"Made a decision already?" His casual tone gave no indication as to what he wanted her to do.

"Are you sure?" The spare bedroom? What exactly did he have in mind?

"I'm positive."

Alice hesitated before blurting, "Separate bedrooms?" She wanted to make sure they understood each other from the start.

"Only if that's what you want," he said. "I thought you might like a room to keep your things."

She beamed. Okay, that was clear. "Thanks. I'll be the perfect housemate."

"I'm not here for much longer and I need someone to housesit for me anyway. I'd prefer someone I know."

*And maybe not.* The reminder of his fast-approaching departure date took the shine off his offer. Pride bade she keep her thoughts concealed, her smile intact. James had never promised happy ever after.

Wanting a future was her dream, her problem, not his.

"Thanks," she managed, even though the word almost choked her. *Her problem.* "Will you look at the budgets? I'm spending the morning in the office before heading out to the fete. I promised Lindy I'd help her deliver her cookies."

"I need to make a few calls first and I want to check on dispatch to make sure there aren't any problems with the orders due to ship. I might not make it to see you this morning."

She nodded, maintaining an impassive expression to cover her hurt. He didn't believe her. Fine. She'd gather her facts and present the evidence. She hurried down the passage to her office, noting at the back of her mind that the moss-green carpet needed replacement.

Laughter from the boardroom slowed her steps. She peeked through the partially open door and saw everyone present apart from Richard. The scent of coffee and cinnamon floated in the air. Alice inhaled deeply and stepped inside, giving into temptation. Cinnamon buns. Oh boy.

"Ah, here she is!" The tinge of glee in Harriet's voice halted Alice. She scanned the faces of the other board members—Joseph, Ben and Katarina. Even Rita bore a smirk.

"I have to make an important phone call." Cinnamon buns or not, there was a joke here at her expense. Alice backed toward the door. She'd have a coffee later.

"Not so fast, missy," Ben said. "Pour the girl a coffee, Harriet. She's looking a mite tired. A jolt of caffeine might wake her up."

Alarm heightened. This was a mass attack.

"Alice, sit here." Joseph waved her to a seat beside him.

Feeling like a mouse facing a nest of snakes, Alice perched on the edge of the chair ready for a quick getaway. A cup rattled in its saucer as Harriet placed a black coffee in front of her. Ben handed Harriet the milk and sugar, and she set these in front of Alice too.

"She might enjoy a cinnamon bun," Katarina said.

Those pale eyes were predatory.

"What is going on?" Alice made eye contact with Rita, Ben and Harriet. Her stomach roiled when her gaze moved on to Joseph. Why did they have to pick on her? At least she knew it wasn't condom related since they didn't have any of those handy-dandy penis models on the table. At least she hoped it wasn't condom related...

"Isn't James here?" Joseph asked with a glance at the door. If Alice weren't mistaken, his expression held disappointment.

It was something about the two of them. Oh heck. It *was* condom related.

"James shouldn't miss this," Ben agreed, springing to his feet. "I'll go and get him."

Perhaps she didn't feel like a mouse after all. No, she was a special exhibition at the Auckland museum. Alice forced herself to reach for her coffee instead of fidgeting. She added milk and half a teaspoon of sugar. Her hand shook, although she didn't think it was too noticeable. She sipped her coffee and waited for the oldies to spring their trap.

Voices sounded in the passage outside the boardroom. Alice wondered who else Ben had rounded up to witness whatever humiliation the board wanted to heap on them.

"After you," Ben said in a loud voice.

They all straightened, a signal the show was about to begin. Alice darted a glance at the door and set her coffee cup down with a thump. "Steven. What are you doing here?"

"He's come to set your wedding date," Ben said in a gleeful tone.

Alice jumped to her feet. "We'll have this discussion in private. Come to my office." She seized Steven's arm and tugged but Ben blocked their way.

"Have a coffee and a cinnamon bun," Katarina suggested. "No need to hurry. James, here's your coffee."

Alice glanced at James. He didn't give a hint of his emotions, and she could only guess at his thoughts. When he neared, a flicker of emotion darkened his eyes, vanishing almost as quickly as it appeared. He stepped past and dropped into an empty seat at the far end of the boardroom. Meanwhile the board members shuffled along so Steven could sit next to her. She muttered under her breath and stomped back to her chair.

"You're in the local paper today," Joseph said, breaking the uneasy silence.

Alice's stomach flipped uneasily, a version of butterflies but ten times worse. Her gaze darted to James. His blue eyes widened briefly and his head moved in an imperceptible shake. He had no idea what they were on about either.

"James, you're mentioned as well."

"Stop prodding and tell us what you're talking about," James snapped. "We're busy and don't have time for your shenanigans."

"Not too busy for a little rumpy-pumpy," Harriet said in an arch tone.

"You know we're testing the condoms." James vibrated with anger, his eyes glowering and his mouth compressed into a flat line. His gaze scorched as it flitted across Steven before grazing over her face. He thought she'd lied to him.

"Testing condoms? You? And Alice? Together?" Steven's brows rose toward his retreating hairline.

"Yes." Irritation built inside Alice. She aimed it at James for his lack of trust—although why it mattered when he intended to leave anyway. She aimed it at Steven for informing everyone they intended to get married, and she aimed her displeasure at the board members for stirring trouble. Their board powers had zapped to their heads. They thought it was fun to play with other people's emotions.

"Oh well. What's done is done. Alice will return home with me. I've booked the church and ordered your wedding gown."

James ignored the pompous idiot sitting beside Alice and concentrated on Harriet. It was either that or hit the man. "What the hell are you talking about? What have Alice and I done to hit the headlines?" He cast about for a plausible reason and alarm bells wailed. The oldies were up to something. James glowered at each of them in turn. "Tell us now."

Ben produced a copy of the *Sloan Gazette* and handed it over. "Ms. Knowall's column."

"What page?" James glanced at Alice's ashen face. "Do you have another copy?"

Katarina handed her paper to Alice. "Page three."

James flipped over to page three and stared in shock. Ms. Knowall had a full page spread instead of her normal column, and she'd used the entire page to report on Fancy Free, its manager and new owner. The article covered private stuff that most people wouldn't know about him and pictures taken outside his house. *Last night*.

"I feel sick." Alice appeared numb. She glanced at him before turning back to study the photos on the page, the photos of them having sex on the car hood.

"Alice, I forgive you," Steven said.

Harriet sniffed, showing what she thought of his magnanimous offer.

"It doesn't matter. We can work something out," Steven added. "No one will see this two-bit paper."

"Don't say another word," Alice snapped.

James snorted in contempt. The man kept digging himself a deeper hole.

"Is any of that true?" Joseph's grizzled gray brows arched to punctuate his question.

Alice stood abruptly drawing everyone's attention. "Yes, it's all true. But I have no idea what Ms. Knowall hopes to gain by my public embarrassment or why she's determined to blacken our names. I have work to do and a fete to attend."

Pride filled James as she stalked out, head held high. She wasn't apologizing for spending time with him. She wasn't ashamed of his profession or lack of one. A smile played across his lips. Alice didn't judge people or assign them with labels. No, that wasn't her style.

"Where is she going?" Steven demanded.

The oldies gave him the look that said he was a worthless sack of shit and didn't deserve Alice while James suppressed a curse. The man was clueless. James unclenched his fists, shook his head and followed Alice. No wonder she'd decided to stay in Sloan. Only a fool would think Steven equated security.

She stormed down the passage in front of him, her head held high, looking neither left nor right. The slam of her office door was the only hint of a temper she displayed.

James grinned. What a woman. He paused outside, hand hovering at the doorknob, before he decided he'd wait. Give her time to cool down about Ms. Knowall's article. Meantime, he intended to confront the author in person. This time Ms. Knowall had gone too far and given herself away.

J ames strode past the kitchen window and entered the rear door of the house without a polite knock. It was like time traveling to his teenage years. The house hadn't changed. The same beige carpet and fussy décor, the scent of lavender furniture polish, a vase of white daisies on the sideboard. Each surface in the kitchen gleamed with not a thing out of place.

"Hello, Mother," he said.

"Ah, I thought you might come to your senses." Satisfaction coated her voice and seeped into her expression. Some might call it smug.

"Yes, I have." A sense of hurt ached in his chest, and he wondered why he cared. Thoughts of Alice floated into his mind. They had more in common than he'd realized. Much more.

"I'll call Melissa. You can start at the law firm next week. You'll need a few days to organize suits and cut your hair."

"For the last time, I'm not going into law. I don't enjoy it and I only qualified to please you and Dad."

"Not... Then why are you here?" Suddenly his mother seemed old and unsure of herself. Probably a temporary situation, but in that moment, he knew his mother loved him even if it was misguided. They'd probably never see eye-to-eye about the way he chose to live his life. It didn't matter. James realized they argued because they were alike. In his own way, he was just as determined.

"I want you to stop picking on Alice. She doesn't deserve her name blackened along with her reputation."

"But—"

"No." James held up his right hand to emphasize his order. "You tell Ms. Knowall to lay off Alice or else I'll take steps to ensure she never works in this town again."

His mother's face paled before she rallied. "She's not good enough for you. I thought I recognized her name. Her father is the man who ripped off his customers and would have continued if he hadn't declared bankruptcy."

"Alice is a qualified accountant," James snapped. "She's too good for me, which is why I'm leaving town once she fulfils the terms of the will."

"You're leaving?"

"Isn't that what Ms. Knowall wants? Haven't you and your nom de plume been angling for me to leave all along?" His eyes narrowed on his mother, not holding back his irritation. He'd suspected all along but hadn't cared enough to call her on it until she'd blackened Alice's name along with his.

His mother tottered over to the table and drew out a chair. She sank down, her face so pale James started to worry.

"Are you all right?"

"Do you intend to tell everyone?"

"It depends on what you do next. Most of Sloan citizens enjoy your column, but that's because you write in a clever way that isn't offensive. You've stepped over the line with Alice. Skulking in the shadows to snap photos is wrong. I'm not a kid. I don't need you to supervise my love life."

"So what are you going to do? You won't tell people about Ms. Knowall. *You wouldn't.*"

"Try me. I will keep seeing Alice while I'm in Sloan. The minute Ms. Knowall starts on more veiled references to Alice, I'm writing a letter to the editor of the *Gazette* to let everyone know her real identity. You will apologize to Alice in person. Clear?"

"Yes." His mother nodded, albeit grudgingly.

James narrowed his gaze as a nasty thought occurred. "While you're at it, Ms. Knowall should write a column featuring Esmeralda Bates and her daughter Melissa. Spread it around a little." Maybe it would knock his sister off the pedestal she lived on, take away her air of superiority because he'd bet Melissa didn't know what their mother had been up to. "Deal?"

His mother grimaced. "I will do as you ask."

"But you still don't agree about the way I choose to live my life."

"Couldn't you—"

"No." He glared at his mother and she shriveled at his stern expression. "I intend to live my life the way I choose."

"You're making a mistake." She swallowed hard but lifted her chin to meet his gaze.

"Possibly. But it's my mistake to make." James left the house the same way he'd entered, his mood lighter. If his mother thought he wouldn't act, she didn't know him as well as she should.

Her carefully planned secure life was falling around her ears. Ms. Knowall had splashed details of her private life across page three of the *Sloan Gazette*. A lot of it was innuendo with enough truth to bring acute embarrassment.

Steven was treating her like a commodity in front of everyone and worst of all, James intended to leave town. He mightn't be marriage material, he mightn't be the perfect man to give her security, yet he was the man she'd fallen for—the one she loved.

Talk about a mess.

Alice brushed a tear from her eyes and bit her bottom lip hard to stem a crying jag.

She sat on her blue swivel chair and tried not to let the sense of helplessness overwhelm her. Although she'd taken a step forward today with James inviting her to move in with him, he still intended to leave and her savings were nil since she'd used them to prop up the company.

She had nothing.

No money, no reputation and no man.

*Zilch*.

Her gaze fell upon the printouts and her thoughts narrowed to one thing. Her godmother had left her Fancy Free for a reason. She'd trusted Alice to do the right thing and that didn't include letting the company fail.

Time for her to return the trust her godmother had given her. She started going through the figures, manually checking totals and percentages instead of relying on the spreadsheet program to do the calculations. Alice took her responsibilities seriously.

She might ultimately fail, but damn if she'd go down without a fight.

Two hours later, she thought she'd worked out the problem with the budgets. As she'd expected, someone had altered the formulas, which had thrown everything out, resulting in the bottom profit line appearing far less than it was. No wonder the bank manager had baulked at another loan. Alice placed the evidence in a folder and went searching for James.

Rita sat at her desk and Alice studied her with new eyes. She'd never have guessed she and Alicia were lovers. Somehow, that had to be the key to why she'd attempted sabotage.

"Hi, Rita. Is James in his office?"

"Yes, I think he's on the phone."

"I'll go in and wait for him to finish his call." Alice held her head high. She refused to cower because of Ms. Knowall's article.

Rita nodded and Alice walked past her, tapped briefly on the door and entered James' office. She took a seat.

While she waited, Alice thought about her godmother's will. She couldn't remember if Rita had received a bequest. The reading of the will had been so surreal—she didn't remember much of the day. James might know and failing that, the lawyer would know.

James concluded his call and hung up. His blue eyes held sympathy and more that she was frightened to decipher. When it came to James, terror and anxiety stopped her assumptions. He was still going to leave. That hadn't changed.

"You okay?"

Alice shrugged. "I feel a bit battered and bloody. I'm sure it will pass."

"You want to go out for a coffee?"

Alice shuddered even though she knew showing her face in public would help the gossip die down more quickly than if she acted the hermit. "All right. I have time before I need to go to Lindy's to help with the fete. I want to show you something first." She opened the folder and produced her budget printouts. "Someone has fiddled with the formulas. It's been done very cleverly and isn't obvious unless you sit down with a calculator and check everything manually."

"But only three of us have looked at the budgets."

"Yes. I was sure this had nothing to do with the dog and the clown." A rush of fear tiptoed down her spine. "I'm sure they're cult members who want to scare me."

"I'll get Rita to explain herself," James said in a tight voice.

"Wait," Alice said. "What did Alicia leave Rita in her will?"

"Their house."

"So there's no reason Rita would feel slighted?" It was the only thing that made sense.

James tapped his pen on the printouts in front of him. "I don't know. Let's confront her. I'd hate to see Fancy Free fail because of dirty tactics."

"I'll ask her to come into the office." Alice stood and opened the door. "Rita, can you come into the office please?"

Rita's welcoming smile faded. For an instant she looked like an animal caught in vehicle headlights but rallied quickly. "I was about to go to the bank."

"This won't take long," Alice said firmly. "James is waiting."

Silently, Rita entered the office. Alice followed and shut the door, indicating she should sit. Once Rita sat, she dropped into a seat beside her.

Their admin assistant scanned James then Alice, her expression holding a touch of defiance. "What's this about?"

"I think you know." Tension rippled in Alice's tone.

"The budgets. Rita, what's going on?" James spoke curtly and Alice knew he was determined to resolve the matter.

Rita's chin shot upward, her dark eyes glittering with challenge. "I haven't done anything."

"That's not true," Alice snapped. "Someone amended the budgets before they were sent to the bank. James didn't do it. I didn't do it, so that leaves you."

"So what if I did?" Rita responded, abandoning all pretense. She tossed her head in a gesture of defiance.

"Why?" James demanded. "What the hell are you playing at?"

The fight seeped from Rita and she suddenly looked her age with lines bracketing her mouth and gray circles beneath her eyes. "It was my idea to start Fancy Free. Alicia supplied the money. I thought she'd leave the company to me when she died." Rita paused to sniff and glowered at Alice. "She left the company to you."

"I knew you helped Alicia at the start. Surely the company means as much to you as it did to her." James' face never softened as he spoke, remaining unyielding and stern. "Did you interfere with the orders? And leak details of the X-100 to the opposition?"

Alice studied Rita and knew, just knew she lay at the bottom of Fancy Free's problems. She shook her head in pure disbelief. "All of this because Alicia didn't leave you the company? Because of greed."

"It wasn't greed." Rita eyes spat fire and her lips set in mulish determination. "It's the principle. I gave my all for this company and Alicia threw it in my face."

"Alicia left you the house. Wasn't that enough?" James asked.

Rita stiffened at his challenge. "It's not about money. I don't care about the money." She waved her hand in a dismissive manner, "All I want is recognition for my contribution to the company."

James rose and prowled to the window. He stared out for a moment before turning to face them. "Have you done anything else we haven't discovered?"

"Nothing else." Rita dipped her head in tiredness and defeat, as if she knew her run had ended. "I don't know how you did it or where the money came from but the overdraft is back under the limit and the bank is happy. You fixed the order I pretended was canceled." She covered her eyes with trembling hands. "I'm sorry."

"Yeah, we know. Just go, Rita." James opened the door.

"Go?" Rita glanced at Alice for clarification.

"We can't work with someone we don't trust," Alice said.

"You can't do that! Fancy Free is my life. I don't have anything else." Anger turned Rita's face blotchy. Her hands clenched and she cast them a look of hatred. "Oh, look at you. You're both judging me, but you don't understand. I loved Alicia and she treated me like a possession. She didn't give me credit for having the idea for Fancy Free. She owed me, dammit!"

"Goodbye, Rita," James said in a terse voice. Implacable determination stamped his face. Alice shivered, fiercely glad his anger wasn't directed at her.

Rita met his gaze for an instant before storming from his office. She paused at her desk and opened a drawer.

James followed. "Don't bother to clear your desk. We'll have everything sent to your house this afternoon."

Rita grabbed her handbag and marched from the office, fury apparent in every line of her stiff back. A woman scorned. Alice shivered again. Thank goodness she hadn't confronted Rita on her own, which had been her initial reaction.

James sighed. "God, I had no idea all that festered under the surface. Rita was the last person I suspected."

"I'm sorry."

"It's not your fault." He wrapped his arms around her and drew her close. Alice needed no persuasion to sink against his muscled chest and take the comfort he offered.

"I feel as though it is."

"Don't. Alicia knew exactly what she was doing. She left Fancy Free to you for a reason."

"I don't know why. I don't even remember her well since I only saw her a few times when I was a kid." Alice pulled away to meet his gaze.

James cupped her face with his hands. He stroked her cheek with his thumb. "It seems to me she picked the right person for the job. You paid off the overdraft."

"Yes," Alice whispered, trying not to think about her empty savings account. Her heart blipped in alarm anyway. She'd risked her security for Fancy Free. Maybe she had something of Alicia in her after all.

"That was a brave thing to do, Alice. You won't regret it. Fancy Free is a solid company. It might not look like it at present, but now that we've discovered Rita's tricks, we'll make headway. You'll get your money back." James pressed a quick kiss to her lips. "We'd better inform the board members."

"They've gone to prepare for the fete."

"No problem. I'll call an emergency meeting for tomorrow."

Alice sighed at the loss of his protective heat but nodded at his suggestion. "I'll start clearing Rita's desk."

"We make a good team," James said before striding away.

Alice forced a smile. They did make a good team. Too bad it was only temporary because she'd fallen hopelessly in love with the dashing and dangerous James Bates.

# Chapter 15

"Alice?" Steven appeared in front of Rita's desk. "We need to talk."

"I thought you were leaving. I won't marry you because I don't love you."

"But we're good together," he countered. "We're perfect for each other."

"No, that's only when I do everything you say and go along with whatever you want. I'm not willing to be your doormat any longer." Alice said the words without a stutter, without backing down. "No, Steven, I won't marry you." A feeling of accomplishment filled her once the words were in the open.

The stunned expression on his face made her want to laugh. She'd never spoken to him like that before, with such firmness and honesty.

"Are you sure?"

A snort escaped her. "I'm positive. You might as well go home."

"Are you going to marry him?"

"No, James is going overseas in two months." She didn't want him to go but she wouldn't beg him to stay either. One thing she'd learned while living in Sloan and helping to run Fancy Free was that she could cope with anything that came her way. Money didn't equate with security. Security came with the discovery of a comfortable niche. Sloan and Fancy Free were hers. A man in the equation might be nice but it wasn't necessary.

Oh heck. Who did she think she was trying to kid? She wanted James. When he left, he'd take her heart.

"If you change your mind, you know where to find me," Steven said.

Alice pushed aside her irritation and graciously inclined her head. "Thank you, but I won't change my mind."

For the first time since she'd known him, he appeared uncertain. He raised his hand before dropping it again. "I guess I'll go."

"That would be best."

"Are you still here?" James growled, appearing without warning.

"Steven was just leaving," Alice said. "I'm ready for a coffee." *Or something stronger.*

They had a quick coffee and a blueberry muffin at the cafe before James dropped her off to help Lindy.

"That wasn't so bad, was it?" he asked when he pulled up outside the bed and breakfast.

"No, it felt worse," Alice muttered. "Everyone stared."

"Tomorrow we'll be yesterday's news."

"I don't know if I'll survive until then."

"Course you will." James leaned over and took possession of her mouth, moving his lips slowly, deliberately over hers. Stealing her breath. His hands cupped her head, holding her still. When he finally pulled back, they were both breathless. "You'd better go before Lindy comes outside to see what's holding you up." He ran his thumb over her swollen lips. "Take care at the fete. Luke told me he intended to discuss the matter with the cult leaders and put the fear of god into them. His words, not mine."

"I hope it works. I'm jumping at shadows and I hate feeling that way." She climbed from the SUV and waved when he drove away.

"Lindy. I'm here," she called, tapping on the door.

"About time," Lindy grumbled, unlocking the door to let her inside.

The scent of orange and spice filled the kitchen. Several tins were sitting on the table ready for transport to the fete. "Do you need a hand with anything? Luke said I could go back into my room. I'm going to move in with James so I thought I'd pack."

"I couldn't bear cleaning up in there," Lindy confessed. "I hired commercial cleaners from Auckland. They threw away anything damaged beyond repair. I hope that was all right."

"That's fine," Alice soothed, relieved she wouldn't need to face the task herself.

Working together, they packed the last batch of muffins and loaded the tins inside Lindy's car.

The school grounds bustled with parents and excited children racing in all directions. The fete started officially at one, and it was almost that when Lindy stopped in the drop-off zone. They unloaded and Alice and two eager students carried the tins of home baking to their allocated stall while Lindy parked the car.

A familiar face reigned at the cake stall.

"We're organized here, dear," Harriet said. "Why don't you stroll around the stalls? Grab some bargains."

Alice was happy to oblige. She wandered past a variety of stalls—one selling secondhand books, the white elephant stall sold all shades of weird, a plant and flower stall and one for clothes. The scent of coffee, candy floss and flowers filled her senses.

A large bouncy castle wobbled in the soft breeze. Over the far side of the field, several parents organized games such as egg and spoon, wheelbarrow and three-legged races for the children. A group of adults took turns hurling a gumboot through the air. Alice noticed the judging was very serious indeed. A loud shout of pain rent the air when one of the fathers struck his thumb with a hammer in the nail-driving contest.

An hour melted away as Alice wandered aimlessly, fascinated by the activities. There were displays inside the classrooms. Children had constructed animals from vegetables and decorated saucers with a floral theme. Excited children bounced up and down and shrieked when they saw their exhibits had won coveted prizes.

Another open classroom door beckoned and she strolled inside, stopping several steps into the empty room. She'd come to the end of the exhibits and was about to retrace her footsteps when the door slammed behind her. Alice whirled, her eyes widened and she backed up, fear spiraling through her gut.

The clown and the dog.

Oh god. They had her trapped.

Alice opened her mouth, ready to scream for help.

"Don't bother calling for aid," the dog growled. "Don't give me reason to inflict pain." Something about the voice struck a familiar note. The awareness seeped away when she noticed the outfit came complete with tail. It swished from side to side each time the dog moved, making it look friendly. Alice knew better.

"How nice to see you," the clown said, his voice at odds with his beaming, oversized grin. At least Alice thought the clown was a male. It was difficult to tell.

The dog didn't utter another word, merely strolled over to another door and opened it.

Alice saw it was a storage cupboard with a key on the outside of the door. Her legs developed a tremor and she thought she'd buckle and fall. Dammit, she should've listened to Luke and not wandered off, but she hadn't thought anyone would hurt her at the school with so many people present.

"Inside," the clown ordered. "Leave your handbag."

A growl rumbled when she failed to comply, and Alice imagined the dog's hackles rising.

"Hurry," the clown snapped. "Inside. Now."

Alice dropped her bag on a child-size desk, sidled past and entered the storage cupboard. The door slammed shut and she found herself in total darkness. The key turned with a scraping, mocking click.

She waited for an instant, listening intently for any sound to give her a clue about the activities in the main classroom. Nothing. She couldn't hear a single sound apart from her rapidly pounding heart and panicked breathing.

Once her eyes adjusted to the darkness inside the storage cupboard, she checked out her surroundings. Her fumbling fingers found something wet and gluggy. Glue by the smell of it. And that was a jar of paint brushes. She was locked in with the art supplies.

Apprehension unfurled from the tight ball inside her stomach. What were they intending to do? Frighten her? Because they'd managed that. But what if they intended to do worse? Like set the classroom on fire. Her panic rose then, seizing her tightly and making her hyperventilate. Alice grasped the edge of a wooden shelf, desperately concentrating on her breathing, just as the specialist had shown her all those years ago. She would not slip into her old habits and have a panic attack.

She refused.

Time elapsed. Alice wasn't sure if it were five minutes or fifteen.

Slowly, she regained control over her breathing. It remained noisy and raspy but she regulated her inhalations enough for her to concentrate on escape. Alice placed her head next to the door and listened carefully. She gave the door an experimental thump. It rattled but remained closed. Half expecting it to open without warning, she waited. Either they'd left or they waited outside entertaining themselves at her expense.

Alice banged on the door. "Help! Help! Someone help me." She paused. Nothing bad happened. The clown and the dog didn't protest her cries for help.

"Probably because there are so many people about," she mumbled. "They'd risk discovery if they hung around here."

But what if they intended to come back once everyone had left? "Help!" Alice shrieked. "Help!" She rattled the door with her fists and kicked it for good measure. "Somebody help."

Alice screamed until her throat turned raw. With no idea of how much time had passed, her terror grew. She'd offered to help on the baking stall, but Lindy had told her to enjoy herself. No one would miss her. "Help! Somebody help me!" Alice beat her fists against the wooden barrier.

A thud came from the other side.

Alice froze, hope surging in her hard and fast. "Hello?" Her voice emerged as a low croak. "Help!" The second attempt wasn't much better. Panicked, Alice kicked and beat her fists on the wooden door. After another frenzied series of thumps, she paused to listen.

"There's someone in there." The voice sounded far away.

Another voice sounded, young and high in pitch, but she couldn't understand the words.

Alice thumped the door again. "Please let me out," she croaked. They had to release her. She didn't want to wait for the clown and dog to return. No telling what they'd do next.

The key scraped. The handle turned and the door opened. Alice blinked at the surge of afternoon sunlight that struck her face. Half blinded, she stumbled from the storeroom, blinking rapidly to focus. She turned to thank her rescuers. One glimpse and fear gripped her tightly. A scream of terror rippled from her strained throat and she backed up rapidly, her body hitting a wall. The three clowns stared at her, their smiley mouths gaping and red button noses jiggling.

Alice screamed again and again and again.

Dimly, she was aware of the sound of running feet and that her screams had made the clowns scatter.

Finally, the clowns parted and she focused on a familiar face. *Luke*. Luke was here. He'd make the clowns leave. Alice pushed away from the wall and threw herself at him. She shuddered as his strong arms closed around her. *Safe*.

She knew she was safe. Luke would make the clowns go away.

"Alice. Alice, it's okay. You're all right," Luke murmured.

She cuddled into his muscular chest, inhaling his musky scent. His blue uniform shirt felt soft under her cheek and his steady breathing soothed the ragged edges of her fear. Gradually her tremors receded.

"Did you arrest the clowns?" Her voice came out low and raspy and it hurt to speak.

"Alice, they were kids. There's a face painter here at the fete and they're selling clown noses. Lots of the children are wandering around dressed in clown suits."

"The clown and the dog locked me in the storage cupboard." Lord, it hurt to talk.

"Okay, come with me. We'll get you a cup of tea while I search the school grounds. Can you tell me what they looked like?"

"The same as before."

Luke nodded and guided her from the classroom. Once they walked farther down the corridor, the noise from the people attending the fete increased. Alice heard the excited shrieks of the children and the strident words from a parent when she repeated her instructions not to touch the exhibits.

With the amount of noise it was no wonder her cries for help had gone unheeded. Alice's mouth tightened. It also explained why the clown and dog had left her alone. They'd assumed she would remain there until their return.

"Alice, there you are. I wondered what had happened to you," Lindy said.

Luke spoke up. "She's had a bit of a scare. She needs a cup of tea and a quiet place to sit. Can I leave her here with you?"

"Sure thing, Luke." Lindy's freckled face creased in distinct worry. "Does she need to go to the doctor?"

"No, I think it's just shock." Luke pushed her down into the chair and crouched to talk to her. He smoothed a lock of hair behind her ear and studied her intently, concern in his brown eyes. "Do you want me to call James?"

"He's busy," Alice said. "I'll be fine now that I'm out of the cupboard." Her voice was scarcely louder than a whisper, and she swallowed to ease the throb inside her throat.

"Okay, sweetheart. Just as long as you're sure." With a final smile he stood. Alice watched him until he disappeared. Tears stung her eyes while each movement of her throat caused a twinge of pain that echoed in her heart. Why couldn't James be more like Luke? Oh, she knew James cared for her, but he still intended to leave.

"Here's a cup of tea," Lindy said. "What happened?"

Alice sipped a mouthful of tea, the warm liquid easing her throat. She swallowed more tea before attempting to answer. "I was looking at the exhibits, going from classroom to classroom. I walked into a classroom right down the far end of the corridor, not realizing it was empty. After I walked inside the clown and the dog followed—"

Lindy cut in with a scowl. "The ones who Luke thinks broke into our house?"

"Yes. They locked me in a storage cupboard and left me there. Luckily some of the children heard me and let me out."

"Alice." Lindy squeezed her arm in sympathy.

"I hope Luke catches them. They're making my life miserable."

"But why? What have you done?" Lindy asked.

Alice sighed, lingering traces of anxiety bringing a tremor to her hands. After wiping at the tea she'd sloshed on her skirt, she frowned. She'd probably dream about clowns tonight. "I don't know. It seems tied to the company and the cult, but honestly, contraception isn't that big a deal." Scorn laced her voice. "The culprits need to focus on bigger issues. Maybe world peace."

The emergency board meeting they held the day after the fete went well. They hashed out a plan and James assigned jobs and responsibilities. Alice loved the way they took the problem in their stride, treating Rita's betrayal as a hiccup rather than a full-out disaster, although not one of them understood her attitude.

"Are you clear on what you need to do?" James asked.

Everyone nodded.

"What do we do if Rita has done other things we haven't discovered yet?" Katarina asked.

"We deal with them," Alice said. "Aunt Alicia believed in this company and you obviously do too otherwise you wouldn't be here. We give one hundred and ten percent and that's what will make this company a success."

Ben started clapping and the others joined in the applause.

James' grin widened to broad and he closed the distance between them to draw her into a crushing hug. "That's my girl!

Are you sure you're well enough to be here? Luke said you were in a bad way yesterday and you weren't well this morning."

"I'm fine. It was a bit of a scare, that's all." She'd had nightmares about cupboards, and feeling ill this morning wasn't so hot, especially since she'd realized she hadn't had a period for some time. The more she thought about it, the more she worried. James wouldn't be happy if she were pregnant. Alice attempted to push her worry aside and concentrate on Fancy Free. The other...if it eventuated...well, she'd have to deal with it.

A dark slice of humor slithered through her. She'd wanted security and a family, a place to call her own. She'd received everything she wanted, but jumbled and out of order.

"Has Luke learned anything else about the clown and the dog?" Ben asked.

They turned to Richard, and he snorted. "He has reports of clowns coming out his ears. Every man, woman and child sighted clowns yesterday. No dog sightings at this stage."

"You need to take care, Alice." Katarina reached over to pat her forearm, but a tiny pucker between her eyes highlighted her unease.

Harriet's knitting needles clacked in a comforting manner. "Don't go off on your own."

A shudder of remembered horror hit Alice. Her stomach roiled without warning. "Believe me, I intend to be very careful. It was horrid being locked inside the cupboard."

"I'm off to ring around more companies," James said. "Take care, huh?" He stooped and pressed a chaste kiss to Alice's lips, unconcerned with the presence of the oldies and the fact they were witnesses to the intimacy. He strode from the boardroom seemingly unaware of the silent speculation he'd fired to life in the board members.

Not one of them said a word until James' footsteps faded.

"What's up with you and James?" Joseph asked.

"Besides the obvious," Harriet added. "We know you're doing the wild thing but that was for work purposes."

Richard groaned. "The wild thing? Where did you get that from?"

"It's a modern term. You should get with the times," Harriet said with a delicate sniff.

Alice rolled her eyes. Maybe she could sneak from the boardroom and they wouldn't notice? She stood, ready to escape the approaching torment.

"Where do you think you're going, missy?" Ben asked.

"To my office." Alice took two steps toward the door.

"It's not safe for you to work on your own," Katarina said. "Come back right now. You can do your assigned tasks in here. Harriet and I will keep you safe."

It sounded more like a prison, being babysat by the two oldies. She frowned but the oldies nodded and smiled at her in a friendly fashion. Some of the smiles bore a distinct predatory flavor in her opinion, but she knew when she was beaten. Alice returned to her seat as Ben spoke up.

"Tell us about James."

"There is nothing to tell. Don't you have jobs to do?" Alice added pointedly.

"You and James are more than work buddies," Harriet said.

Bother. They weren't listening in the slightest. "We test the condoms together. That's it. Period." Alice flinched, wishing she hadn't mentioned that particular word. The truth—she was crazy in love with James and since he'd made his views clear, she intended to store up crumbs to remember on the nights when she lay alone in bed.

"You went out for dinner the other night." Harriet watched her closely for the slightest reaction. "You were caught having sex outside on the car and now you've moved out of the bed and breakfast and you're living with James."

"I have my own room," Alice snapped. Even if it was only used for her clothes.

"Maybe, but I'm thinking it's used for storage. I bet you share a bed with James every night." Harriet finished with a smirk, her eyes sparkling with shrewd insight.

Was Harriet a mind reader? She would not blush. *She would not.* "It's none of your business," Alice said finally, rushing in to fill the blooming silence. A tinge of color had crept into her cheeks. She could feel the glow of heat that blazed from her face. Every single one of the oldies regarded her closely. Too closely.

"Ah-ha!" Joseph said, clicking his fingers. "That blush and those downcast eyes look like proof to me. Alice and James are officially a couple. Okay, guys. Pay up." He held out his right hand and waited with clear expectation.

"I'm not convinced." Ben scratched his bald pate.

"Bah, you're just a bad loser. James and Alice are a couple. I know it. You know it. Time to pay up."

"He's right." Harriet beamed. The clack of her knitting needles seemed to highlight her glee. She finished her row, bent to rifle through her knitting bag and pulled out a black purse. After perusing the contents, she extracted two five-dollar notes and placed them on the table.

"Aw, all right." Richard tugged his wallet from his rear trouser pocket and pulled out a ten-dollar note. He tossed it into the middle of the table.

Alice watched open-mouthed while several of the other oldies tossed money onto the boardroom table.

Joseph raked up the notes and placed them in a pile, sending a wink in her direction. "Thanks, Alice."

"But I'm not with James. James is leaving soon. We're not a couple I tell you."

"Methinks she argues too much." Joseph winked again.

"Lots of things can happen in a few months," Katarina said. "The writing is on the wall."

Huh? If there was writing somewhere stating James and she would get together, she hadn't seen it. Besides, if James learned she was possibly pregnant, he wouldn't be thrilled. In fact, she could picture him racing from the rabbit hole called Sloan, dust clouds obscuring his form while he ran for cover.

"Nice doing business with you all," Joseph said. "You coming?" He prodded the two men. "We need to sort out those extra orders for James and deliver them. Have a business to run you know."

The men trooped out leaving Alice with Katarina and Harriet. She didn't feel any more secure when the men left. Deciding businesslike was best, she said, "What do you want to tackle first? Going through the results for Rodney or trying to organize the packaging and final color combinations?"

Harriet started a new row, using bright yellow wool. "Let's do the color combinations first. Those men are hopeless when it comes to color sense. We know that women like to see something smart, a combination that's modern and snappy."

Alice pulled out the latex color swatches and spread them. Gold, silver, turquoise, royal blue, bronze, red and green along with white and natural. "I like the original discussion we had about using the color grading of gold, silver and bronze."

"It would make it easy for customers to recall which version they prefer," Katarina said.

"The outer packaging plus the foil packaging should match the condom inside," Harriet said. "We already have condoms with racing stripes and colored dots. I think we should stick with plain and stylish with the Vibration."

"We could market a combined pack and call it the box of champions," Alice suggested. "Or something along those lines."

"Love it," Harriet said, her hands moving the entire time, working on her knitting. She cackled. "Appeal to the male psyche, the need to go out there and win."

"That would be a great marketing angle to introduce the product," Katarina agreed. "Maybe we could con some Olympic champions into promoting our product."

"Never mind Olympic champions," Harriet said. "We need some All Blacks."

"Pooh, that young man you're always spouting about is the same age as your grandchildren," Katarina said, but there was a sparkle in her eyes.

"But he was very good in the underwear ads." A smile pursed Harriet's lips.

Alice blinked.

"What's the matter, missy? We might be old but we're not dead. That young man is very fine and he'd be perfect in our advertising promotion," Harriet said.

"What she said," Katarina said. "We like sex. No need to be ashamed of it. We were young once."

"And we're still young at heart," Harriet snapped.

"But...but...I think they earn enough money from their professional sporting status without needing to display...ah..."

"A penis," Katarina said.

"Yes." Alice cursed the warmth crawling across her face. She blamed the lack of sleep the previous night. Every time she closed her eyes, she'd seen clown faces smirking at her. When she'd finally fallen asleep, it had seemed only a matter of minutes before James woke her. "Yeah, I doubt any of the All Blacks would want to display their nude bodies even with parts clothed in our products."

"She's probably right, dang it," Katarina said.

Harriet cocked her head. "We could always ask."

Alice stared, her gaze moving from Harriet to Katarina and back. "You're winding me up. You are!"

The two oldies grinned at each other before Harriet spoke. "Of course we are, dear, but it's good to see a little color in your face again."

"That wasn't very nice. I'm meant to be in charge," Alice said.

They roared with laughter and Alice gave up trying to maintain an impassive expression. Her lips quirked before she gave in and chuckled with the oldies.

The click of the door closing drew Alice's attention.

"Well, well, this is cozy."

Alice gasped. "How...how did you get in here?"

The clown cocked its head to the side and made a *tsk-tsk* sound. "We walked in of course."

"What do you want?" Harriet demanded. "Going around and frightening people is wrong."

"You need to get a life," Katarina snapped. "Go and bother someone else—someone who cares."

"Shut up," the dog snarled.

Alice's heart pounded. Every time she looked at the clown a shudder zapped down her spine, but she took courage from Harriet's and Katarina's presence. Three against two. That was good odds if it came to a struggle. "What do you want?"

The dog let out a bark of rusty laughter.

Alice frowned. She knew that laugh. Beneath that tan and white dog suit was a person she knew, but she had no idea who among her acquaintances hated her enough to persecute her in this manner.

"We want you, missy." The clown produced a gun from its pocket and pointed it directly at Alice. "You're coming with us."

All thoughts of fight left Alice then. The addition of a gun made a difference. She couldn't put Harriet or Katarina at risk. They had families. Children and grandchildren.

218

"All right." Alice's voice sounded surprisingly level considering her knees knocked so hard. "I'll come with you."

"No, Alice," Harriet snapped. "They'll hurt you."

"Shut up," the dog commanded.

"You, sit there where we can see you, and you, missy, are coming with us," the clown ordered.

The gun never wavered.

"What has Alice ever done to you?" Katarina demanded.

Alice found herself nodding. That's what she wanted to know.

"She shouldn't have come to Sloan," the dog snarled. "She doesn't belong here."

"You," the clown snapped, pointing to Katarina. "Get in the storage cupboard."

"There's mice in there," Katarina said, giving a theatrical shiver. "I think the dog should go first. Scare them away so an old lady doesn't have a heart attack."

The dog snarled again, and Alice caught a glimpse of shiny white teeth.

"In the cupboard." Pure agitation shaded the clown's voice and it contrasted sharply with the big red smile. Alice hated the way the gun had started waving all over the place. To her way of thinking, the clown appeared unstable while the dog, although it seemed in better control, had started to snap and snarl.

"Oh, all right." Katarina used a put-upon voice.

"Well, I can't go yet. I need to finish my row."

"Put the freakin' knitting down," the clown roared.

The dog strode over to Harriet and grabbed the knitting.

"Now!" Katarina sprang at the clown while Harriet wielded her knitting needles like weapons. She jabbed the dog in the thigh.

Alice froze before her wits returned. She grabbed a fiberglass penis sans condom and thumped the clown over the back of the head. The sound of the penis connecting with the clown's scalp sent horror through her but she did it again. A dull thud. Alice repeated the move and the clown dropped to the floor. Katarina immediately turned her attention to the dog and Alice followed suit.

Harriet jabbed at the dog with her knitting needles. The dog howled when she connected. Katarina bent to pick up a chair. She wobbled unsteadily and Alice grabbed it from her, indicating with a jerk of her head that she should move around the front to distract the dog. Alice bypassed the chair by in favor of the bin. She scooped it up and crept closer before raising it above her head.

Without warning the dog turned. Alice stomped on the dog's foot and a few seconds later Harriet poked it in the butt with a knitting needle. When the dog howled in pain, Alice decked it with her rubbish bin. This time she took great satisfaction in the crunch that sounded when head and bin connected. The dog crumpled like a popped balloon.

Harriet set her knitting aside with a scowl. "Damn fool dog made me drop a stitch. Call Luke, Alice. We'll throw their asses in jail. Look at my knitting!" Harriet shook her fist at the dog and kicked it in the ribs. "They've ruined my scarf."

"Who are they?" Katarina asked, hobbling over to stand by the clown.

"Are you both okay?" Alice demanded. With shaky hands, she reached for the phone and dialed the police station. Luke promised he'd be in a few minutes, and she hung up.

"No, I'm not fine. My knitting is ruined," Harriet muttered.

A sound from behind had them whirling to face the door. At the back of her mind Alice noted with amusement that the elderly women wore belligerent don't-mess-with-me scowls.

"What the hell happened here?" James asked. "Is everyone all right?"

"No, I'm not. That stupid dog ruined my knitting," Harriet snapped.

Alice grabbed her before she kicked the dog in the ribs again.

"Have you called Luke?" James asked. "Where's Richard?"

"Yes, I've called Luke," Alice said.

"Luke shouldn't be far away because he told me he had paperwork to do today." Richard stood in the doorway. His gaze took in the dog and the clown, both unconscious on the floor. "You haven't killed them, have you?" As he spoke, Richard stooped beside the clown and checked for a pulse.

"We should have. They ruined my—"

"Harriet, that's enough about your knitting," Katarina snapped. "We're in shock. We need a strong cup of tea with a shot of whiskey."

"No whiskey for me," Alice said hastily. "But I'll make tea."

"Who are they?" James demanded.

"I don't know," Richard said. "But we'll find out." He jerked the red wig off the clown's head. "It's one of the guys from the cult."

They turned to look at the still body of the dog. James stalked over and crouched beside it. He tugged on the head and eased it off. "Hell, it's Rita."

Alice literally felt the shock and sense of betrayal that rippled through the room.

"Rita! That double-crossing witch," Katarina said.

Harriet glared at the silent, still figure. "She ruined my knitting. Damn, I should have jabbed her a little harder with my knitting needle."

Luke walked into the boardroom. "Everyone all right? Is that Rita?" His gaze moved to the man in the clown suit. "That looks like one of the cult guys."

Rita started to stir.

"Tell me what happened," Luke said.

They all started to talk at once.

"Stop." Luke held up his right hand in a stop gesture and scanned their faces. "One at the time. Alice. You first."

Alice took a deep breath. James moved closer and wrapped his arm around her waist, giving her silent reassurance. "Harriet, Katarina and I were working in here. The clown and dog walked in and started issuing orders. They wanted me to go with them and intended to lock Harriet and Katarina in the cupboard. I didn't think much of the idea and I picked up the penis model and hit the clown on the head. I took the clown by surprise. They didn't expect us to fight back."

Luke's mouth quivered, and his eyes danced with silent humor. "A penis, huh?"

"Yes." Alice stared back, silently daring him to make a smart-arse comment.

Beside her, James risked a laugh. "Must have been a hard one."

The men snickered. Every one of them. Alice started quivering, but it wasn't with laughter. Her stomach danced and roiled and tears poured down her face. "It wasn't funny. They wanted to hurt me."

"Sweetheart." James pulled her into his solid embrace and held her tight.

"They're going to have headaches but they have strong pulses. I'll call the doctor to come and check them out," Richard said.

Luke nodded at his father. "Looks as if Rita is waking. I'll need to take formal statements from you all."

"Can Alice come down to the station later? She doesn't look well," James said.

"That's fine. In fact, you can all go and I'll catch up with you later this afternoon for statements," Luke said.

James guided Alice from the boardroom. She heard Harriet's strident demands that Luke add a charge about destruction of property. Her knitting was property, wasn't it? Alice tried to smile, but her mouth refused to cooperate. Her legs didn't want to follow her directions either. Her footsteps wavered, making her glad of James' help.

"I was right," she muttered. The entire affair appeared so surreal. The bizarreness fit right in with her initial impressions of Sloan.

"Right about what?"

"Sloan is a rabbit hole. We're all living in a parallel universe. A rabbit hole just like Wonderland."

James chuckled, the sound reverberating through her. One of comfort. Familiarity. Lord, she wished James would stay in the rabbit hole with her instead of leaving. But on the other hand, a person could go crazy in a place like this—if they stayed too long. Maybe that was why he intended leaving.

"You might be right, sweetheart. Some days Sloan sure as hell feels like a rabbit hole."

# Chapter 16

James helped Alice climb into his SUV, a surge of protectiveness filling him. Every freckle stood out in stark relief on her face. He wondered if he should take her to the doctor since she'd had a shock. *A rabbit hole*. Damn if he didn't think she was right. He settled behind the wheel and noticed she'd fallen asleep. Probably the best thing for her.

She slept for the whole journey, only waking when he pulled up outside his house. He helped her inside and removed her shoes and outer clothing before putting her to bed. He frowned, worried about her lethargy and paleness. James touched his hand to her forehead. Normal. Maybe she just needed to nap because she hadn't slept well during the last week, the shadows under her eyes confirming her fatigue. Perhaps all she needed was rest.

Alice snoozed through the afternoon and early evening, waking briefly when he joined her in bed.

"Go back to sleep," he whispered.

She rose and wandered to the bathroom before returning. "I'm not tired." Alice stripped off the rest of her clothes, the ones he'd left on when he'd undressed her, and slipped between the sheets naked.

James pressed a kiss to the tip of her nose, prepared to cuddle and do nothing else. Alice accepted the first kiss and sought more. Her lips were soft beneath his, teasing yet purposeful. Hell, he could take a hint. He wrapped his arms around her, stroking the smooth fragranced skin and fitting their bodies together.

His breath eased out. He'd become used to this, to having Alice in his bed each night. Sometimes they didn't need to test condoms, but they made love anyway.

He tried not to think about what that meant. Alice hadn't commented so he didn't either. He went with the flow, enjoying the closeness and the feminine presence in his life.

The time on his contract was almost up and he'd leave soon. He'd taught Alice everything he knew about running the company. She didn't need him anymore. James cupped Alice's head and took the kiss deeper. He explored the interior of her mouth but kept it slow and easy. Their tongues twined, and he savored the rub of her breasts against his chest, the soft, fragrant hair beneath his hands. He loved the groans of pleasure and appreciation she made, her floral scent that he'd remember at the strangest of times.

"James, make love to me."

Her hand crept between their bodies to pinch his nipple, teasing it until it burned, reverberating in his cock, his balls. James swallowed and nuzzled her neck. A sudden urge to mark her, to show the world she belonged to him blindsided him. He still intended leaving.

Sloan wasn't for him.

He didn't fit with the other people who chose to live here. Rabbits, to hear Alice talk. Nah, he was a traveler and soon he'd leave. That was his problem. He had itchy feet. This strange restlessness would fade once he left Sloan.

"Are you sure you shouldn't go to sleep?"

"That would be a big, fat no," Alice said. "Oh well. I guess I can seduce you. Just lie back and I'll try to tempt you."

James spluttered. God, he loved her sense of humor, the funny things she came out with, the way she handled the oldies. He didn't like the way Luke looked at her...

Before he could take that thought any farther, Alice pushed him back on the mattress. Her hands trailed over his body, confident and cool, bringing a shudder of heat, a ripple of awareness. She kissed his mouth before moving down the bed. Her warm breath feathered across his collarbone and her teeth nibbled a path across his chest. His hips jerked at the sting of teeth, not because it hurt but because it felt so damn good. She teased one nipple, worrying it with her mouth until darts of pleasure rushed through him. Alice nipped his belly, unhurriedly making her way to his groin.

James tried to recall when a woman had taken such care with him, taken so much pleasure in exploring his body--giving instead of taking and gifting herself.

She blew across the tip of his shaft before tracing the length with her finger. She teased the sensitive underside, squeezing a groan from him. The reaction seemed to be something she wanted. The knowledge that she wrung him inside out with each touch. She cupped his tight sac, rolling his balls gently beneath her fingers and clenching his dick in her fist.

"Alice."

"Shush," she said. "Just enjoy."

Alice crawled on top of him and guided his cock to her entrance. Slowly she pushed downward, impaling herself one slow increment at the time. He clenched his teeth to hold back a groan. The sweet, tight grip of her pussy felt amazing. James stared up at her and watched the play of emotions over her face. The flicker of pleasure. The sultry passion in her brandy-colored eyes. Steadily, she rose and fell on his cock, riding him and gripping him sweetly. She rocked, her breasts bouncing with each move. A prickle of awareness started at the base of his spine, building sweetly.

She whimpered, her hands moving upward to pinch one of her nipples. Another moan resounded in the bedroom. It was a sexy sound that made his cock jerk. He reached for her then, slipping his fingers between her legs. Slick dampness met his touch. He strummed her swollen clit and fought to hold back his impending climax. The pending explosion built higher and higher until it reached the point of no return. Semen rushed up his cock just as she keened again. Her vagina contracted sharply, clutching at his dick while he spurted into her with violent contractions.

Minutes later, she slipped off his body before rearranging herself at his side, cuddling into him like a sleepy kitten. James pressed a kiss to her cheek and gathered her close before falling into sleep.

He woke with his heart pounding. Something had woken him. He leaned over and groped for the bedside lamp, hitting the on switch on his second attempt. The bed beside him was empty. His gaze darted to his watch. Six thirty. Almost time to climb out of bed.

"Alice?" The unmistakable sounds of retching came from the en suite. James climbed from bed and went to investigate. After tapping on the door, he walked into the bathroom, the light gray tiles cool beneath his bare feet.

Another series of retches started along with a sob and a pitiful groan. When the noise abated, he pushed open the door to the toilet.

She stood, her shoulders slouched in fatigue. She wiped the back of her hand across her mouth and offered a weary smile. "I'm not feeling too good."

"I noticed." He went to her and pushed a lock of hair off her forehead. Clammy heat met his touch. Alice shivered and spun away from him, lurching for the toilet. Helplessly, James watched unsure of how he could help her.

When her shoulders stopped heaving, she stood and turned slowly to face him. "I need to tell you something."

Pronounced shadows highlighted her extreme paleness.

"I think you need to return to bed."

"No—"

"You can't go to work in this condition."

"James, will you listen to me?" Alice's voice emerged in a sharp snap and demanded his attention.

"At least go back to bed."

"I think I'm pregnant."

He stared, his mouth dropping open in shock. "What did you say?"

"Pregnant. I think I'm pregnant."

"But how?" He chastened himself for asking the stupid question as soon as it emerged. It was obvious how it had happened, but it shouldn't have. "You're on the Pill."

Her chin lifted, her eyes flashing irritation. "Yes."

God, this couldn't be happening. He wasn't cut out for fatherhood. He didn't do relationships, dammit. He was a traveler, a wanderer.

"And before you make things worse, I've taken the pills religiously." Alice snorted, a derisive sound, and pushed her way past him.

He followed a little more slowly trying to make sense of the riotous emotions that swamped him. With Alice at his side, Sloan didn't seem quite as claustrophobic. Maybe...

Nah. No way.

He wasn't going to get sucked into the family trap where he'd have to take up law again and live a responsible life. He didn't intend to become his father.

"I'm not asking you to marry me," she snapped. "I'm merely doing you the courtesy of telling you." Her eyes flashed, and color seeped back into her cheeks.

"How long have you known?"

"I've missed my period and haven't felt well." She slipped an oversize T-shirt over her head, screening her body from his gaze.

"What did the doctor say?" James swallowed, emotions rioting out of control. Fear—no, panic—stalked his mind, worry that he was handling this situation wrong. He wanted to apologize, to start again, to tell Alice...

Hell, he didn't know what he wanted to tell her.

That was the problem.

"I haven't seen a doctor yet. I thought I'd go today." Alice grabbed a set of clean clothes and returned to the en suite. She shut the door with a defiant click. A solid clunk confirmed she'd locked him out.

James dragged his hand through his hair. "Well, hell." He grabbed a pair of jeans and stepped into them before heading to the kitchen. Maybe a cup of coffee would help settle his confusion. It tangled inside him, flaring with hints of anger and regret.

A child. Bloody hell.

Alice didn't appear until he drank his second cup. He lifted his head and studied her, trying to see if she looked different. She didn't. "What do you want to do?"

Her shoulders lifted in a shrug. "Who said anything has to change? I thought we'd carry on, me running Fancy Free and you traveling overseas."

He gave a curt nod, feeling rejection instead of relief. Didn't she even want him to stick around? To help her?

"I'm going to work now. There's a lot to do, and I still need to see Luke to give him a statement."

A flare of jealousy struck James. Was that why she wasn't worried about him leaving? Because she had Luke waiting in the wings? His hand curled to a fist and the tension from wanting to lash out pounded through him. "Let me finish my coffee and I'll drive you."

"Thanks, but I want to walk. The fresh air will help clear my head." Alice collected her handbag, slipped on her shoes and stepped outside, shutting the door behind her with a soft click.

James scowled at the wooden door. He didn't believe it. She didn't expect him to do anything except leave. Alice hadn't worked through everything yet. She'd change her mind and try to trap him. She wasn't any different from his mother, sister and the woman they'd tried to hitch him up with. Yeah, she'd sing a different tune once reality set in.

A few hours later, a tap on her office door made Alice start. Her pen dropped on to the floor and she scrambled after it, belting her head on the corner of her desk before she had the pen back in her hand.

"Ouch." Alice rubbed the rapidly forming bump on her head, a rueful smile on her lips. An interruption to drag her back to the present, something to divert her thoughts from a possible pregnancy, James' departure and her procrastination in ringing the doctor to make an appointment. She sighed inwardly. Another tap on the door sounded—a little louder this time. "Come in."

The door inched open and Rodney stuck his head through the gap. "Do you have a moment?"

"Sure. Take a seat." She gestured at the upright chair on the other side of her desk.

Rodney bore a worried frown that made her wonder if she shouldn't worry herself. "Um...er...I..." He hovered in front of her desk instead of sitting.

Alice's stomach flipped briefly before it settled. She wasn't sure if it was because of morning sickness or because of the unease she sensed in Rodney. She regarded him intently, attempting to read his body language. Stuttering. Blazing red face. General reluctance to sit on the seat she'd indicated. It didn't bode well. "Is there a problem with the Vibration?" *Surely not. Not after all they'd been through so far.*

"No, no. Everything's fine. The first orders should roll out at the end of the month as planned."

A sigh of relief whistled through her teeth. She consciously relaxed. Leaning back in her chair, she picked up her pen and prompted him again. "Then how can I help you?"

Rodney hesitated. He ran his hand through his hair and adjusted his frameless glasses, shoving them farther up his nose. "I want to hand in my notice," he blurted.

"Why?" Caught off guard, she fumbled her pen again. It shot across the floor, ending up by Rodney's foot. Things were finally going well at Fancy Free now that the dog and clown were in police custody. The company had managed to claw away at some of their overdraft and had hired extra people to help in the dispatch department to keep up with the new orders. But Rodney leaving—this was one possibility she and James hadn't factored into the equation.

Rodney couldn't leave.

Alice tried not to think about James' imminent departure. "What are you going to do? Do you have a job with another company?"

"I've been listening to James talk about his trip. It made me think. I've never been out of New Zealand." Rodney handed Alice her pen and fussed with his glasses again. "I've purchased my plane ticket. I'm going to Europe. I want to run with the bulls in Pamplona." Spots of pink appeared on his cheeks when he added, "And drink beer in Munich."

Panic struck, searing through her stomach with acidic sharpness. The company would fail if they lost Rodney. Because it was a small company, losing key personnel meant a huge upheaval. They didn't have a backup plan. Alice glanced at her pen but refrained from picking it up. It would only end up on the floor again. Rodney couldn't do this to her. Oh boy. That wasn't very businesslike if her first thoughts were of how Rodney's departure would impact her personally. Her throat ached with tension and a sharp pang started up in her chest.

Just when she'd begun to feel more secure, Rodney pushed her back out of her comfort zone into panic and uncertainty.

Heck, was it always going to be like this—her life out of control and her running behind to pick up the pieces?

Alice licked her lips, noticing at the back of her mind how dry they were. She swallowed and coughed to clear her throat but the anxiety continued to grow. She stood and paced.

Breathe.

Think.

Then it hit her.

She was a selfish cow. This wasn't about her. This was about the company and the board members who had become friends. They'd been through so much and worked together for the success of Fancy Free. When James left, she took full responsibility for the company. She had to sort out this problem. But how?

Inspiration hit and suddenly she knew what to suggest. "Rodney, what if you take a leave of absence? Go over to Europe and explore, and when you return home, your job will be waiting for you?" She beamed at him, pleased with her idea. Yes, the initial panic had hit and brought familiar insecure ghouls from the closet but she'd come up with a solution. Yes! She really had changed.

A knock sounded on the door an instant before it opened. James strolled inside, his familiar grin absent. Alice's gaze skimmed his body before heading back to his face, regretting the tension between them. Last night he'd woken her from a sensual dream that had rapidly become reality. Skin sliding across skin. Wet, warm mouths. Drugging pleasure. She sighed. His grin flared and one blue eye closed in a wink, bringing forth a blush. Maybe he wasn't angry with her after all.

James glanced at Rodney. "Is there a problem?"

"Rodney is going on his big overseas experience."

"You're leaving?" James cast her a worried look.

"I was just asking Rodney if he'd consider taking time off and coming back to Fancy Free in say six months." Alice peered at Rodney in clear expectation. *Please let him agree.* Otherwise the company would lag behind their competition while they searched for a suitable candidate. Six months was the maximum time they could wait before employing a replacement. "Rodney?"

"I'm not sure. I'll need to think about it," Rodney said.

Alice wanted to shake the bespectacled man. How much thought did it take? She'd given up everything for Fancy Free. Alice forced a gracious smile, reminding herself that no one had compelled her to accept the conditions of her godmother's will. "That's fine. Can you let me know by the end of the week? If you decide to leave, I'll need to start searching for a replacement."

"Thanks. I'll come and see you on Friday."

Alice smiled again and watched him scurry from her office. James walked over to the door and shut it before closing the distance between them. He drew her near, seemingly forgetting about their words this morning.

"I'm proud of you," he whispered against her hair. His large hand glided down her spine and came to a rest on her bottom.

Alice dwelled on the loss of Rodney for a few seconds longer. Somehow, she'd cope. The company would survive.

"Thanks." Humor surfaced without warning and she pushed his chest so she could move from his grasp and view his face. She couldn't resist stroking his cheek and savoring the rasp of stubble beneath her fingertips. "Did you know Rodney wants to do the run with the bulls in Pamplona? I should have reminded him to take out travel insurance."

"I don't want to discuss Rodney." James placed his hand over hers and stopped her exploration of his face.

"No?"

"Have you made an appointment to see the doctor?"

"Not yet."

James picked up the phone and handed it to her before rattling off the number. With a trembling hand she dialed and spoke to the receptionist.

"Well?"

"They have a canceled appointment in half an hour."

"Good," James said. "I'll come with you."

"No!" Alice remembered last time, the whispers, the gossip. Her embarrassment. "I'm capable of going by myself."

"Fine." His eyes narrowed, and leashed masculine power simmered in his face, giving her no illusions as to his mood. He was pissed and that knowledge fired her temper.

"It's not my fault. I've done everything you asked and taken those stupid pills religiously."

"Stupid pills?"

"A figure of speech," Alice snapped. "I will be out for an hour." She picked up her purse and strode for the door, eager to escape his brooding gaze.

"Alice?"

"What?"

"You'll tell me what the doctor says?" Anger tinged his voice and the set of his face emphasized his mood.

"Yes, I'll tell you." Alice flashed her own version of irritation with a searing gaze. "Not that it will make the slightest difference to our situation. I'm staying here and you're leaving. It's quite simple really."

He stared after her, for once failing to enjoy the saucy twitch of her butt. Shit. He dragged his hand through his hair while his mind chased in circles. If Alice were pregnant, he couldn't leave. He couldn't walk away and leave her with a child. Their child. Torn, he returned to his office. He slumped into his chair and put his feet up on his desk.

Trapped.

Damn, he felt cornered like a snared rat. Logically he realized this wasn't Alice's fault. Deep in his gut, he knew she was honorable and would never attempt to trap him. But he couldn't help his panic. The idea of having to stay in Sloan, having to conform and seeing the smug expressions on his mother's and sister's faces when they saw him with the child.

"Bloody hell," he muttered.

"James, I've brought in a cake for morning tea. It's in the boardroom," Harriet said. "Where's Alice? She's not in her office."

"She's gone to the doctor." He cursed silently the minute he realized what he'd said.

"Why?" Harriet cocked her head, reminding him of an inquisitive bird. "Is she pregnant?"

James glowered at Harriet.

"Goodness gracious!" Harriet's eyes glittered with genuine amusement. "Didn't you use contraception? You know Fancy Free sells condoms, right?"

"Go away," he growled.

"I'm going," Harriet said gleefully. She hotfooted it from the office, ready to spread the juicy gossip. James didn't care. He was more worried about Alice. Yeah, he was ready to remain in Sloan and do the right thing, but what if Alice remained firm and didn't want anything to do with him?

He attempted to work but couldn't concentrate. Instead, he found himself staring at the blank wall of his office, willing Alice to return.

Finally, two hours later she appeared at his office door. Her face looked pale and tear tracks marked her cheeks. James leaped from his chair and strode around his desk. He wrapped his arms around her and drew her into a comforting hug. She was pregnant.

"It's all right. You don't need to worry."

"But—"

"I'm not pregnant. The doctor said it's likely stress that's messed up my body."

Instead of elation, a pang of totally unexpected disappointment hit him. Alice wasn't pregnant. He wasn't sure what to say or how to act. "Why don't you head home for the rest of the day?"

"I..." Alice trailed off before nodding. "Okay."

James grabbed his keys. "Come on. I'll drive you."

T he next day Alice returned to work after tiptoeing around James at the house. They hadn't talked. Instead, they'd watched a detective show on television and retired for the evening. They'd shared a bed but hadn't made love. Suddenly, everything had changed with a mile-wide chasm between them. Alice couldn't believe how devastated she'd been after the doctor had confirmed the negative test.

Alice checked through the mail she'd collected from the post office on the way to work. She regretted upsetting James. She loved him, but knew how much he needed to leave. Making him stay would be like keeping a wild animal caged. His desire to travel and explore was every bit as important as her urge to nest and make a home. Neither way was wrong.

"Hi." James stepped into her office. "Do you have anything important happening in the next half an hour?"

Alice shook her head, mystified by the twinkle in his eyes but glad. She wanted to enjoy their remaining time together. "No, nothing more important than sorting the mail."

"Good. Let me introduce you to the delights of an office quickie." His eyes glowed a darker blue and they danced with mischief. "Take off your panties."

"Here?" Intrigue laced the shock in her squeaky voice.

"I dare you."

"Oh well. In that case." Maybe everything would be all right, after all.

Alice took a step backward and lifted her short black skirt until it rested halfway up her thighs.

"Nice legs, sweetheart," he said in a husky voice. Alice noticed his gaze remained riveted to her thighs. He'd persuaded her to add to her wardrobe during the last couple of months. The proprietress of the local fashion store had helped her choose classic items that suited her body type and went with the rest of her wardrobe. While she mightn't be the height of fashion, she had her own style now and had managed it without spending heaps of money. Coming to Sloan was one of the best things she'd ever done. She might not have a bank account full of money and the security of owning her own home, but she had made friends and learned about herself. She peeked at James through lowered lashes. Best of all, she'd learned about her sexuality.

"Thank you, James." Alice wouldn't think about his departure. She'd promised herself she wouldn't cry and cling even though she ached inside. Alice let her hands skim beneath the hem of her skirt and peeled her silky black panties down her legs. One hand shot out to hold on to him for balance while she shimmied from her panties.

"Very nice." James bent to pick up her underwear and with a wicked grin, tucked them into the rear pocket of his jeans.

"Are...are you giving those back?"

"Nope." He crowded her against the wall then unfastened the top three buttons of her pale blue shirt and slipped a hand into her bra. His mouth lowered, and he kissed her deeply, at the same time as he dragged her bra downward. Alice's pulse pounded at the naughtiness of making love in the workplace. Their kiss seared her. Fiery hot. Perfect.

His hands wandered everywhere. Under her skirt. Tweaking her nipples. Smoothing across her belly. Parting her folds. He delved between her legs, sliding one leg between hers. Fire whipped through her, sending nerve endings wild, pleasure swamping her. He stroked his tongue into her mouth while his fingers explored.

The hard bulge of his cock bumped her hip. She unfastened his jeans and tugged on the zipper until a wide V of flesh showed. He probed her cleft again, brushing his fingers across her moist flesh. Oh god. This was unexpected. So pleasurable. Who'd have guessed? She scooped his cock from his briefs, his hot, hard erection springing into her hands. Warm strength pulsed beneath her touch.

"Lift your leg and curl it around my hip," he ordered.

Alice found herself obeying and the next instant he pushed into her tight channel. She sucked in a breath, releasing it on a moan when he pressed deeply, impaling her until she felt impossibly full, until she felt him pulsing inside her. His hands cupped her naked bottom. James took her weight and thrust with steady strokes. A rich tapestry of scents surrounded them. Aftershave, perfume, sex. Alice's hips jerked when the long, thick shaft massaged her inner muscles. She grew slicker, the wet sounds of arousal filling the air.

Forced against the wall, she couldn't move, all she could do was feel. The pleasure. The smooth strokes. A rough growl vibrated deep in his chest.

"Touch yourself," he ordered. "I want to see you come."

A few months ago she would have baulked. Not today. She savored the leashed power in his strokes, her pulse racing as the sensations grew. Slipping her finger between their bodies, she rubbed her clit in a steady circular motion. Her head fell back against the wall. The bliss grew, swelling until it coalesced in a violent spasm of pleasure. Alice groaned. She bucked in his hold. James gripped her butt more firmly and stroked into her in short, choppy plunges before stilling. His eyes were closed, an expression of almost pain contorting his handsome face. He took her mouth in a passionate kiss that made her channel clench his cock in another series of flutters.

"Oh James. My heart is thumping so hard I think I might expire."

He opened his eyes and brushed a gentler kiss across her lips. "It's not you. Someone's at the door."

"What?" Alice shrieked. They separated, and she planted both feet on the ground. Her gaze fastened on the door behind James with something akin to horror. In slow motion it opened.

Katarina stepped inside. She paused, her eyes growing round. Then she giggled and slapped her hand to her mouth.

"What's...? Oh!" Harriet said from behind her. "We're interrupting. We'll come back later."

They backed out with an agility that belied their years. Alice heard their giggles as they hurried away, probably to tell the men they'd caught James and Alice in the act.

Alice straightened her skirt and did up her shirt with clumsy fingers. "I can't believe that just happened." She shot a glance at James. His bottom lip quirked, the movement echoed in his eyes. Alice snorted and found herself laughing too.

"We'd better go and see what they want." James straightened his shirt.

"I'm not sure I'm ready to look them in the face," Alice said, her tone wry. "I'll stop by the ladies' room first. Can I have my underwear please?"

"Not now." He strode to the door and paused to waggle his brows at her.

"What? James, you can't!"

He returned to her side and finger-combed her disheveled hair. "You look beautiful. Do this for me." He placed his fingers beneath her chin and tilted her head. Their gazes met and her pulse jumped. Unable to look away, she drowned in his sexy blue gaze. "Please," he murmured.

The smoky quality of his voice tugged at her emotions. She had to clear her throat to reply. "But why?"

James winked. "That's why I like you so much. You're always asking questions, gathering information." He traced her lips with a forefinger. "Because it will turn me on."

"But...but..."

James winked. "I'll see you in a few minutes." Before she could raise a decent argument to reclaim her panties, the man disappeared. A jaunty whistle followed in his wake.

"James," Alice shouted. "Come back here." She hurried to the door, hoping to catch him but found him talking to Rodney.

Damn and blast. James shot her a Cheshire cat grin along with a friendly wave and patted his backside. Rat! Alice stuck her nose in the air and hurried to the ladies' room.

After she'd cleaned up, she traipsed to the boardroom. Laughter and the low rumble of male voices greeted her. Joking at her expense, no doubt. Embarrassment collected in her cheeks and seeped down her neck. Her entire body glowed with heat and the swish of skirt fabric around her bare limbs brought intense awareness. What happened if she tripped and sprawled flat on her face? What happened if everyone noticed she wasn't wearing knickers? Drawing a deep breath, Alice sailed into the boardroom with her head held high. She would murder James while he slept. Her eyes narrowed when she spotted his smirking face. Or at least slap him around a little to show her displeasure. Alice paused. Okay, so she wouldn't really do that—not for real. In her imagination now, that was another matter.

"Alice is here," Joseph said.

Alice forced a smile in place and waited with trepidation.

"I hear Rodney is going on his big overseas experience," Ben said. "An OE will be good for him."

Harriet and Katarina giggled. One glimpse of their faces told her their laughter was at her expense.

"You shouldn't enter my office without knocking," she said.

"If you're that worried," Harriet said in an arch tone, "you should have locked your door."

"Leave Alice alone," James ordered, earning brownie points. "What did you want to speak to us about?"

"My niece has had a wonderful idea," Katarina said. "She suggested we branch out and do parties that feature our products."

Rodney cleared his throat. When he had their attention, he fiddled with his glasses. "I have a friend who designs sex toys. Maybe you could hire him."

"That's a wonderful idea," Harriet said. "Let's vote."

"Before we vote." Alice cut in before the oldies signed and sealed the idea. "I think it's an excellent suggestion but first we're going to do more research. Rodney, please ask your friend to ring me and we'll talk. I'll take care of the monetary angle and the costings. I want the rest of you to check out the existing businesses and see how they do things."

"You want us to spy?" Ben demanded.

Alice hid a smile. "Yes, but keep it legal. You have a week. We'll check in every morning so we're all in the loop. And remember not to discuss the details with anyone except each other."

With a burst of chatter the oldies hurried off, eager to start their research. Alice exhaled slowly.

"See you tomorrow," Rodney said. "And thanks. I've made up my mind. I want to come back to work for you. I'll take six months." With a nod at James, Rodney left, leaving them alone.

Time for a little payback. Alice stalked toward him. The man grinned and stood his ground. Two could play at that game. Alice narrowed her eyes and poked him in the chest with her finger. "Give me back my underwear, you...you...panty thief!"

He chuckled. "Make me."

"I could withhold privileges."

The humor faded from James. "I'm leaving soon. Anything but that. I could buy you more lingerie."

Alice sobered. She'd miss James so much. She didn't think she'd want to look at another man, not for a long, long time. At least she had Fancy Free and her friends to keep her busy. James was right. She didn't want to fight or even disagree.

Alice linked their arms and tugged him from the boardroom. "Deal." She cocked her head to the side. "I'd like a fire engine-red G-string."

# Chapter 17

## Departure day

"Do you want to come to the airport with me?"

Alice swallowed. Unshed tears glistened in her beautiful brandy-colored eyes while her mouth pursed tight. She was trying not to cry and it made his chest ache. Recently, they'd cruised along and avoided discussions of the future. Even after the condom testing ended they'd continued to sleep and live together. They'd talked about Fancy Free and local stuff. James had never liked a woman as much as he did Alice. He'd never had so much trouble leaving Sloan before. In the past, he couldn't wait to shake the dust of Sloan from his shoes. But today...today was different.

His throat felt so damn tight it hurt to swallow.

"I have a meeting with Rodney's friend about his toys. I'll say goodbye here." She gave him a bright smile that didn't quite reach her eyes. "Do you have everything? Your passport? Money? Tickets?"

"Alice?" He had everything except Alice. James wondered if he was making a huge mistake.

"Yes," she whispered.

"Can I have one last hug?"

She threw herself at him, knocking him back a step before he regained his balance. The lump in his throat grew larger and he couldn't have spoken if he'd tried. Instead, his arms wrapped around her and he held her tight. James breathed in her scent of flowers and knew he'd never forget her.

A horn tooted outside.

"That's the cab," James said.

"Send us a postcard or two." She pulled away from him and forced another one of those false smiles that twisted his insides into knots. At least she hadn't started crying. Yet.

James couldn't resist leaning in for one last kiss. It was short, sweet and not nearly enough. The cab driver tooted again and regretfully he picked up his backpack and grabbed his smaller daypack before smiling at Alice and walking away.

It was the hardest thing he'd ever done.

# Chapter 18

## Three weeks later

The phone rang five minutes before the start of the board meeting. Alice grabbed it and answered almost absently, her attention on the array of sex toys that littered her desk.

"Alice Beasley."

"Alice, it's Max in production. Our bloody machine is stuffed. Excuse the language."

Stuffed? As in working to produce lots of condoms to keep up with the orders? Judging from the tone, Alice thought not. A series of small problems seemed to have hit them recently, problems that cost money to fix. "Have you called the repairman?"

"He's here now."

*Uh-oh.* That didn't sound good. "I'll be down in a few minutes."

After a quick phone call to Harriet, she speed-walked to production. The huge warehouse sounded unusually silent. Several employees loitered outside, taking the opportunity to have a cigarette. Alice strode inside to see the rest of the workers standing around the silent machine.

"What's the problem?" She studied the repairman, who had his hands and head stuck inside the bowels of the condom-manufacturing machine. He backed up and grinned at her. His face bore grease splotches where he'd rubbed his cheek.

"What isn't? I told Alicia she needed to upgrade soon."

When Alice cast a questioning glance at Max, he nodded. *Great*. "Can you patch up the machine until I arrange a replacement?" More money spent. Alice had given up the idea of retrieving her money and had poured more into the company to fix the latest round of glitches. The good thing was that with the packaging and dispatch problems sorted out, they were at full capacity and looking to hire more workers for the sales department.

How would James deal with this? A sense of loneliness assailed her. With James gone it felt as though she were missing an arm. Alice clenched her jaw, imposing an iron control on herself. She'd cried enough in the privacy of his bedroom while holding one of the T-shirts he'd left behind.

The man shrugged. "I've patched it before."

"Good. I'll research a replacement machine."

He scratched his nose and left another greasy mark. "It'll cost you."

"Yes, I know." There were more important things in life than money. And her idea that money equated security—well, James had blown that one away. Security was a state of mind. She knew that now. Alice turned to Max. "I have a meeting. I'll be in the boardroom if you need me. Get a couple of the workers to help in dispatch while they're waiting. I want the smaller room at the back cleared out. We need to use that space in the toy production."

Max nodded and returned to work, issuing a stream of instructions to his crew.

Alice hustled back to the boardroom. All the board was present apart from Richard, who had gone on holiday. Tony, the sex toy inventor sat beside Harriet. His brow crinkled when she brought out her knitting but he didn't say a word. Joseph's daughter had taken on the position of administration assistant and she waited with her pen poised to take notes of the meeting.

"Sorry I'm late. There was a problem in production." Alice took possession of an empty seat.

Ben turned a shrewd gaze on her. "Another expensive problem?"

"I'm afraid so, but we're going to be okay. Orders have increased since we've done our marketing and our debtors are paying. That's the important thing. Can we start? I have a busy afternoon."

Tony stood and placed a bag on the table. He opened it and pulled out his wares. "This is a board game, some dice, I have mini vibrators that fit on a finger and some dildos."

Alice suppressed a smirk when the oldies leaned forward and paid careful attention.

"How does this work?" Joseph picked up a mini vibrator and held it up.

"Those? Oh, you flick the switch and massage nipples, the clitoris or anus." Tony picked one up and switched it on. It produced a tinny buzz before he turned it off and passed it to Joseph.

"A board game. Can we play it now?" Katarina asked.

Tony's mouth dropped open. A croak of dismay escaped, and his head jerked toward Alice, his eyes holding panic. "They can't!"

"Why not?" Ben asked.

"Because...because..."

Alice laughed, taking pity on him. The young male had visions of naked oldies dancing through his mind. It was as obvious as the nose in the middle of his face. "I don't think they're going to take off their clothes." Alice narrowed her gaze on the oldies sitting opposite her. "At least they'd better not be thinking along those lines."

Harriet sniffed. "James would have let us. You spoil all the fun."

The mention of James brought a pang of sadness and thoughts of yet another empty night. Alice ran a hand through her hair, ostensibly to smooth her curls but in reality to gain control over her wayward emotions.

"Do we need to test all these products?" Ben asked.

"Rodney said the board liked hands-on tests," Tony replied. "I've designed a checklist and have written instructions for everything."

"My wife enjoys testing our products," Joseph said. "You know we should go in to books. There's this company in America that sells sexy books. Forget the name. Some foreign place." He frowned then clicked his fingers without warning. "A cave...Majorca's Cave," he finished in triumph. "That's it. Majorca's Cave."

That's not a bad idea," Alice said. "We could market entertainment packs complete with a book, toys, a game and our condoms. Make them themed."

"That's a fantastic idea. I'll get my wife to ring you tomorrow with the info of that company. I like it when she reads their books. She gets frisky." Joseph turned a little pink but bore a pleased smile at the same time.

"Alice, who will you test your samples with?" Harriet asked. "Maybe you should ask Luke."

The boardroom went quiet. The oldies stared at her, and disconcerted, Alice crossed her arms and scanned her clasped fingers. As much as she enjoyed spending time with Luke, they were only friends. She'd given her heart to James. "I don't think—"

"Alice won't be testing sexual aids with anyone but me." It was a familiar voice.

"James?" Alice whirled around, half standing at the same time. "James, what are you doing here?"

"I missed you like hell," he said gruffly. With two rapid steps, he closed the distance between them, grabbed her and spun her around. His mouth covered hers hungrily despite the interested audience. He trembled, his heart pounding against her breast when he stilled and took the kiss deeper. Alice held on tight, unable to believe he was here, holding her as if he'd never let her go again.

Gradually, she became aware of the applause. James lifted his head and let her stand on the ground again but retained physical contact with an arm around her waist.

"Oh, don't stop now," Harriet said.

"Yeah, we thought you were going to demonstrate the new products for us." Ben smiled. "Give us some tips."

James grinned, making his cute dimple flash. "Give you lot more ammunition to torture us with? Not bloody likely."

Alice couldn't take her eyes off him. He sported a healthy tan that brought out the blue in his eyes. His hair curled over his collar. She reached up to test the stubble on his cheek to reassure herself he truly stood in front of her. For the first time since James left, she wanted to be alone instead of surrounded by people. Alone with James of course.

"Are there any more questions for Tony? Is everyone clear on what they're doing with their samples?" Alice paused and waited for questions. There weren't any—just lots of sly grins. "Excellent."

"Will you be in a meeting this afternoon?" Katarina's left eyelid dipped in a wink.

Oh boy. "Stop with the innuendo," Alice said. "I intend to go home for the rest of the afternoon. Don't ring me unless the sky is falling." She grabbed James' hand and dragged him from the boardroom.

"Yoo-hoo! Don't forget your sample pack. Yoo-hoo!" Harriet's bray of laughter trailed them after Alice ducked back to get the pack of samples.

James drove them to his house. Alice kept sneaking glances at him while her heart rejoiced. He was here. He'd come back. She didn't understand why, but she could hope.

He pulled up outside his house. Her house now. James switched off the ignition and turned to look at her.

The expression in his blue eyes—it stole her breath. It made her hope they might have a future. Just that one glimpse of the emotions flickering in his eyes soothed away the rough edges left by loneliness and doubt. Her palms felt suddenly moist and sweaty and her stomach fluttered inside. She wanted him, but she wasn't going to settle for crumbs.

"Why are you here?" The question emerged as a croak.

"I couldn't stop thinking about you. I missed you. Can we do this inside?"

Alice nodded and climbed from the car. Her heart ached with the need for him to hold her close again, to feel the solid security of his arms and the warmth his presence brought. Footsteps behind her indicated James followed. Apprehension collided with gratitude as she turned the doorknob. Why was he here? She didn't understand and was afraid to hope even though she'd seen something in his eyes.

"Let me." James opened the door and pushed her gently into the kitchen before turning her to face him. "I love you, Alice." He paused to fish something from his pocket. "Will you marry me?"

Alice stared at the ring in his hands. "Marry?"

"Yes, please. I missed you from the moment I left Sloan." James ran his hand through his hair and shoved his hand back in his pocket. He cleared his throat, a look of uncertainty on his face. "I thought...hoped you felt the same way."

"Marry?"

His shoulders slumped. "Sorry. Forget I asked. It seemed like a good idea at the time." He turned away.

"No!" Alice grabbed his upper arm, terrified he'd leave before her shock subsided. She hadn't thought James would want marriage. "Don't go. You've taken me by surprise."

"So you might be interested?"

Alice smiled. "James, I missed you too." She moved into his arms and clung to him. "I love you. I have for a long time."

"Why didn't you say something?"

Alice shrugged. "I knew you weren't happy here. You enjoy being footloose and fancy free. I couldn't make you stay against your will. It would be like caging a beautiful bird."

"I'm happy when I'm with you." He gave a derisive snort. "I had to leave Sloan to work that out. I went to the Gold Coast in Australia. All those beautiful girls in bikinis and I didn't feel a thing. All I could think about was you and how my freedom didn't make me feel better. The gloss has worn off my fancy-free status. I missed you so much. Will you marry me?"

"Persistent."

"Yes. I know what I want." He cupped her face with his hands. "I want you."

"What about your wanderlust?" Alice wanted everything clear before she said yes. Not that she worried about security any longer. Her life was so different from what she'd planned and dreamed about from childhood. She loved life in Sloan. "Are you sure?"

"Very sure. The company is important to you. I know that, but once things are running smoothly, there's no reason why we can't take a few weeks off now and then. A honeymoon for a start."

Alice grinned broadly. "Yes."

"Yes?"

"You're my security, James. When I'm with you, I feel as though I can do anything. Can I have my ring now?"

"Of course." James kissed her tenderly before he took her left hand and pressed a sapphire and diamond ring onto her finger. "Now what do you say we take this through to the bedroom?"

"A splendid idea." She stood on tiptoe and touched her lips to his, sealing the promise.

Engaged to Mr. Hottie. Wow! Strange things occurred in this rabbit hole called Sloan, but she wouldn't have it any other way.

**B**reaking News! Read *Festive*, book 4 and a stand-alone, in my Fancy Free series as part of *Wanted: Mistletoe*. This anthology is due out on 1 November 2022 and is currently on pre-order for 99c. Get it today at this bargain price!

# Note to Readers

I hope you enjoyed reading *Protection*, the first book in the *Fancy Free* series. The next book in the series is *Romp* where you'll make a return visit to Sloan and Fancy Free. It's a threesome romance, which I know isn't to everyone's taste.

No problem! I have an alternative option for you.

*Safeguarding Sorrel* (book three in my *Military Men* series) is set in the same small town of Sloan. You'll revisit Alice, James and the oldies on the board and meet some new characters. This is a stand-alone story, and it won't matter if you haven't read the other books in the *Military Men* series.

*Safeguarding Sorrel* also features characters from my *Alien Encounter* series. The eagle-eyed among you might have already recognized Richard and Luke Morgan from this series.

**Fancy Free series**
Protection
Romp
Buzz
Festive (Wanted: Mistletoe Anthology)

**Military Men**
Innocent Next Door

Soldier With Benefits
Safeguarding Sorrel
Stranded with Ella
Josh's Fake Fiancée
Operation Flower Petal
Protecting the Bride

**Alien Encounter**
Janaya
Hinekiri
Alexandre

Also, I want to ask a huge favor. Word-of-mouth is crucial for an author to succeed. If you enjoyed *Protection*, please consider leaving a review at your favorite review sites. Even if it's only a few lines, it would be a tremendous help.

Now turn the page for a glimpse of *Safeguarding Sorrel* and an excerpt from *Romp* the second book in the *Fancy Free* series.

Happy reading,
Shelley

P.S. To keep up with new releases and book news please join my newsletter or follow me on Bookbub.

# Excerpt

## Safeguarding Sorrel

S orrel Thyme peered through the scratchy bushes, desperately trying to ignore the sand flies making a meal of her bare arms. This had to be one of the world's most uncomfortable ways to score a job interview.

The man and woman she was spying on started to kiss—a passionate no-holds-barred kind of kiss. Horrified, she watched hands steal beneath clothes, gulped as busy fingers squeezed and caressed.

The amount of flesh on display increased, and she squirmed, heat whooshing through her body to explode in her face. Talk about embarrassing. She wasn't sure what to do, where to look. Alice and James Bates, the owners of the Fancy Free condom company, didn't have a mere picnic on their minds. Oh, no. They were busy tearing off each other's clothes, right in front of her.

Aghast, she squeezed her eyes shut, her skin crawling from exposure to the bugs. It was the only way to explain the edgy sensation blooming inside her, prickling across her skin, irritating her breasts.

The sharp evergreen scent of the totara and manuka trees wafted to her, refreshing and aromatic. Her stomach let out a feisty rumble of complaint, and she jerked in panic. The bushes concealing her rustled, and her eyes flew open. She froze, horror filling her at the risk of discovery.

Alice and James continued their amorous activities. Sorrel's breath eased out. She caught a flash of pale breast. At least they were too far away to hear her stomach clamoring for food. Placated by the thought, she eased her weight into a more comfortable position. The bush played a musical tune against her robe, and a branch cracked beneath her right foot.

"What was that?" Alice's voice carried across the clearing.

Sorrel bit back a moan of dismay, her gaze darting this way and that to determine the damage. If she didn't move, didn't answer perhaps they'd decide a restless bird loitered in the trees. *I promise to leave the instant they settle again. Please let them continue.* Maybe she'd manage to retreat with her dignity intact.

This was a bad idea. A stupid one. How she'd ever thought—

"Who's there?" James was on his feet now, putting his jeans to rights and staring in her direction. "I know there's someone there. You might as well come out."

Intent on self-preservation, Sorrel sprang to her feet, adrenaline kicking in big-time. She cried out as cramp struck in a painful surge, staggered two steps. Her robe snagged tight on a bush. Held fast, she panicked, yanking fabric free, frantic to escape.

Then he was on her, tackling her from behind. She hit the ground. A pained grunt escaped, the air exploding from her lungs. A hand closed around her leg, and seconds later, his weight held her in place.

"Let me go." She flailed. Ineffectually, as it happened. James Bates was one big dude.

"Who is it?" Alice called.

"A woman."

He shifted his weight, and Sorrel could breathe again. She sucked in a huge draft of air and gathered herself, ready to flee.

"Not so fast." James grasped her upper arm and yanked her around to face him. His bright blue eyes held an edge of anger that had her quaking in her sandals. He dragged her into the clearing where Alice stood with her arms crossed protectively over her chest.

Sorrel couldn't meet their gazes. She straightened her robe, brushing off the dry leaves and dirt. Her hands trembled while panicked thoughts buzzed through her mind like a swarm of bees in a tizzy about honey theft.

*Job interview.*

*Not going well.*

This was a bad, bad idea.

With escape looming large in her mind, she slid a furtive glance to her left.

"You're from the Children of Nature cult."

*Give the man a prize.* Sorrel twisted her hands together, her grubby robe brushing her bare legs. She had others the same, albeit cleaner, hanging on the rack in the shared wardrobe at the single women's quarters. The white robe was a dead giveaway of her status.

*Cult member.*

*Woman.*

*Trapped.*

"Yes." She aimed for a crisp tone. Instead her reply emerged young and scared. Terrified, which was nothing but the truth because the noose was already around her neck. Day by day it tightened, threatening to choke the life from her.

"Why are you spying on us?" Alice's brown hair stood in tousled peaks, her face pale beneath its sprinkling of golden freckles. "Is this a new angle—another campaign to smear Fancy Free?"

Sorrel swallowed, still prepared to flee the second James loosened his grip. But her legs quivered, her knees threatening to crumple like flimsy paper, not up to the job of holding her weight. She'd give anything to turn back the clock ten minutes. *No.* She had their attention—the opportunity she'd schemed and plotted for. It was time to embrace courage.

She sucked in a fortifying hit of tree-laced air, striving for calm. "I wasn't spying. I have no intention of hurting your company or...or haranguing you about the evils of condoms and birth control." *Better.* Her voice quavered only a fraction this time.

"You were spying through the bushes," James snapped. "Do you have a camera?"

A startled laugh burst from her. "Where would I get a camera? I have no money. I didn't mean to spy. Really, I just wanted to talk to you."

"Most people use the phone," James said.

"You don't know much about Children of Nature, do you?" Sorrel owned the clothes on her back—her sole possessions—and even then she wasn't sure she always received the same white robes back from the communal laundry.

"What did you want to discuss?" Alice's tone carried a generous helping of suspicion.

"I've invented a cream. It's similar to a...an aphrodisiac. It enhances sexual pleasure. I want to sell it to your company, in the hope I can raise enough money to strike out on my own and leave Children of Nature." Once she'd started, the words poured from her, one almost running into another in her haste to get them out. "But you can't tell anyone I've offered it to you. You can't tell or they'll steal it from me. You have to promise. You have to promise me you won't tell."

"Shush," Alice said, visibly calmer now. "Have you eaten?"

"I..." Sorrel's stomach let out an embarrassing rumble, forcing the truth from her. "No."

"James, release the girl." Alice offered a kind smile, which settled some of Sorrel's unease. "Come and have something to eat. You can describe your product while we have our lunch."

"I thought we were going to have a private picnic." James scowled, his brows drawing together in displeasure. His longish dark hair gave him a disreputable air as did the stubble on his face.

Alice reached out and ran her fingertips over his cheek. "I'll make it up to you tonight."

"Promise?"

The clear intimacy between the couple brought discomfort, and Sorrel shuffled from foot to foot, debating whether she should grasp this opportunity or try to make an appointment for a later date.

"With a cherry on top." Alice winked at her husband. "Come." She grasped Sorrel's hand and tugged her to their tartan picnic blanket. "Do you work in the Children of Nature store?"

"No." Sorrel's mouth compressed into a tight line. She used to take her turn working in the store and had enjoyed interacting with the town's people. But that had been before Brother Rick had taken over the running of Children of Nature from his father. That had—

She broke off her thoughts. "No, I make the soap and other products to sell in the store."

"The cult won't let you leave?" James asked, his eyes narrowed on her as if she were untrustworthy and out to take advantage of his wife. She'd seen the way he looked at Alice, as if she was the most important thing in his world. As a teenager she'd wished someone would gaze at her in that—

Again she put a brake on her thoughts. Thinking of what-if wouldn't help her situation. She had to make her own luck.

"It's difficult to leave if you lack money or contacts in the outside world."

"Sit," Alice said. "Here, you can have my glass. I'll share with James."

Gingerly, Sorrel kneeled and settled herself on the edge of the blanket. Now that she had their ear, fear writhed through her—a ravenous beast. She'd tested her product on herself, but what if her tingly cream didn't work on other women?

"I need to do more tests," she blurted.

"Of course you do." Alice handed her a glass of homemade lemonade and a chicken sandwich. "Eat first, and then we'll talk."

"Who stops you from leaving the cult?"

Alice laughed lightly. "James, do let the girl eat before you decide to grill her."

"They're not trustworthy." James scowled at her. "None of them."

Sorrel's shoulders slumped. "It's all right. I understand your doubts. I'll find another way." Despite her hunger and her disappointment, she placed the sandwich back on the plate and set down the glass of lemonade. "Thank you for listening to me. I'm sorry I interrupted your private time together." She stood and turned away, defeat a heavy sack on her shoulders.

She could hardly blame them. Children of Nature held regular protests outside Alice and James's company, Fancy Free. They organized petitions and talked to everyone who would listen about the evils of condoms—the very product Fancy Free manufactured.

"Wait. You want out." James glanced at his wife in clear speculation. "How far are you willing to go to leave the cult?"

Gasping, Sorrel drew herself up tall, or as tall as a five-foot-three-inch woman could and scowled at him. "I don't do group sex."

Turning away once again, tears of failure smarted at her eyes, but she held her shoulders square and departed. She'd have to find another way, and soon before Brother Rick implemented his plans to partner every woman above twenty-five with a man. There was no doubt in her mind he'd make good on his threats, and her twenty-fifth birthday was a mere two months away. Stars! She couldn't pretend enthusiasm for sex when pregnancy would trap her in the compound.

"We don't participate in group sex, either," Alice said in a wry tone. "One man is more than enough for me to handle. Wait." She jumped to her feet and ran after Sorrel. "Please stay."

Sorrel hesitated, unsure. She cast a doubtful glance over her shoulder, her steps slowing.

"Please, tell us about your cream. Please." Alice smiled in encouragement and led her back to the blanket. "What's your name? You know ours so you have us at a disadvantage."

"Sorrel Thyme. I know your names because I've been part of the picket line outside Fancy Free a time or two." She lifted her chin in faint challenge when they scowled at her words. "It's a change from making products for the shop."

"Glad our condom business offers you rest and relaxation," James muttered.

Alice elbowed her husband and smiled at Sorrel. "Share our food. Tell us what help you want from us."

Learn what happens next in Safeguarding Sorrel...

# Excerpt 2

## Romp

"**Q**uiet!" James Bates hollered the order and waited for the bedlam to subside. All normal for a Fancy Free board meeting. Alice, his wife, winked at him and set down the fiberglass penis she'd been fondling in her hands. Just as well, too. He had a devil of a time concentrating when she caressed the demos, and the saucy wench knew it pressed his buttons.

"I don't see why we needed this special meeting." Richard Morgan placed his coffee mug on the table with a thump.

Sam Glengarry, another of the elderly board members smirked, his face lighting with glee. "You're pissy because you'd rather canoodle with Hinekiri."

"Damn straight," Richard snapped. "Shut up like the man said or we'll be here until Christmas."

"We might as well listen." Joseph Craig indicated the crumb-laden plates in the middle of the table. "The cake's finished."

"I'm ready." Harriet Te Whare's knitting needles flashed like silver swords, yarn twisting this way and that while she completed another row. "Hello, Gabrielle." Her knitting needles ceased their clicking. "Were you looking for me? Can it wait until after my meeting?"

"Hi, Gran." Gaby stepped inside the boardroom and hovered uncertainly.

"Gaby is here for the meeting." James indicated the seat beside him, waving her over. "Come and sit beside me."

She still hesitated. "Should I bring in my bag of stuff?"

James nodded with enthusiasm. "Bring it on."

Gaby disappeared, returning a few minutes later lugging a bulging green fabric bag.

"Do we have a new condom design?" Katarina Wilson straightened, her pale blue eyes sparkling with eagerness. "When do we get to test it?"

The second Katarina mentioned condoms the smart-ass comments and gossip subsided to quiet anticipation. James bit back his amusement. Condoms and the Vibration in particular had made them and the company rich. He couldn't wait to learn what the board made of the product today.

"Gaby approached Alice with this idea last year. We thought her concept held merit and sent her away to develop it into a product."

"What is it?" Ben Kumar leaned forward, a frown creasing his brow. "Surely they can't come up with another condom design? Haven't we done everything? There's ones with spots and stripes, different flavors. They vibrate. Hell, they practically stand up and beg."

Joseph barked out a laugh. "They're no use if something isn't standing."

James ignored the interruption and resulting chortles to continue. "Gaby has developed several sex toys. We intend to choose one and do a Christmas promotion. We'll target the toy as a special gift for the one you love."

"Sex toys are for women," Joseph scoffed. "Stick to condoms. At least both men and women buy them."

James grinned. "Not this one."

"James, perhaps I should explain," Gaby said.

"Someone needs to explain," Sam muttered. "I want to know why we need another new product."

"Hush! That's my granddaughter," Harriet said, the knitting needles halting for an instant while she beamed at everyone. "She's very clever."

"Go ahead," James said drily, yielding the floor to Gaby. "Maybe you can control them better than me."

Gaby winked at her grandmother and lifted the bag onto the table. She made a show of opening the zipper fastening. Each of the oldies craned their necks, leaning forward for a glimpse of the contents. Her nerves subsided at their curiosity and excitement fizzled inside her. James and Alice had seen her invention and taken one of the prototypes home to test.

"I've worked in the research and development department since I joined the company. I started thinking about sex toys and, in my spare time, I tinkered and developed my own." Gaby pulled out her first toy. "This is a butt plug. It's fairly standard in design. I've made the plug from a material that will hold both heat and cold. Once inserted, the toy will gradually acclimate to body temperature."

Richard winced. "That's all I need. A red-hot poker up my arse."

"Look at Joseph." Katarina chortled gleefully. "He's crossing his legs."

The insults started to fly and, like James, Gaby ignored the interruption to continue with her product description. "Notice the flared base. That's for safety reasons because we don't want anyone having to go to hospital to have an item surgically removed from their rectum."

"I should think not," Richard said in a weak voice.

"We didn't have any problems when we tested it." Alice smirked at James. She let out a sudden *eep* of shock and fell silent, color spreading across her face.

Silence fell and speculative glances winged their way around the boardroom.

"James, hands on the tabletop," Richard said sternly. "This is a meeting, not foreplay."

"Doesn't that depend on your mindset?" Alice asked, cocking her head to the side like a curious cat. "How can talking about sex and condoms all the time not rate as foreplay?"

"Ew," Katarina said. "I don't wanna imagine sex with anyone but my husband."

"As it should be," James said, smirking at Alice.

"James said you'd want to test my inventions," Gaby said loudly. Inwardly she marveled at her lack of embarrassment. Not even blunt talk about sex threw her these days. Not even if it was in front of her grandmother.

Maybe her mother was right and she was a lost cause. No man wanted a woman who always talked about sex or constantly thought about the act. Gaby pushed aside memories of the last hurtful conversation with her mother and older sister because they weren't right. Sex was a normal bodily function, dammit. Nothing to get embarrassed about.

"The secret to any sex toy is to make sure your partner is excited and to use lubrication. Lube is our friend," Gaby said in a firm voice.

"Gaby has designed several new lubes for us to test," James added.

"I'm a fan," Alice said. "We need to market Gaby's lubes. We could give away sachets of gels with the condoms to get people used to using them. You'll see when you test them. The lubes make things nice and tingly. They're excellent."

Gaby couldn't help smiling at Alice's enthusiasm. God, she loved her job. Working for Alice and James was the best job ever.

"What else do you have in your bag of tricks?" her grandmother asked.

"Could you pass these around please?" Gaby handed James several bottles of lube and butt plugs. "I've included detailed instructions with each product plus a questionnaire. If you have any questions you can ring me—not in the middle of the night," she added, knowing her grandmother and her friends too well.

Her mother blamed her grandmother for sending Gaby off the rails in the first place. Gaby didn't want to follow the traditional route of her mother and sister with a secretarial job. She liked making things and she liked sex. Nothing odd about either of those factors.

"This is my second invention and, I think, the best choice for Fancy Free to market. It's a vibrator but different from the norm. I've managed to design a long-life battery that lasts significantly longer than most. I've also made several speed settings because everyone requires different levels of pressure and our bodies are diverse in the way we behave to stimulus. There are five different attachments." Gaby reached into her bag and pulled out a vibrator plus her favorite attachment. "Most of you will have noticed the massage chairs they have at the mall. I've designed this attachment to massage either side of the clit. It gives the most delicious Os." She handed the boxes containing the vibrators to James to pass around. "Make sure you read the instructions. I've tried to keep them brief and concise, but I want to know if you have any problems, either in understanding my instructions or working the toys. I can't correct problems or confusion if you don't tell me."

"Does your mother know about this?" her grandmother asked.

"Nope," Gaby said, forcing a smile and ignoring the tight sensation in her chest. "And you're not gonna tell her."

Ben cast her a sly smile. "Do you still bake those cupcakes? The ones with the pink icing."

"Ah! Good point," Sam said. "How many cupcakes will you give us not to tell her?"

Gaby gasped. "That's blackmail."

"You'd better get used to it." Alice glowered at each of the elderly board members. "They're good at blackmail. It was their misspent youth."

Learn more about Gaby's New Invention...

# Other Books by Shelley

*Fancy Free*
Protection
Romp
Buzz
Festive

*Friendship Chronicles*
Secret Lovers
Reunited Lovers
Clandestine Lovers
Part-Time Lovers
Enemy Lovers
Maverick Lovers
Sports Lovers

*Military Men*
Innocent Next Door
Soldiers with Benefits
Safeguarding Sorrel
Stranded with Ella

SHELLEY MUNRO

Josh's Fake Fiancée
Operation Flower Petal
Protecting the Bride

*Bundle*
Military Men

*Alien Encounter series*
Janaya
Hinekiri
Alexandre

*Bundle*
Alien Encounter

# About Author

USA Today bestselling author Shelley Munro lives in Auckland, the City of Sails, with her husband and a cheeky Jack Russell/mystery breed dog.

Typical New Zealanders, Shelley and her husband left home for their big OE soon after they married (translation of New Zealand speak - big overseas experience). A twelve-month-long adventure lengthened to six years of roaming the world. Enduring memories include being almost sat on by a mountain gorilla in Rwanda, lazing on white sandy beaches in India, whale watching in Alaska, searching for leprechauns in Ireland, and dealing with ghosts in an English pub.

While travel is still a big attraction, these days Shelley is most likely found in front of her computer following another love - that of writing stories of contemporary and paranormal romance and adventure. Other interests include watching rugby (strictly for research purposes), cycling, playing croquet and the ukelele, and curling up with an enjoyable book.

Visit Shelley at her Website
www.shelleymunro.com

SHELLEY MUNRO

Join Shelley's Newsletter www.shelleymunro.com/newsletter

Visit Shelley's Facebook page
www.facebook.com/ShelleyMunroAuthor

Follow Shelley at Bookbub
www.bookbub.com/authors/shelley-munro